VISIONS

Also edited by Donald R. Gallo

SIXTEEN: Short Stories by Outstanding Writers
for Young Adults

VISIONS

Nineteen
Short Stories
by
Outstanding Writers
for Young Adults

Edited by
DONALD R. GALLO

Delacorte Press
New York

Published by
Delacorte Press
The Bantam Doubleday Dell Publishing Group, Inc.
1 Dag Hammarskjold Plaza
New York, New York 10017

Manufactured in the United States of America   First printing

Library of Congress Cataloging in Publication Data

Visions: nineteen short stories by outstanding writers for young adults.

   Summary: Nineteen short stories, dealing with teenage concerns, written especially for this collection by well-known authors of young adult novels such as Joan Aiken, M. E. Kerr, Richard Peck, and Colby Rodowsky. Also includes bibliographical sketches for each author.
   [1. Short stories]   I. Gallo, Donald R.
PZ5.V47 1987   [Fic]   87-6787
ISBN 0-385-29588-X

For Mom, who is proud . . .
and
For Dad, who would have been

ACKNOWLEDGMENTS

Thanks are due to George Nicholson for his optimistic support of the concept of this book and to Michelle Poploff for her careful editorial guidance.

Thanks also to those authors who allowed us to read and use their stories in this collection. I appreciated their patience while we compiled the collection and their enthusiasm for being a part of it.

Most of all, thanks are due to the students, teachers, librarians, and parents who have bought and enjoyed this book's predecessor, *Sixteen*. It was your excitement and joy that led to this second volume.

Don Gallo

CONTENTS

INTRODUCTION

Even before *Sixteen* reached the hands of its intended audience of teenagers and preteenagers, it was enthusiastically received by librarians as well as by teachers of English, language arts, and reading. For the first time there were fresh, lively, never-before published stories for teenagers by a variety of respected novelists with reputations for speaking to young adults' concerns and interests.

The enthusiasm of those adults was echoed and expanded by students in middle schools, junior high schools, and senior high schools across the country when they had the opportunity to read those same stories. There was no story that was a favorite of everyone; yet every story in the collection became someone's favorite. In other words there was something for everyone—which is what an anthology should provide.

That kind of response, from both young adults and adults, encouraged us to start a second collection of the same kinds of stories—never-before published short stories written by famous authors for young adults who write about teenagers' concerns. This time we selected nineteen stories that range across the spectrum of teenage interests, again with something—we hope—for everyone.

In this book you will find an eerie ghost story, a fantasy from another time, science fiction from another place, a story of romance, humorous stories about teenagers who are faced with difficult decisions about friendships, responsibilities, and sex, and serious stories about teenagers who face painful problems of child abuse, nonsupportive parents, and death in the family.

You are no doubt already familiar with the novels of many of the authors in this collection. Other writers here may be new to you. In either case you will find a description of their other writings, as well as some additional information about them, following each story, since you will no doubt want to read more of the works by those writers whose stories strike your fancy.

Enjoy!

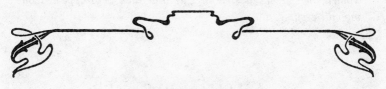

FIGMENTS

She was used to seeing ghosts—in her room, on the stairs, along the hallway—in their old New Orleans house. Usually they were old women, or soldiers dressed in gray. But then Seth appeared one moonlit evening. . . .

SHADOWS

RICHARD PECK

From the very beginning I knew the place was haunted. I wasn't frightened. Far from it. Ghosts were the company I came to count on.

An infant will fear, of course. The newest newborn fears falling and loud noises. But my room was at the top of a long flight of stairs, so I was used to heights. As for loud noises, ghosts are quiet as . . . the tomb.

Better yet, there were no other little girls about me to scream and shriek and tell hair-raising tales. I was a solitary child. I might have been lonely except for my haunts.

I loved the dark. You're never alone in the dark. Or if you are, you can't be sure. Before I was old enough to roam the house, they came to me in my room. Just before sleeping, I'd often watch the closet door open. I'd see the little oval knob turning, blinking in the moonlight. Then hands—I don't know whose—would sort through my baby clothes. I'd drift toward sleep to the faint metallic music of the hangers scraping along the rod.

When I was hardly more than a toddler, things—beings—would pass me in the hall. I suppose I must have thought that even in these modern times there were women who still hid their faces in deep bonnets. And men, booted and spurred.

Only one of my spirits spoke, but that was later.

Every house on the river from here to Baton Rouge had haunts. It was expected, and the tourists liked it. More and more houses were open to the public, who were charged good money to be shown through. At Nottoway plantation they even served the public something called "brunch."

"Brunch," Aunt Sudie said, clamping her granite jaw. "Swilling vodka drinks on Sunday morning when they ought to be in church."

"Live and let live," sighed Aunt Margaret. Being sisters, they hardly ever agreed.

Our house was not open to the public. It was being kept in trust for me, for it seemed that I'd inherited it.

"Catch *me* opening this house to the public so a bunch of rednecks can tramp through and ruin the parquet!" said Aunt Sudie.

"Though heaven knows we could use the money," Aunt Margaret sighed.

"Margaret," Aunt Sudie said unfairly, "you're money crazy. Money is your middle name."

I was so young, I thought it really was.

Aunt Sudie and Aunt Margaret Money were spinsters in the best southern tradition, except they were from New York. In a rare moment of agreement, they'd decided to be Southern. They napped and sipped sun tea through the heat of the day and read the New Orleans *Times-Picayune*. They took up the habit of funeral-parlor fans and sat sniping at Yankees.

I was said to be New York–born too, but I was being brought up as a southern child. Even as a baby I wore a tiny heart-shaped locket, an heirloom that couldn't have come down through the family. And I was allowed to run barefoot well into winter.

Though I never minded the Louisiana heat, the aunts suffered with it. In New York Aunt Sudie had been in charge of something called a typing pool, which had a cool, refreshing sound. Aunt Margaret had skied once, on real snow. Though it had tired her, she never tired of recalling it.

They worked hard at being eccentrics, but how could I know that? I'd met stranger beings than they on the night-time stairs.

One of their oddities was that they were content to appear older than they were. When I first remember her, Aunt Margaret must still have been in her thirties, though she was fading fast. And Aunt Sudie was the sort who'd never really been young.

They let themselves go. Aunt Sudie, who gardened, wore her denim pants, rolled to the knee, even indoors. Aunt Margaret, who kept house in a vague way, wore pink rayon housedresses that zipped up. They both went gray early and did nothing about it.

They weren't really my aunts. They'd been friends of my parents, who were said to be dead. By all accounts my father really was dead. But my mother, always spoken of in the mournful past tense, occasionally wrote to the aunts. Her envelopes were powder blue, and the stamps were sometimes foreign.

I don't believe this ever worried me. With a child's wisdom, I thought a mother who had no time for me wasn't worth missing. And I wouldn't have fretted over the death of a mother. The creatures of my nights upstairs had erased the border between the living and the dead.

Though the neighbors gave us a wide berth, we weren't alone. There was a little house, a dependency, standing out in the cedar swamp behind us. The farmland had been sold off long since to the oil companies, and so this little cabin, steep-roofed in the Cajun way, stood there just at the end of our world. Though I wasn't to go near it, I knew there were people in that house. A very old woman sometimes stepped out to sweep the bald yard and to throw feed at the chickens who lived under the floor.

Never very maternal, the aunts rarely tucked me in. I spent many a night with my chin propped on the windowsill, looking out at the cabin in the trees. Often I went to sleep at my window, watching the flickering glow from the cabin as figures within it moved in yellow lamplight. Sometimes I slept all night at the window, waking in the early dawn, the only really quiet time, after the dead slept and the living hadn't stirred.

I must have been five when my special spirit came to me the first time. By then I was ready for the change of going to school. I'd already explored all the world allotted to me. I'd climbed the forbidden levee and all the trees I could manage. I'd swung upside down from low branches while my skirt settled around my face. I'd taunted dead snakes in the river road with long sticks. I'd even grown a little weary of my ghosts, who were as restless as I.

Then one night, moonlit of course, there was a new shadow in the room. I was used to grown-up ghosts: gaunt women who wept silently, gray military men who stared sadly at their empty sleeves. But this new shadow, dark against the moon-white wall, was hardly taller than I.

I looked for petticoats. Dead daughters were often beautifully dressed for burial. But I saw only the suggestion of bare feet. I looked for a deep bonnet, as my shadows never liked showing their faces. But the moonlight played on white flesh. The eyes were deep-set and dark. I was interested at once. It seemed to be a boy.

He was watching me, but then they all did. He moved along the pale wall. Had he entered from the door or the closet? I hadn't noticed.

I thought he would fade. They often did. I watched his drift. When he crossed before the closet door, he seemed lost in the darkness of walnut wood. But he moved on through a final glare of moonlight to the darkest corner. There he lingered, looking at me. I drew up on my elbows, wondering if his eyes would glow. Eyes in that corner often did.

I looked until I saw him better. No staring revealed his eyes, but I made out the small circle of his mouth. Then I heard the ghost of a sound. It might have been his bare toes curling on the floorboards. It might have been some small creature in the walls. We had plenty of them too.

I tried something new, something not done. "Who goes there?" I said, almost aloud.

I expected no answer and got none, though the room was full of his listening. I knew he heard, and so I slept, satisfied.

He came again and again. Not every night, but often. Once I was just drifting off when the rag rug beside my bed seemed to come alive and move. He was edging out from under my bed, turning his shadowed face up to see if I saw. I saw the mop of his hair, paler than his face. I could have reached down and touched him, but I thought better of it.

Another time he stepped forthrightly out of the closet as soon as I was in bed. At last I expected him there. I even imagined he guarded me while I slept, though I could think of nothing to be guarded against.

I went to school, but it was a disappointment. The children were all too—real. I couldn't fathom the rules of their games. They were forever dividing into teams to defeat each other. But at least I learned to read.

I even read storybooks in bed, but I soon gave that up. The bright light kept all my ghosts away, and so the room was too lonely. I left my lamp dark, and the boy returned. One night when he formed one of the shadows in the corner, I sat up in bed, saying, "What was your name?"

The whole room seemed to catch its breath. Then I heard some sort of answer, unless it was the breeze in the trees.

"Seth," he seemed to say.

"Seth? Seth what? Calhoun? Randolph? Deschamps?" I named all the oldest families in the local graveyard.

"Just Seth," said he or the breeze.

On another night he seemed to settle. He sat in his corner cross-legged in a flowing, old-fashioned shirt. It looked hand-me-down and gravely dingy. His trousers were hardly longer than his shirttails, riding up his white legs. Dressed no better for burial than this, he must have been a poor boy.

Too poor to be schooled, perhaps.

"Seth," I said, "do you know your letters? The alphabet?"

He and the room thought about that for a long moment.

"Teach me," I heard from somewhere.

Proud of my own knowledge, I plumped up my pillow and began, soft for fear I'd frighten him into fading. "A for apple."

I heard an echo.

"B for boy."

I heard it again.

Through nights, seasons, semesters, we worked through the alphabet and simple spelling. When I came to third grade and the multiplication tables, I passed them along to the shadow in the corner. If I was too sleepy for our lesson, I heard in my dreams a distant voice, prompting me: "Seven eights are fifty-six."

In fourth grade we did geography at school. At night I taught world capitals, sketching the shapes of countries in the night air while eyes watched from the corner. "Caracas, Venezuela," I'd say.

"La Paz, Bolivia," the corner answered.

A child dreads changes, but they come. I was a long time noticing that as I grew, so too did Seth. I got longer in the leg, lanky as a colt. In scraps of moonlight I saw Seth's hands resting on his knees. His hands were wider, the knees bigger. When he loomed into the room, he threw the shadow of a man. I hadn't known that ghosts grow, but I never looked for logic in the dark.

In the summer after sixth grade, I got a licking I didn't deserve. In a burst of housecleaning, Aunt Margaret took a feather duster to my room and discovered bits of burned tobacco in the corner.

She reported at once to Aunt Sudie. Lurking somewhere, I heard. "Quite apart from anything else," Aunt Margaret sighed, "she could burn the house down around our ears."

Aunt Sudie said less and went for the yardstick.

She walloped me, and I wept at the injustice of it. They sent me to my room, but that place was meaningless to me during the day. I sat huddled on the stairs, hearing them.

"She is getting to the difficult age," Aunt Margaret sighed. "Now our troubles begin."

"Girls!" said Aunt Sudie, immensely disgusted.

I sulked all day, but I was secretly pleased. The ghost, Seth, had come to the age when boys sneak smokes. But he hadn't smoked in my presence. He was too old-fashioned and courtly for that. He'd smoked only when I slept. Treated like a lady, I heard the first promise of womanhood.

Seventh grade was too much for me, and I gave in to it. At school I joined the other girls clustered around the washroom mirror. We stared at ourselves, hoping our faces would clear and our busts appear. We dreamed of leading cheers and being loved. I began to notice living boys.

But I didn't like them much. They were too loud and never alone. They moved in a pack and would not be taught, even by teachers. How could I say to some basketball-playing boy, "Caracas, Venezuela," and expect the proper reply?

Yet the living boys, the daylight boys, drove my Seth away. He went as quietly as he had come. Or perhaps I stopped looking for him, and so he was not there.

The light began to burn in my bedroom till all hours. I had a little radio now, beside my bed, playing hard rock while I experimented with new colors on my fingernails. I read beauty tips in magazines suspended by my drying fingers. My nights were as bright as my days.

Then it was senior year, and I was all but grown. The aunts flooded the house with the catalogues of distant colleges, hoping I'd go far away so they could have my house to themselves.

I was willing to go. I'd have left that house, that life, without a backward thought, except Seth returned.

On that last night, I'd packed my college clothes and dropped into bed, but it was too sultry for sleep. I found myself at the window, gazing out into the heavy night. Though I'd long ago ceased wondering about the cabin among the cedars, I saw it now. Faint yellow light fell in a square from its open door. I'd never seen that door open at night, or perhaps I'd forgotten.

When I turned back to bed, I knew I wasn't alone. Beside the shape of my piled suitcases was the shadow of a man. His outline was between me and the door. Looking for some refuge, I reached far back and found a name.

"Seth?" I said, hoping it was he.

His mop of hair was pale in the black room. He worked his big hands together. In a voice deep but soft, he spoke. "I couldn't rest easy without saying good-bye."

I'd forgotten what my childhood had taught me, so I was frightened. I went cold, and my teeth chattered when I said, "You knew I was going away."

He nodded. Perhaps he smiled. "We're both going away, but to different places."

He looked down at himself, and I saw he'd outgrown the flowing shirt. Instead, he wore something dark with bright buttons blinking in the gloom.

"I've joined the army," he said.

His uniform should be gray, I thought, Confederate gray. But it wasn't.

"If it hadn't been for you," he said, "I wouldn't have been schooled at all. I'd only have known the swamps and the bayous. But for you, there'd have been no one to learn from, or love."

He turned to go. I heard his boots on the floor, stealthy but real. "Much obliged," he said.

He was at the door now, ready to walk down through the silent house and back to the cedar swamp.

I knew everything then, almost.

"Seth?" I said, too loud.

He stopped, too sudden for a ghost, and turned humanly back.

"Whose son are you, Aunt Sudie's or Aunt Margaret's?"

A light glowing down the hall caught the profile of the living man.

"It don't matter," he said, and smiling, he left me.

RICHARD PECK

After a brief experience as a teacher, Richard Peck turned to a career in writing and subsequently has published a number of novels, several poems, a collection of essays, and three poetry anthologies for teenagers: *Sounds and Silences, Pictures That Storm Inside My Head,* and *Mindscapes.*

Among his earliest novels are *Dreamland Lake, Don't Look and It Won't Hurt, Through a Brief Darkness,* and *Representing Superdoll.* Both *Are You in the House Alone?,* a first-person account of the rape of a teenager and its subsequent effects, and *Father Figure,* the story of an older teenager's relationship with the father who once abandoned him, became made-for-TV movies that have attracted an adult as well as a teenage audience. Those two novels, as well as several of Peck's other books, were named Best Books for Young Adults by the American Library Association.

Next came *Secrets of the Shopping Mall,* a zany story in which two runaway teenagers hide and live within the confines of a shopping mall. Then *Close Enough to Touch,* the sensitive exploration of how a teenage boy copes with the death of his girlfriend and learns to reach out to a new love in his life, and *Remembering the Good Times,* a hard-hitting novel that traces the friendship of three teenagers and the questions that arise when one of them commits suicide, were both named Best Books for Young Adults by the ALA.

Younger readers who have enjoyed the ghostly adventures of Blossom Culp and Alexander Armsworth, first in *The Ghost Belonged to Me* and then in *Ghosts I Have Been* and *The Dreadful Future of Blossom Culp,* will want to investigate Peck's most recent spooky, comic-adventure story: *Blossom Culp and the Sleep of Death,* in which Blossom is threatened with a curse from an ancient Egyptian mummy.

Born in Decatur, Illinois, Mr. Peck, who makes his home in New York City, is also the author of three novels for adults, most recently *This Family of Women.*

*Who is this strange, gorgeous merman in Maddy's haunting dream,
with his blue-green eyes and gold earring? And what is his connec-
tion with the poem that Mrs. Stevens has assigned for English
class? . . .*

SAINT AGNES SENDS THE GOLDEN BOY

CIN FORSHAY-LUNSFORD

When Mrs. Stevens began her little speech on dream motifs in
English literature, none of us was paying much attention. The
majority of the class was staring out the second-story window
watching the snow come down in thick waves and hoping school
would let out early. Of course Marc Finkelstein was the excep-
tion. He was hanging on her every word as usual, and throwing
out a lot of ass-kiss questions to prove he'd been paying attention.
Chances are he'll be named valedictorian when my class gradu-
ates. He'll probably give some typical "God bless our parents, and
our teachers, and America" speech, and I'll be forced to throw up
in one of those caps that looks like an album jacket that sprouted
a tail.

Finkelstein was rattling away about nothing, so I absorbed myself in doodling on the cover of my spiral notebook. Just think, if
school wasn't so boring, I would never have become such a good
artist. My specialties? Unicorns with wide eyes and tangled
manes, roses, feathery-winged butterflies, pointed crosses, and
daggers stuck through hearts.

Mrs. Stevens finished writing the assignment on the board. I
took that as a cue to attempt to pay attention. It wasn't easy. I'd
just put the finishing touches on a heart that read, "Paul and
Maddy," and all I could think was how great it would be if Paul
came crashing through the wall on the hood of a zebra-striped
GTO. The rest of his band would be jamming out in the backseat. I could just picture Paul terrorizing Mrs. Stevens with nasty
guitar riffs, sticking Marc Finkelstein's head in the pencil sharp-

ener, and cranking away till only his rubber duck-hunting boots
would be left. Then he'd sweep me up in his arms and we'd take
off amidst screaming guitars and applause. How come stuff like
that only happens in music videos?

Mrs. Stevens adjusted her bra strap. "Today we will be reading
a poem by John Keats entitled, "The Eve of Saint Agnes." I've
chosen this particular poem because tonight, January twentieth,
is the actual Eve of Saint Agnes. Saint Agnes, in the Catholic
religion, is the patron saint of young women, young virgins."

The classroom erupted into laughter.

"Okay, that's enough," she said. "It's nice to see I finally have
your attention. As I was saying, according to legend, if a girl
adheres to a specific ritual, Saint Agnes will reveal to her a vision
of the man destined to be her true love while the girl sleeps."

I quit drawing. This was getting interesting.

"The young girl in this poem is named Madeline."

Everybody turned around to look at me, because that's my
name, too. What is this, kindergarten?

"Madeline abides by the ritual. She goes without eating, un-
dresses in the dark, and stares straight ahead, praying to Saint
Agnes. She dreams about her boyfriend. Of course, that is only
the premise to this poem." Mrs. Stevens smiled. "The actual
story it tells is much more symbolic and complicated. . . ."

I went back to drawing a Harley-Davidson insignia with bat
wings coming out of it. Then I turned the notebook over because
it was getting a bit cramped. On the back I began to write, over
and over, "Maddy and Paul, tru luv 4 eva."

I missed him so bad. I hadn't seen Paul since Christmas. Almost a whole month. It wasn't his fault really, considering he
lives almost two hours away. Plus he has to practice his guitar,
and rehearse with the band all the time. He wants to be something. That's why I love him so much. Like the night I met him,
he was doing a show at Paddywacks. Me and my girlfriends stood
right in front of the stage. Paul had such grace, such charisma, it
took my breath away. He played with his hips thrust forward and
his back arched, whipping his head around like a gyroscope. You
could tell he really loved his guitar, loved the things he could
make it do. His facial expression changed from smiles to sneers,

to grins, to lip biting with every chord change. Then he saw me looking at him and he strutted over and leaned down, playing just for me. He held me with his eyes, and I knew I'd always be his lady.

I traced a heart so deep in the cardboard that the penpoint went all the way through to the other side. I glanced up. Jack Mason was leaning over to see what I'd been drawing. I tried to hide all the *tru luv*'s and *4 eva*'s with my elbow. Jack smiled at me. I felt incredibly stupid.

"Now," Mrs. Stevens was saying, "let's go around the room in order, and everyone read a stanza. Nancy, would you please start?"

"Saint Agnes' Eve—Ah, bitter chill it was!"

Jack Mason looked around the room, counting heads, then made a mark next to the stanza he'd have to read. Then he went back to what he was doing. He'd been doodling too, but on the desk. He was a very good artist. I guess he thought school was even more boring than I did.

I'd watched him work since the first day of school. He'd started with the upper left-hand corner of the desk, working his way down. He sketched in pen, and sometimes in black marker. Three fourths of the desk was crawling with dragons, demons, wizards, skulls, and cobras. Once he'd come to class and the custodians had scrubbed the desk clean. For a split second this hurt look passed over his face. Then he'd wiped the powder grit off with the sleeve of his denim jacket and started all over again.

Our class didn't finish reading the poem that period. Mostly because Marc Finkelstein had to comment on every other line. So, thanks to Ein(Finkel)stein, we had to finish it for homework.

"Don't pack up your books yet," Mrs. Stevens yelled over the conversations that burst out at exactly twelve twenty-six. "I want a short essay from you tomorrow also."

There were immediate groans and protests. Suddenly the entire classroom was overwhelmed with a touching sense of school spirit. There was an urgent need to attend hockey practice, Spanish club meeting, drama production rehearsals—any semilegitimate excuse to postpone an English paper.

Mrs. Stevens held her hands over her head like a referee.

"Okay, guys! That's enough. I'm not asking you to read *War and Peace.* Just finish the poem. There's only one page left. The assignment is on the sheet I'm passing out."

The paper she gave us said, "In 'The Eve of Saint Agnes,' by John Keats, the heroine's future is affected by her dream/fantasy. In a brief but well-constructed essay (three to five paragraphs should suffice), describe a dream or fantasy you have had. Would you want it to come true? Why or why not?"

I gathered up my books and glanced out the window. It had stopped snowing, my boyfriend was a hundred miles away, and I had another lousy homework assignment to do. There is no justice in the universe, on any level.

As soon as I got home from school, I called Paul's house. His mother answered the phone. I put on my telephone voice.

"Hi. Can I speak to Paul, please?"

"Jeanie?" Paul's mother asked brightly.

"No," I said suspiciously. "It's Maddy."

"Oh. Maddy." She hesitated. "Hold on a minute. I'll see if Paul's in."

A few moments later she came back on the line.

"Honey, Paul's in the shower. I'll tell him to call you back later."

"Thanks." I hung up the phone.

I paced around the kitchen wondering who Jeanie was. I shrugged it off. Probably just a friend or a cousin or something. At five thirty, when my mother came home from work, I made a fire in the fireplace, and before dinner she whipped up two mugs of vin chaud—warmed wine spiced with cinnamon, cloves, and slices of orange and apple.

By six o'clock Paul still hadn't called back, so I decided to phone his house again. This time he answered.

"Paul?"

"Yeah."

God, did he sound sexy! Even just saying "yeah."

"Hi, babe. I called you before. Didn't your mother give you the message?"

"No," he said. "I guess she forgot."

I penciled a heart on the kitchen wall by the phone.

"It's so good to hear your voice," I told him. "I miss you so much, you don't know. Do you think you'll be able to come down soon?"

"Oh, I don't know. I doubt it. I've been really busy with the band and all. . . . You know how it is."

I tried not to sound disappointed.

"Yeah. Sure, it's okay. I understand. Did you get the card I sent you? And the picture?"

"Yeah," Paul said. "Thanks. I was going to write you back . . ."

A funny sort of tinge to his voice curdled the edges of his words. I cut him off.

"Listen—Paul? I was thinking. If you can't make it down here, maybe I could come up there and visit you. I could take the bus. I bet my mom would say yes, if your mother says it's all right."

There was a long silence on the other end.

"Paul? Did you hear what I said?"

"I don't think it's such a good idea, Maddy."

"Why not?" My voice came out too soft.

For the first time since I'd known him, Paul Matthews, budding rock musician and all-around champion talker, was actually having trouble with his public image. The monarch of social butterflies was at a loss for words.

"Uh . . . Maddy? Look, I've been meaning to talk to you," he finally managed to say. "You're a really nice girl. I know you deserve someone who's going to pay more attention to you. . . ."

I rubbed out the heart I'd drawn by the phone.

"Right now I just need a little time. I need to think, to get myself together. You understand, baby, don't you?" He stumbled on. "I want to explore my feelings . . ." (Long, cowardly pause.) "Maybe see other people . . ."

I smashed the receiver down. My mother walked into the kitchen and put the glass mugs in the sink. She started babbling about nothing, then stopped when she saw my face.

"Maddy? What's wrong? What happened?"

"Stupid, conceited idiot! I hate him! I do, Ma. I really can't stand his guts."

"Who? Paul? Wait . . . don't tell me. He's hocking your an-kle bracelet to buy a new amplifier."

"Ma!" I snapped. "It's not funny. You think it's a joke? Paul just broke up with me. I don't find it amusing at all. I don't . . ."

Her face went all soft, and she held her arms out to me. And suddenly I crumpled from the inside out.

She did what she could to make me feel better. My mom's very patient. She nodded a lot and said, "Yes, yes, he is an idiot. I know." She got upset when I told her I didn't want dinner, but I had no appetite. Instead, I lay on my bed, listening to albums that reminded me of Paul.

I got sick of that after a while, and I tried to do my homework to get my mind off things. I read the rest of the poem for English, but I had a hard time concentrating, so the ending didn't make much sense to me. When it came down to writing an essay, I was at a total loss. I had nothing to say. All my dreams and fantasies had been strangled with a phone wire. I hated everything.

Finally I couldn't take it anymore. At nine-thirty I picked up the phone and dialed Paul's number.

A girl's voice answered this time.

"Who is this?" I demanded.

"Jeanie," she snapped. "Who is this?"

I hung up.

I sank down on the floor of my bedroom, staring blankly in front of me. Twinkle, my Siamese cat, tiptoed over and gingerly tried to sharpen her claws on my lap.

"Get off!"

I pushed her away. Then I felt guilty, and I gathered her up in my arms. She flicked her ears at me, annoyed that I was crying. She doesn't like for her fur to get wet.

Then I didn't feel like crying. I felt like breaking things. My brain hurt. My English book was lying on the floor next to me, and that seemed as good an inanimate object as any to take out my aggressions on. I reached for it. Even through the blur of tears, the footnote stood out. I read it over and over.

"It was within Saint Agnes's power to reveal a girl's true love to her during a sleeping vision."

True love. Was Paul my true love? Had he ever been? I'd written it enough times. I guessed wishing wasn't enough to make it true. Saint Agnes! Ha! If Paul's not my true love, who is? Yeah, who is? So the idea crept into my mind like mist taking shape. This is crazy, I thought to myself, as I pulled down the shades and turned out the bedroom light. There's no such thing as saints. I kicked off my shoes and pulled off my socks by stepping on the toe of the sock with the heel of the opposite foot and then wriggling out of it.

"Saint Agnes' Eve—Ah, bitter chill it was!"

I unzipped my jeans.

There is no Saint Agnes. Just like there's no Santa Claus, or tooth fairy. My jeans were now lying in a crumbled heap on the floor. Maddy, you're ridiculous. It's not going to work. I pulled my sweater off over my head. Give it up, kid. Don't forget not to look around the room. Just climb in bed. What does a saint look like, anyway? Probably like a kid. Like a young girl with pale skin and china-blue eyes. She'd have ripples of gold hair, like an angel, blush-pink cheeks, a sweet, timid smile.

Okay. No dinner, a dark room, no clothes, and no peeking around. That's my end of the bargain, Saint Agnes, I thought to myself. Your turn now.

I woke from the dream with a start. When I turned on the light, strands of seaweed that had been wrapped around my bare legs turned out to be the damp, twisted sheet bunched at the foot of my bed. The great gray house was gone, and the lake had disappeared like vapor. I put my hand to my face and brushed back the tendrils of hair that stuck to my cheek. I looked down at my pillow, half expecting to see that a garland of purple sea lilies had fallen out of my hair onto the bed. But the sea lilies were only a dream like the rest of it, and my skin was damp with sweat, not sea brine. So Golden Boy, too, was only a figment of my imagination.

It was the weirdest dream I'd ever had, frightening, yet tempting and beautiful at the same time.

I'd dreamt I was with a group of friends. I don't know who they were specifically, but we were visiting my uncle, who'd just bought a new house. It was more like a mansion, really—a great gray stone building with tiny windows and massive chimneys. The house was set back from a lake. Eerie, tangled trees overhung the water. Jagged black rocks jutted out of the green-gray surface at odd angles. One of them was shaped like the crown piece of a human skull.

On the left side of the lake a waterfall gushed and bubbled, but no mountain rose behind it. The water simply defied gravity, foaming up like a geyser on one side of the rock formation, and tumbling down the other in a silvery curtain.

Something glistened under the surface of the water. Goldfish, I thought to myself. But they were huge, more the size of small porpoises. They swam around the back of the rocks and came tumbling down the waterfalls. One of them was a muddy green-ish brown, the other a shimmering gold.

I walked to the edge of the lake. My friends called me to come away. They begged me to go back to the house with them. All they kept saying was that it was dangerous, that something evil lurked beneath the calm water. I laughed, plunging into the lake to look for the strange creatures I'd seen sliding down the water-fall. I just had to get a better look at them.

I swam into a cave, a high tunnel of rock eight or nine feet long. Surfacing under the canopy of rock, I found that the water wasn't all that deep. I could stand flatfoot and the water just covered my eyebrows, tiptoe and it only reached my chin. The cave was dank and cool, droplets of water dripping from the glistening ceiling two feet above my head, making ripples in the still water.

Suddenly, something brushed against my leg. I gasped and spun around in the water. It surfaced with a great splash. I was too shocked to move or scream. The waves his body had made calmed around him, and he stared at me with slanted green-blue eyes, the water dripping from his chin.

He was the most beautiful creature. His face was almost human. Almost. The bone structure was feline, with sculpted cheek-bones and a solid jaw that looked like it could snap jugulars with a nip and a twitch. His eyes were like a cat's too: huge, almond-shaped, with a slit of black pupil. He looked like a very attractive guy who was being mystically transformed into a lion and, as yet, had made it only halfway there. His mouth, nose, forehead were all normal. He even had a gold hoop earring in one ear. A mane of long gold hair floated in the water around his shoulders and hung in his eyes. His skin was golden, translucent almost. So much about him seemed touched by a pale light, the name immediately came to me: Golden Boy.

"Don't be afraid," he whispered.

He held out his hand to me. His fingers were long and bony, ending in pointed fingernails like claws. I took his hand and he dove under the water, dragging me down with him. That long under water, I should have been dead. But the water was like air in my lungs, and I moved freely and saw everything clearly.

Aside from the human face with feline characteristics, he had a man's body, sleek and muscular. A spiky gold fin ran the length of the back of his neck to the small of his back. His human limbs ended at the knees, where his legs seemed to melt together, a huge fish tail waving underwater where his ankles should have been.

Something inside told me not to be afraid of him. He swam around me in graceful circles, brushing shyly against my legs. Then he swam away from me and I panicked, thinking he'd left me. Out of nowhere, he came up behind me and put his arms around my waist, curling his body into my back. I turned to him. He smiled, touched my face. Softly, he nuzzled into my neck, rubbing his face against my throat the way a kitten would.

I bent my head to his and showed him what a kiss was. He seemed to like it a lot. I laughed at his eagerness to try it again. Under water, laughter sounds like windchimes.

After we swam the length of the lake, we lay on a rock in the dying sunlight. Golden Boy had a friend, like him but a muddy brown color. He frightened me though. He wasn't sleek and handsome like Golden Boy. He was emaciated. It looked like the skin was pulled so taut over his skeleton that the sinews and knobby bones would burst out like tree roots from the earth.

Patches of scraggly black hair sprouted from the back of his skull, and his skin was mottled, diseased.

But he dove under the water, bringing up armfuls of sea lilies, which Golden Boy wove into a garland and set on my brow like a crown. From the shore my friends called to me to come back to them before it was too late. The muddy brown creature hissed at them, and they drew back.

"Just a few more hours," I yelled to them.

Golden Boy took my hair in his hands.

"Don't go back," he said earnestly, "Don't leave me."

Beautiful, rare creature—how could I ever leave him?

It was then that I looked down at the murky water and the rotted skull bobbed to the surface. I drew back, terrified. Suddenly the muddy brown creature grabbed my leg and sunk his teeth deep into the flesh of my ankle.

I cried out.

"Swim! Swim away!" my friends screamed to me. "They're evil, like ghouls or vampires. They devour people who come too close to the water's edge."

Horrified, I looked down at my ankle, expecting to see flesh torn away, exposed bone, flaps of bloody skin. But my ankle was fine. Not a scratch. The muddy brown creature shook his head and laughed, as if it had all been a joke. I looked over at my Golden Boy. He was laughing too. Relief passed over me like a wave. I smiled back at him. He was still graceful and handsome. He drew his lips back when he smiled, and for the first time I noticed the small, sharp fangs.

That's when I woke up. I rehashed the dream in my head, trying to hold on to it. It seemed so real. I wanted desperately to fall back to sleep and finish it, find out what would have happened next. Would I have stayed? Was he beast or human or good or evil? I wasn't ready to return to the dreamless world where mercreatures were an absurdity. I sat at my desk and headed the paper and began to write.

The next few days I didn't think about Paul as much as I figured I would. Now and then I caught myself scheming up fiendish plots to torment Jeanie, but that was all harmless fun. Mostly I wondered about Golden Boy, and what the dream meant. I wondered about saints too. What kind of twisted sense of humor could this Saint Agnes have, to put terrifying, yearning visions in a young girl's sleepy brain?

When Mrs. Stevens read my essay out loud to the class later that week, it sort of overwhelmed everyone. I guess because it was so weird. Even Marc Finkelstein was at a loss. She wouldn't tell who wrote it, and I noticed several people looking casually around the room for telltale signs of the author. I kept my head down throughout the ordeal, diligently scribbling out the "Paul and Maddy" hearts.

The bell rang. Jack Mason grabbed my arm.

"This is for you," he said, holding out a sheet of white sketch paper. "I drew your friend."

Golden Boy was in the water, smiling enigmatically, holding a seashell. The waterfall was behind him, and the rocks, and the faint lines of a tree on the shore.

I sucked my breath in through my teeth.

"How did you know it was me?"

He shrugged. "I just did."

Neither of us really knew what to say. He smiled awkwardly, "I liked your story a lot. Especially when you said how you'd have stayed with him anyway, even though you didn't know if you could trust him. That part was cool. All of it was cool."

"Thanks," I said.

For the first time I took a good look at Jack Mason. His hair wasn't as long and wild as Golden Boy's, but it was a nice shade of blond. There was something else, but I couldn't put my finger on it. Maybe the way his blue-green eyes lifted up at the corners.

"What did you write your paper on?" I asked him, because I didn't know what else to talk about.

He fidgeted with his gold hoop earring. "You really want to know? I wrote about this fantasy I have, about this girl who sits next to me in English. Well, tell you what: take a walk with me to the coffee shop after school and I'll tell you all about it."

I smiled at him, pulling on my fingers because my hands were shaking.

"You've got a deal."

He smiled back at me, a wide reckless grin. It was then that I noticed the teeth. . . .

CIN FORSHAY-LUNSFORD

Walk Through Cold Fire was Cin Forshay-Lunsford's first published book, and it earned her first prize in the second annual Delacorte Press contest for the Outstanding First Young Adult Novel. She began writing it when she was a seventeen-year-old senior at Lynbrook High School on Long Island, New York.

Like Cin, who moved out of her parents' home and into a studio apartment in Long Beach, New York, before graduation, the sixteen-year-old heroine of *Walk Through Cold Fire* leaves her middle-class father and new stepmother and enters a very different world when she takes up with a gang called the Outlaws. From the wreckage of broken loyalties and lost love, Désirée Valentine searches for something to live for and believe in, and struggles to realize her own uniqueness.

Forshay-Lunsford says she had no lack of inspiration for this autobiographical novel, for the story came "partly from my frustrations with a society bent on creating followers, partly from my diary excerpts, and partly from my imagination. My heroine echoes my sentiments on love, frustration, anger, and friendship. Other characters are based in part on my view of the more interesting people I've encountered who have fought to be different.

"Written in the first person, the novel is a confession of my own weaknesses and strengths, a raw attempt to contact other people who want more from life than what is given." She wants to tell young people "that it is not only okay to be different, it is desirable. So many creative things can come from turning one's back on convention and tending to the realm of imagination."

Forshay-Lunsford continues to tend to her own imagination as a young writer in Long Beach, where she lives with her two parakeets (Biker and Davide), a mutt named Nigel, and a revolving door for the friends who continue to entertain and inspire her.

Being a receptionist for a publishing company got boring awfully fast for sixteen-year-old Becky. It isn't a very exciting way for an aspiring writer to spend the summer. Then obnoxious Mr. REM pops into her life. . . .

DREAM JOB

MARJORIE WEINMAN SHARMAT

I got my summer job because my mom and dad knew the right person. Mr. Lamb, my boss at Garth Publishing Company, is a good friend of my parents and a fan of my smile. He said, "Becky has a sunshine smile, and that's what we need at our front desk."

So all I have to do is sit at the front desk and not chew gum and look older than I am, which is sixteen, and not offend anybody, and above all else, SMILE! Mr. Lamb's regular receptionist, Miss Ding, took her thirty-year-old sunshine smile on a six weeks' rest tour of the Orient. I get paid $6.25 per hour for taking her place. In just two hours I can smile my way to $12.50. I wish that Mr. Lamb would acknowledge my brain, my imagination, my gift for fantasy, and all the other things I value about myself. But they are worth zero to him.

For the first couple of weeks the job was interesting, which is a word most of the people who come to my desk avoid using because it's not an interesting word. They are writers. Published. Unpublished. Famous. Unknown. Yearning. Arrogant. Humble. Hungry. Overfed. You name it, it showed up at my front desk.

But the job got boring fast. Smiling all the time might be an easy way to make a living, but it's not my line of work. I'm going to be a professional writer, specializing in fiction. Wild, crazy, weird, unreal stuff based on everything that has ever happened to me or could happen to me. But now, for $6.25 an hour, I am letting my imagination and my identity go down the drain.

By the first day of the fourth week my mind was failing from disuse. Imagination atrophy, a disease unknown to medical science because it was just invented by me, set in. Nobody was around, so I turned off my smile, leaned back in my chair, closed my eyes, and wondered how to rev my imagination back to life.

Then, suddenly, Raunchy Ezra Moore, known to the American public by his initials, REM, appeared in front of my desk. He had written one of the most disgusting books ever, so of course he is famous. It was called *And America Came Tumbling After*, and Garth Publishing Company had published it. It was a literary dud, but the book jacket was a fabulous success. The public had to buy the book in order to get the jacket. On the jacket REM had been photographed against a background of used-car lots, neon lights, garish road signs, seedy motels, and a huge blowup of a decaying tooth. He was reclining in a leather chair which had been placed on top of a bulldozer, and he wore a Deep Thought expression as if he were fighting a mental battle against encroaching Junkdom.

Now here he was in person, with his frizzy bright red hair, his blotchy face, and teeth that seemed to reflect the raging pink of his gums. He was wearing the same T-shirt that he wore on the book jacket picture. It had the slogan BABY, I HAVE MET THE ENEMY AND THEY BOUGHT ME.

He was looking me over. "You're new here?"

"Yes." Smile.

"I'm REM. *And America Came Tumbling After*."

"Yes, I read the book jacket. I mean, I haven't read the book yet."

"You have no plans to read the book, sweets."

Sweets is a sexist word I think. I'm not sure. Maybe it's just friendly.

REM kept talking. "You're too busy with your smiling young life to read books. Allow your head to wake up, sweets. You must have a few ideas buried in the mothflakes of your mind, waiting patiently for their airing. But they'll never see the light of day."

"Now just a minute . . ."

"Do you have any mints? The other girl had a thing for mints. A homey touch. You've got a clean desk. Decay comes in many forms. A clean desk says emptiness to me. Think about emptiness, sweets. That's what I'm writing about now. *America the Empty.* It's only a working title."

"I am not empty, and you don't have an appointment here, Mr. REM."

"An *appointment?* Appointments, schedules, and such blunt me. They take the edge off the creative flow. You don't know anything about creativity, do you, sweets?"

I made a quick financial summary of my life. My parents had furnished me with a roof over my head, clothes, food, and an allowance. I didn't really need the books and records I was going to buy with the money I made at this job. I didn't *need* this job.

I am far more creative than you and you are a nasty person, Mr. REM.

I said it in my head. My mouth, however, smiled. My mouth said, "I'll see if Mr. Lamb can see you."

"He will, sweets, believe me." REM started to walk past my desk.

"You can't walk past my desk without my permission," I said.

"*Your* permission? You're just a teenager who was placed in that chair to smile. That is your function, sweets. That is *you!*"

REM kept on walking. I stood up and looked around for help. I found it. I picked up a vase of plastic leaves that belonged to Miss Ding, and I brought it down—SMACK!—on REM's frizzy red head.

"I hereby quit this job!" I said. "And, excuse the pun, REM, but this is a smashing way to do it!"

Had I just mortally wounded another human being? No. He kept right on walking! He hadn't even felt anything. I was powerless against REM. What was wrong with me? No verbal power, no physical power.

I ran from the floor. I ran from the building. I had to go home and tell my parents everything. They would understand. They did not raise me to be a smile.

I was on the street. I had no money. I had left my purse in my desk drawer. I couldn't go back. And I couldn't get home. Home was twenty-six miles away, out of the city. It costs money to get transported twenty-six miles.

"Taxi!"

I would go home in style. My parents would pay for it at the other end.

A taxi stopped. It stopped for me. I was important. I was a person a taxi would stop for. So there, REM!

I scrambled into the backseat, trying to hide my face in case the driver hadn't already gotten a good look at it. He might not willingly have picked up a teenager. People with briefcases and aristocratic faces and polished shoes and hundred-dollar haircuts give bigger tips than teenagers do.

"Where to?" the driver asked without turning around.

It was a woman's voice. The driver was a woman.

"Uh . . . out of the city . . . toward the suburbs, please."

She'll refuse. She'll want to get paid in advance or something.

"Fine, miss."

She accepted me. She was respectful. I was Miss, not Sweets.

She started up her cab. The taxi motor was steady and supportive. The click of the meter was soothing and dependable. We glided along. It was a winged chariot. Maybe this was my destiny, to be driven around by a polite charioteer.

I huddled in the corner, still not wanting to raise my head. I wondered if she was someone I could confide in. "Ma'am, I just hit somebody over the head with a vase. See, I'm a creative person and the guy I hit said I wasn't."

"I'm sorry, miss. You deserve much better. It is difficult for me to convey a sincere message through a slot in the bulletproof partition that separates you from me, but you deserve much better."

"You really think so? I took this summer job and all I did all day long was smile. It made me lose my identity."

"Your identity? You can have it back, miss. Just smile and say please, and you can have it back."

"What are you talking about?"

"Look, miss, there's an underground market in these things. Everybody is looking for the best identity possible. Now, you be a good girl and say please and smile and you can have your own identity back."

Was she kidding? Was she for real? I slowly looked up. I stared at the back of her head. It revealed nothing. Her hair was frizzy bright red. *Frizzy bright red.* It was a coincidence, that's all.

"What is your name, ma'am?" I asked like an interrogator.

"My name and face are on my identification card. Can't you see it?"

I was afraid to look at it.

"Very well, you want me to tell you my name, miss? It's Ramona Eunice Metcalfe, miss. Sometimes my husband calls me REM. You know, R for Ramona, E for Eunice, and M for Metcalfe. Now, what do you want to do about your identity? I'll give it to someone else if you don't smile and say please."

She stopped for a red light and turned her blotchy-skinned, pink-toothed face back toward me!

I bolted out of the taxi. I ran three blocks. Then I stopped, out of breath. I leaned against a building. I kept my eyes down. I knew that if I looked up I would see that I was surrounded by people with frizzy bright red hair, blotchy faces, and pink gummy smiles, and their initials would all be REM.

I know exactly where I am. I am in a nightmare. I fell asleep at my desk at Garth Publishing Company, and I am in the REM phase of sleep. REM stands for rapid eye movement. During REM sleep the eyes are in motion and this is when dreaming occurs. Raunchy Ezra Moore is REM. Ramona Eunice Metcalfe is REM. What a neat package of a dream.

But I want out of my nightmare before it gets any worse. I'm looking down at my feet. My feet, in shoes only recently purchased at a Fourth of July clearance sale, will soon be stuck to the ground. Helmeted troops with barking dogs will close in on me. I'll find myself in a maze, running up and down in the twisting ribbons of it, looking for a sign, a landmark. I'll be a child in an old-fashioned yellow-and-white checked dress, sitting on the slatted porch of a rotting farmhouse while generations of people march by, through endless time, while I frantically wave, unnoticed, imprisoned in eternity. Armies will mass to the heavy beat of drums, facing each other, long steely lines, waiting across a hideous sweeping plain. I'll hide in a cellar from the Inquisition. If I sneeze, they'll catch me.

I wish Mr. Lamb would shake me and wake me up. I'm not

anxious to go through the feet-stuck-to-the-ground business and the maze and the massing armies and all that stuff. And how many blotchy-faced, red-haired, pink-toothed REMs will I have to meet before I wake up? Why can't I have the kind of creative imagination that dreams about hot fudge sundaes and the captain of the hockey team?

It isn't easy being a creative person. It isn't easy having a fabulous imagination that nobody pays you for and a stupid smile that earns $6.25 an hour. It isn't easy living with my acne and my frizzy bright red hair and my pink-gummy smile that Mr. Lamb thinks is sunshiny. But I accept it. I mean, I, Rebecca Eloise Montgomery, future writer, will probably have to suffer through *Everything* before I achieve creative success.

Meanwhile, Mr. Lamb, could you please wake me up. You're paying me $6.25 an hour to sleep on the job. And no surprises, please. Just remember, your initials couldn't possibly be REM, and you have silver hair, a flawless complexion, and simply dazzling white false teeth.

MARJORIE WEINMAN SHARMAT

At the age of eight, Marjorie Sharmat published *The Snooper's Gazette* with a friend in Portland, Maine. She is now best known to younger readers for her more than eighty children's books, including the popular *Nate the Great* and *Maggie Marmelstein* series, several of which have been Junior Literary Guild selections, and *Gila Monsters Meet You at the Airport*, on which the pilot for the PBS-TV *Reading Rainbow* series is based. One of her other books, *I'm Not Oscar's Friend Anymore*, was featured on a CBS-TV special starring Dick Van Dyke. Her books have been translated into thirteen languages.

Marjorie Sharmat entered the young-adult field in 1982 by writing the novelization of the hilarious CBS-TV situation comedy *Square Pegs*. She followed that with her own first novel for teens, *I Saw Him First*. Some of her other young-adult novels are *How to Meet a Gorgeous Guy, How to Meet a Gorgeous Girl, How to Have a Gorgeous Wedding, He Noticed I'm Alive . . . and Other Hopeful Signs,* and *Two Guys Noticed Me . . . and Other Miracles.* Under a pseudonym she also wrote the novelization of the movie *Supergirl.* Her most recent work is the young-adult series *Marjorie Sharmat's Sorority Sisters*, which includes *For Members Only; Snobs, Beware; I Think I'm Falling in Love;* and *Fighting Over Me.*

Mrs. Sharmat lives in Tucson, Arizona, with her author husband Mitchell, with whom she has collaborated on a three-volume textbook project. The Sharmats have two sons: Craig, a musician, and Andrew, a real estate appraiser, and a retired dog, Fritz Melvin, who doesn't do much of anything.

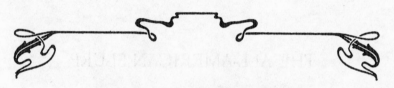

ADJUSTMENTS

Adjusting to a different culture is never without its problems. Even how you eat can be embarrassing. . . .

THE ALL-AMERICAN SLURP

LENSEY NAMIOKA

The first time our family was invited out to dinner in America, we disgraced ourselves while eating celery. We had emigrated to this country from China, and during our early days here we had a hard time with American table manners.

In China we never ate celery raw, or any other kind of vegetable raw. We always had to disinfect the vegetables in boiling water first. When we were presented with our first relish tray, the raw celery caught us unprepared.

We had been invited to dinner by our neighbors, the Gleasons. After arriving at the house, we shook hands with our hosts and packed ourselves into a sofa. As our family of four sat stiffly in a row, my younger brother and I stole glances at our parents for a clue as to what to do next.

Mrs. Gleason offered the relish tray to Mother. The tray looked pretty, with its tiny red radishes, curly sticks of carrots, and long, slender stalks of pale green celery. "Do try some of the celery, Mrs. Lin," she said. "It's from a local farmer, and it's sweet."

Mother picked up one of the green stalks, and Father followed suit. Then I picked up a stalk, and my brother did too. So there we sat, each with a stalk of celery in our right hand.

Mrs. Gleason kept smiling. "Would you like to try some of the dip, Mrs. Lin? It's my own recipe: sour cream and onion flakes, with a dash of Tabasco sauce."

Most Chinese don't care for dairy products, and in those days I wasn't even ready to drink fresh milk. Sour cream sounded perfectly revolting. Our family shook our heads in unison.

Mrs. Gleason went off with the relish tray to the other guests, and we carefully watched to see what they did. Everyone seemed to eat the raw vegetables quite happily.

Mother took a bite of her celery. *Crunch.* "It's not bad!" she whispered.

Father took a bite of his celery. *Crunch.* "Yes, it *is* good," he said, looking surprised.

I took a bite, and then my brother. *Crunch, crunch.* It was more than good; it was delicious. Raw celery has a slight sparkle, a zingy taste that you don't get in cooked celery. When Mrs. Gleason came around with the relish tray, we each took another stalk of celery, except my brother. He took two.

There was only one problem: long strings ran through the length of the stalk, and they got caught in my teeth. When I help my mother in the kitchen, I always pull the strings out before slicing celery.

I pulled the strings out of my stalk. *Z-z-zip, z-z-zip.* My brother followed suit. *Z-z-zip, z-z-zip, z-z-zip.* To my left, my parents were taking care of their own stalks. *Z-z-zip, z-z-zip, z-z-zip.*

Suddenly I realized that there was dead silence except for our zipping. Looking up, I saw that the eyes of everyone in the room were on our family. Mr. and Mrs. Gleason, their daughter Meg, who was my friend, and their neighbors the Badels—they were all staring at us as we busily pulled the strings of our celery.

That wasn't the end of it. Mrs. Gleason announced that dinner was served and invited us to the dining table. It was lavishly covered with platters of food, but we couldn't see any chairs around the table. So we helpfully carried over some dining chairs and sat down. All the other guests just stood there.

Mrs. Gleason bent down and whispered to us, "This is a buffet dinner. You help yourselves to some food and eat it in the living room."

Our family beat a retreat back to the sofa as if chased by enemy soldiers. For the rest of the evening, too mortified to go back to the dining table, I nursed a bit of potato salad on my plate.

Next day Meg and I got on the school bus together. I wasn't sure how she would feel about me after the spectacle our family made at the party. But she was just the same as usual, and the only reference she made to the party was, "Hope you and your folks got enough to eat last night. You certainly didn't take very much. Mom never tries to figure out how much food to prepare. She just puts everything on the table and hopes for the best."

I began to relax. The Gleasons' dinner party wasn't so different from a Chinese meal after all. My mother also puts everything on the table and hopes for the best.

Meg was the first friend I had made after we came to America. I eventually got acquainted with a few other kids in school, but Meg was still the only real friend I had.

My brother didn't have any problems making friends. He spent all his time with some boys who were teaching him baseball, and in no time he could speak English much faster than I could—not better, but faster.

I worried more about making mistakes, and I spoke carefully, making sure I could say everything right before opening my mouth. At least I had a better accent than my parents, who never really got rid of their Chinese accent, even years later. My parents had both studied English in school before coming to America, but what they had studied was mostly written English, not spoken.

Father's approach to English was a scientific one. Since Chinese verbs have no tense, he was fascinated by the way English verbs changed form according to whether they were in the present, past imperfect, perfect, pluperfect, future, or future perfect tense. He was always making diagrams of verbs and their inflections, and he looked for opportunities to show off his mastery of the pluperfect and future perfect tenses, his two favorites. "I shall have finished my project by Monday," he would say smugly.

Mother's approach was to memorize lists of polite phrases that would cover all possible social situations. She was constantly muttering things like "I'm fine, thank you. And you?" Once she accidentally stepped on someone's foot, and hurriedly blurted, "Oh, that's quite all right!" Embarrassed by her slip, she resolved to do better next time. So when someone stepped on *her* foot, she cried, "You're welcome!"

In our own different ways, we made progress in learning English. But I had another worry, and that was my appearance. My brother didn't have to worry, since Mother bought him blue jeans for school, and he dressed like all the other boys. But she insisted that girls had to wear skirts. By the time she saw that Meg and the other girls were wearing jeans, it was too late. My school clothes were bought already, and we didn't have money left to buy new outfits for me. We had too many other things to buy first, like furniture, pots, and pans.

The first time I visited Meg's house, she took me upstairs to her room, and I wound up trying on her clothes. We were pretty much the same size, since Meg was shorter and thinner than average. Maybe that's how we became friends in the first place. Wearing Meg's jeans and T-shirt, I looked at myself in the mirror. I could almost pass for an American—from the back, anyway. At least the kids in school wouldn't stop and stare at me in the hallways, which was what they did when they saw me in my white blouse and navy blue skirt that went a couple of inches below the knees.

When Meg came to my house, I invited her to try on my Chinese dresses, the ones with a high collar and slits up the sides. Meg's eyes were bright as she looked at herself in the mirror. She struck several sultry poses, and we nearly fell over laughing.

The dinner party at the Gleasons' didn't stop my growing friendship with Meg. Things were getting better for me in other ways too. Mother finally bought me some jeans at the end of the month, when Father got his paycheck. She wasn't in any hurry about buying them at first, until I worked on her. This is what I did. Since we didn't have a car in those days, I often ran down to the neighborhood store to pick up things for her. The groceries cost less at a big supermarket, but the closest one was many blocks away. One day, when she ran out of flour, I offered to borrow a bike from our neighbor's son and buy a ten-pound bag of flour at the big supermarket. I mounted the boy's bike and waved to Mother. "I'll be back in five minutes!"

Before I started pedaling, I heard her voice behind me. "You can't go out in public like that! People can see all the way up to your thighs!"

"I'm sorry," I said innocently. "I thought you were in a hurry to get the flour." For dinner we were going to have pot-stickers (fried Chinese dumplings), and we needed a lot of flour.

"Couldn't you borrow a girl's bicycle?" complained Mother. "That way your skirt won't be pushed up."

"There aren't too many of those around," I said. "Almost all the girls wear jeans while riding a bike, so they don't see any point buying a girl's bike."

We didn't eat pot-stickers that evening, and Mother was thoughtful. Next day we took the bus downtown and she bought me a pair of jeans. In the same week, my brother made the baseball team of his junior high school, Father started taking driving lessons, and Mother discovered rummage sales. We soon got all the furniture we needed, plus a dart board and a 1,000-piece jigsaw puzzle (fourteen hours later, we discovered that it was a 999-piece jigsaw puzzle). There was hope that the Lins might become a normal American family after all.

Then came our dinner at the Lakeview restaurant.

The Lakeview was an expensive restaurant, one of those places where a headwaiter dressed in tails conducted you to your seat, and the only light came from candles and flaming desserts. In one corner of the room a lady harpist played tinkling melodies.

Father wanted to celebrate, because he had just been promoted. He worked for an electronics company, and after his English started improving, his superiors decided to appoint him to a position more suited to his training. The promotion not only brought a higher salary but was also a tremendous boost to his pride.

Up to then we had eaten only in Chinese restaurants. Although my brother and I were becoming fond of hamburgers, my parents didn't care much for western food, other than chow mein.

But this was a special occasion, and Father asked his coworkers to recommend a really elegant restaurant. So there we were at the

Lakeview, stumbling after the headwaiter in the murky dining room.

At our table we were handed our menus, and they were so big that to read mine I almost had to stand up again. But why bother? It was mostly in French, anyway.

Father, being an engineer, was always systematic. He took out a pocket French dictionary. "They told me that most of the items would be in French, so I came prepared." He even had a pocket flashlight, the size of a marking pen. While Mother held the flashlight over the menu, he looked up the items that were in French.

"*Pâté en croûte,*" he muttered. "Let's see . . . *pâté* is paste . . . *croûte* is crust . . . hmm . . . a paste in crust."

The waiter stood looking patient. I squirmed and died at least fifty times.

At long last Father gave up. "Why don't we just order four complete dinners at random?" he suggested.

"Isn't that risky?" asked Mother. "The French eat some rather peculiar things, I've heard."

"A Chinese can eat anything a Frenchman can eat," Father declared.

The soup arrived in a plate. How do you get soup up from a plate? I glanced at the other diners, but the ones at the nearby tables were not on their soup course, while the more distant ones were invisible in the darkness.

Fortunately my parents had studied books on western etiquette before they came to America. "Tilt your plate," whispered my mother. "It's easier to spoon the soup up that way."

She was right. Tilting the plate did the trick. But the etiquette book didn't say anything about what you did after the soup reached your lips. As any respectable Chinese knows, the correct way to eat your soup is to slurp. This helps to cool the liquid and prevent you from burning your lips. It also shows your appreciation.

We showed our appreciation. *Shloop,* went my father. *Shloop,* went my mother. *Shloop, shloop,* went my brother, who was the hungriest.

The lady harpist stopped playing to take a rest. And in the

silence, our family's consumption of soup suddenly seemed un-naturally loud. You know how it sounds on a rocky beach when the tide goes out and the water drains from all those little pools? They go *shloop, shloop, shloop.* That was the Lin family, eating soup.

At the next table a waiter was pouring wine. When a large *shloop* reached him, he froze. The bottle continued to pour, and red wine flooded the tabletop and into the lap of a customer. Even the customer didn't notice anything at first, being also hyp-notized by the *shloop, shloop, shloop.*

It was too much. "I need to go to the toilet," I mumbled, jumping to my feet. A waiter, sensing my urgency, quickly di-rected me to the ladies' room.

I splashed cold water on my burning face, and as I dried myself with a paper towel, I stared into the mirror. In this perfumed ladies' room, with its pink-and-silver wallpaper and marbled sinks, I looked completely out of place. What was I doing here? What was our family doing in the Lakeview restaurant? In America?

The door to the ladies' room opened. A woman came in and glanced curiously at me. I retreated into one of the toilet cubicles and latched the door.

Time passed—maybe half an hour, maybe an hour. Then I heard the door open again, and my mother's voice. "Are you in there? You're not sick, are you?"

There was real concern in her voice. A girl can't leave her family just because they slurp their soup. Besides, the toilet cubi-cle had a few drawbacks as a permanent residence. "I'm all right," I said, undoing the latch.

Mother didn't tell me how the rest of the dinner went, and I didn't want to know. In the weeks following, I managed to push the whole thing into the back of my mind, where it jumped out at me only a few times a day. Even now, I turn hot all over when I think of the Lakeview restaurant.

But by the time we had been in this country for three months, our family was definitely making progress toward becoming Americanized. I remember my parents' first PTA meeting. Fa-ther wore a neat suit and tie, and Mother put on her first pair of high heels. She stumbled only once. They met my homeroom teacher and beamed as she told them that I would make honor roll soon at the rate I was going. Of course Chinese etiquette forced Father to say that I was a very stupid girl and Mother to protest that the teacher was showing favoritism toward me. But I could tell they were both very proud.

The day came when my parents announced that they wanted to give a dinner party. We had invited Chinese friends to eat with us before, but this dinner was going to be different. In addition to a Chinese-American family, we were going to invite the Gleasons.

"Gee, I can hardly wait to have dinner at your house," Meg said to me. "I just *love* Chinese food."

That was a relief. Mother was a good cook, but I wasn't sure if people who ate sour cream would also eat chicken gizzards stewed in soy sauce.

Mother decided not to take a chance with chicken gizzards. Since we had western guests, she set the table with large dinner plates, which we never used in Chinese meals. In fact we didn't use individual plates at all, but picked up food from the platters in the middle of the table and brought it directly to our rice bowls. Following the practice of Chinese-American restaurants, Mother also placed large serving spoons on the platters.

The dinner started well. Mrs. Gleason exclaimed at the beautifully arranged dishes of food: the colorful candied fruit in the sweet-and-sour pork dish, the noodle-thin shreds of chicken meat stir-fried with tiny peas, and the glistening pink prawns in a ginger sauce.

At first I was too busy enjoying my food to notice how the guests were doing. But soon I remembered my duties. Sometimes guests were too polite to help themselves and you had to serve them with more food.

I glanced at Meg, to see if she needed more food, and my eyes nearly popped out at the sight of her plate. It was piled with food: the sweet-and-sour meat pushed right against the chicken shreds, and the chicken sauce ran into the prawns. She had been taking food from a second dish before she finished eating her helping from the first!

Horrified, I turned to look at Mrs. Gleason. She was dumping rice out of her bowl and putting it on her dinner plate. Then she ladled prawns and gravy on top of the rice and mixed everything together, the way you mix sand, gravel, and cement to make concrete.

I couldn't bear to look any longer, and I turned to Mr. Gleason. He was chasing a pea around his plate. Several times he got it to the edge, but when he tried to pick it up with his chopsticks, it rolled back toward the center of the plate again. Finally he put down his chopsticks and picked up the pea with his fingers. He really did! A grown man!

All of us, our family and the Chinese guests, stopped eating to watch the activities of the Gleasons. I wanted to giggle. Then I caught my mother's eyes on me. She frowned and shook her head slightly, and I understood the message: the Gleasons were not used to Chinese ways, and they were just coping the best they could. For some reason I thought of celery strings.

When the main courses were finished, Mother brought out a platter of fruit. "I hope you weren't expecting a sweet dessert," she said. "Since the Chinese don't eat dessert, I didn't think to prepare any."

"Oh, I couldn't possibly eat dessert!" cried Mrs. Gleason. "I'm simply stuffed!"

Meg had different ideas. When the table was cleared, she announced that she and I were going for a walk. "I don't know about you, but I feel like dessert," she told me, when we were outside. "Come on, there's a Dairy Queen down the street. I could use a big chocolate milkshake!"

Although I didn't really want anything more to eat, I insisted on paying for the milkshakes. After all, I was still hostess.

Meg got her large chocolate milkshake and I had a small one. Even so, she was finishing hers while I was only half done. Toward the end she pulled hard on her straws and went *shloop, shloop.*

"Do you always slurp when you eat a milkshake?" I asked, before I could stop myself.

Meg grinned. "Sure. All Americans slurp."

LENSEY NAMIOKA

The subject and tone of "The All-American Slurp" are quite different from most of Lensey Namioka's most popular books. Most readers know her for her tales of adventure and terror experienced by two young samurai warriors, Zenta and Matsuzo, in feudal Japan. In *White Serpent Castle,* for example, the young samurai attempt to wade through the intrigue caused by the struggle of rivals for control of the mysterious serpent-shaped castle. The adventures of Zenta and Matsuzo continue in *The Samurai and the Long-Nosed Devils, Valley of the Cherry Trees,* and *Village of the Vampire Cat. Island of Black Ogres* is the most recent title in that series.

Ms. Namioka was inspired to write about feudal Japan by the history of her husband's family. Her husband, a college math professor, was raised in the castle town of Himeji, Japan. She, however, was born in Peking, China, and has lived and traveled all over the world. They now live in Seattle, Washington.

Her background provided much of the knowledge she used to write two travel books, one on Japan and the other on China.

In addition, Lensey Namioka has written a humorous young-adult novel about an Oriental teenager called *Who's Hu?,* and a young-adult mystery-suspense novel set in China before the Mongol invasion called *Phantom of Tiger Mountain.* She is working on an autobiographical book about the adjustments her Chinese family had to make when they came to America. ("The All-American Slurp" is based on one of those incidents from her past.) Her family's name is Chao, and the book will probably be called *Life With Chaos*—a sort of Chinese *Life With Father.*

He's handsome, witty, sophisticated, romantic, sensitive—at least in his fantasies. And Jason has plenty of fantasies, especially about women. . . .

JASON KOVAK, THE QUICK AND THE BRAVE

JEAN DAVIES OKIMOTO

I knew when the phone rang that it would be Bert with the bad news. It was Saturday morning and I was having too nice a time for it not to get wrecked. I was sitting in the living room in my underpants, scratching the hairs on my chest (I have five of them), and reading the ads all these women put in the personal column of *The Weekly.*

The Weekly is this local Seattle paper my parents take that's mailed to our house. Mom and Dad were out of town—they went to Walla Walla, Washington, for parents' weekend at Whitman College. That's where my older brother Jeff goes. I always have a nice feeling of freedom when my parents are out of town, and today I was really enjoying reading the personal column without anyone around to bother me. I really get off on reading the personal column. It's fantastic imagining all these wonderful women out there advertising for men. So far I haven't found any from a woman who desires meeting a romantic, sensitive, caring sixteen-year-old male—but I keep reading them anyway. This one ad really caught my eye:

IMMATURE, IMPULSIVE, uninhibited woman, 36, professional, trim, petite. Want to join my post-divorce, adolescentlike rebellion? Bring dirty jokes, cheap wine, chocolate. PO Box . . .

Most of the ads say what age guy they want but this one didn't. This lady wanted an adolescentlike rebellion—I wonder what she'd do if a real adolescent showed up? If I, adolescent

Jason Kovak, showed up with dirty jokes, cheap wine, and chocolate? I was thinking about this when the phone rang. Damn. I don't know how, but somehow I knew it would be old Bert. He's my boss at Wendy's and he hadn't put me on the schedule so I didn't have to work this morning like I do most Saturdays. I had been glad of that because this morning I was enjoying not having to put on the blue-and-white striped Wendy's uni shirt and that terrible hat they make you wear and go and cut up lettuce, which is what I always do there. I hate cutting up lettuce. I put the paper down to answer the phone.

"Hello?"

"Jason?"

"Yeah."

"Can you come in to work? Mike called in sick and I gotta have someone here."

"Oh."

"Jason?"

"Yeah?"

"Well—can you?"

"I guess so."

"Well, get over here as fast as you can—the whole salad bar has to be prepped."

"Okay."

I hung up the phone and went downstairs to my room in the basement to get dressed. I pulled on my black slacks that I had left folded over the back of the chair. That's what they make you wear at Wendy's—black slacks. As I zipped my pants, I wondered why I hadn't told old Bert that I had plans. When he called I could have said, "No way, Bert. I was just walkin' out the door. I got plans—sorry, man." I could have just said that and then hung up. How would Bert ever know that I was just sitting around in my underpants? I mean the guy doesn't have X-ray eyes or anything. Old Bert can't see through the phone.

I put on the striped shirt and got my name tag where I had left it under a bunch of junk on top of my bureau. You have to wear your name tag at Wendy's. It says JASON right on top of the face of this freckle-faced kid with red hair in pigtails. I guess she's supposed to be Wendy. Big deal.

As I pinned the name tag on my shirt, I stared at my face in the mirror. I am a tall guy, skinnier than I'd like to be in spite of these weights I have. I have a terrific Joe Weider weight set but all I can press is 85 pounds, and only a few times—maybe 150. I'm not what you'd call Olympic material. After I work out I always check out the bod in the mirror and it always looks like the same old set of bones. I have dark hair like my dad, and brown eyes. This girl in my homeroom, Georgette Hector, told me her best friend, Karen Jacobsen, thought I was good-looking and wanted to go out with me. But do you think I ever did anything about it? No. And I'll tell you why. It's for the same reason that I didn't tell old Bert that I had plans today. The cold, hard, naked truth is . . . I'm a wimp.

The real problem is that I can't talk to people. A lot of people have trouble talking to parents, or to teachers—stuff like that. But I can't think of anything to say when I talk to almost anyone —people that is. I can talk to animals fine—dogs, cats, birds, you name it—just not people. It's not that I don't know any words, or that I stutter or something. In fact I think of all kinds of things I'd like to say, but when people talk to me—I lose it. I'm like a jock who chokes in a big game—all that flows from my mouth are things like "I guess so" or "I don't know" or "Maybe." I've got those clever phrases down, no problem.

So what if I didn't have any plans and all I was doing today was reading the personal column? I'd rather do that than be going to cut up lettuce. But it's always the same. I always just seem to go along with stuff. Passive, that's what I am. I am a completely passive person, which is probably just a passive way of saying that I'm a wimp.

I glanced at my watch. Bert would be pissed if I didn't get there pretty soon. I took one last look at the personal column and then I closed the door to my room, but halfway up the basement stairs, I had to go back because I forgot my Wendy's hat. I hate that hat—it makes me look like even more of a wimp. I went back and got it, but I didn't put it on. I never put it on until I get to work. There's no point in walking around in public like that.

When I got to work, Bert was flying around all bent out of shape. Old Bert's like that. He's this real jittery guy. Actually,

Bert's probably only thirty but he just seems old—you know how some people decay earlier than others. He has stringy blond hair and blue eyes, very light blue eyes that kind of bug out when he's extra jittery. His face also gets red sploches on it around his nose. Bert was all uptight even though there was no one in the place. No customers, I mean. Jill and Henry were in the back. Jill Washington's a junior at my school, Ingraham High School. She's black, and real pretty. She looks wonderful in the Wendy's uni and you know a person has a great body if they look good in a Wendy's uni—even the hat looks nice on her. I've never talked to her much. Can you believe that, we've worked together at this same Wendy's for a year and I've hardly said two words to her. It's pitiful. Henry is Henry Ramos. He goes to some Catholic school. Henry is shorter than me but a very muscular guy. I don't think he has a Joe Weider weight set either. Henry just grew that way with natural muscles. Henry and Jill talk a lot and I hang around and listen.

Jill was cutting up tomatoes for the salad bar and Henry was getting the meat out of the freezer and putting it in the refrigerator next to the grill. You know, I've worked here for over a year, as I mentioned, and I still think it's not right to have square hamburgers. But do you think I'd ever say something about it? No.

I signed in on the time sheet and headed to the back, where we prep the stuff for the salad bar. ("Prep"—that's as in "prepare," like "prepare salad"—you gotta know the language if you're gonna work in a restaurant.)

I knew that's what Bert would want me to do. He always has me on lettuce. I guess I must just have that look or something. He sees a guy like me and he just thinks "lettuce."

"Jason!" Bert yelled as I walked behind the counter and headed toward the back.

"Yeah?"

"Cut up the lettuce."

"Okay." I went back to the big walk-in refrigerator and got an armload of lettuce heads and carried them to the sinks in the back. They were cold and a little bit slippery. I put them on the counter near the tomatoes Jill was cutting.

"Hi, Jason."

"Hi." I looked at Jill for a minute and then started washing the lettuce.

"You're working for Mike?"

"Yeah."

"He calls in sick all the time—but it's just 'cause he's out partying the night before. He's too hung over to come to work."

"Yeah, maybe," I said as I started to chop the lettuce.

"Bert ought to fire that boy," Henry said. He was opening the bun boxes.

"He sure should," Jill said to Henry, while I chopped.

"Too bad you had to come in, Jason."

"Yeah." I liked it that Henry sounded sympathetic. I loaded the chopped-up lettuce into a bowl and listened to the two of them talk.

"No one comes in this place this early Saturday morning anyway," Jill said to Henry.

"Especially when the Huskies are playing—like today."

"Who're we playing today, Henry?"

"Stanford. We'll kill 'em."

"That's good—that's real good." Jill put her tomatoes in a bowl. "Jason—you taking that lettuce out there?"

"Yeah."

"Take these for me, too—will ya?"

"Sure." I took Jill's bowl of tomatoes with my lettuce and went to the salad bar in the front.

Bert was wiping the counter near the cash register. "Hurry up and get that filled, Jason."

"Okay."

I was putting the stuff out on the salad bar when we got some customers. Two guys came in, a black guy and a white guy. The white guy went in the bathroom and the black guy went up to Bert and started ordering.

"I'll have two hamburgers, two cheeseburgers with everything, ten fries—"

"Ten orders of fries?"

"Uh-huh. And three Cokes, and two frosties, and the salad bar —and—"

When I heard that I ran to the back and got the blue cheese dressing from the walk-in refrigerator. There are these huge bottles of salad dressing that you dump in the containers on the salad bar. Bert had filled all of them except for the blue cheese—blue cheese is very popular. I guess he forgot that. I unscrewed the top of the jar and took the dressing bottle out to the front. When I got back, I couldn't believe it—the guy was still ordering.

"Four orders of chili—"

I dumped the salad dressing in the container. That guy must be starving.

"Oh, God!" Bert yelled.

I looked up and the salad dressing jar I was holding slid right through my hands. Glass shattered and the blue cheese dressing flew everywhere.

Standing there with a sawed-off shotgun was the white guy—he had come out of the bathroom and he was standing there and pointing it—pointing that gun, a real gun—pointing it right at Bert.

The black guy turned to me. "You. Get over here."

I just stood there. It was like I was frozen.

He came over to me and picked up one of the chairs with one hand and shoved it in my back. "I said, move, man!" he yelled and shoved the chair in my back again.

I don't know if it hurt—because I felt like I was somebody else, like I, Jason Kovak, had left my body or something and I was out there in space watching this guy shove the chair in my back while I got where he wanted me to go behind the counter next to Bert and stood there while the other guy pointed the shotgun at us.

Nothing seemed real except the salad dressing. It had splattered on my hat and it dripped down in my face in big plops.

The next thing I knew, Henry and Jill and I were all tied up together in a heap on the pantry floor. Everything was all a blur and it had kept on being like I was somewhere else while I had watched the robbers shove us and poke us with the gun and make us get down on the pantry floor while they tied us up. All my senses were screwed up. I heard this rushing sound in my head, sort of like blood going through my brain, and I thought I heard the robbers in the office with Bert making him open the safe but

I couldn't tell for sure with the rushing noise in my head. Then I heard this other voice.

"Who peed?"

"What?" Jill whispered.

"Who peed?" Henry hissed again through his teeth.

"Huh?" I whispered to Henry. I wasn't sure I had heard him with that noise in my head.

"There"—Henry nodded toward the floor—"See?"

"They're gonna kill Bert—then they'll kill us," Jill whispered.

"Which one of you peed?" Henry hissed again.

I looked in the corner. Tipped over on its side was a huge jar of pickles—it must have gotten knocked over when they shoved us in the pantry. "It's pickle juice," I whispered to Henry, as the yellow stuff seeped under us.

"What?"

"Pickle juice."

"None of you guys peed?"

I shook my head.

"They're gonna kill us," Jill whispered again. Her hands were tied together behind her back like mine and Henry's, but her fingers were free and I felt them curl around mine. "It's been nice workin' with you, Jason—it's been nice knowing you."

I hadn't stopped feeling numb. The whole thing still seemed like a dream or something, but when I felt Jill's hand holding on to mine, while the rope cut into my wrist, my heart started to pound like crazy. . . . I might die. I might really die. They might shove Bert in here and then shoot us all so there wouldn't be any witnesses. People do stuff like that. There are rotten people in the world who do stuff like that.

"I'm scared. Jason, I'm so scared!" Jill's voice cracked.

"Me, too," I said, holding on as tight as I could.

"Henry, say something," Jill whispered. "Don't tell me you're not scared."

Henry's hands were tied up to my legs. He turned and tried to look at Jill, who was tied up with her arms tied up to mine. Henry just nodded.

It seemed to me that I should say something if I was going to die—like good-bye or something. I didn't know what to say, so I just said what Jill said. "It's been nice knowing you, Jill—nice knowing you too, Henry."

"Likewise," Henry mumbled.

My hand was so sweaty, Jill's probably was too. It was hard to tell which sweat belonged to which person the way our hands were stuck together. Then it occurred to me that I could be about to die and the heaviest relationship I'd ever had with a girl would be right here in this pantry, huddled up to Jill, holding hands, sitting in pickle juice with Henry Ramos tied to my legs. It was pitiful to think about. But it seemed that that's probably what I deserved. If you live like a wimp, you die like a wimp.

I thought I heard them coming out of the office. It could be over—it could be over in just a few minutes. I heard their footsteps. One of those guys must have been wearing boots or something—it sounded like loud thuds. Or was that my heart making the thuds? I listened to that loud pounding noise, and it was right then and there that I made myself a promise. Jason Kovak, I said to myself, if you get out of this alive—you must try with all your might to quit being a wimp.

As the thuds got louder, I thought about the promise I had just made to myself. Even the promise wasn't very forceful—it was a wimpy promise. I didn't say "I'LL QUIT BEING A WIMP!" All I said was "I'll try and quit being a wimp." I was thinking about this and getting discouraged about ever having hope of moving away from the wimp stance in life when the robbers opened the pantry door and shoved in Bert. Bert's face was very white. Veins stuck out on his neck like a roadmap. When they shoved him he slid on the wet floor and crashed down on top of Henry's shins.

"Not one a you say nothin'!" The white robber stood there pointing the gun at us while the black guy made Bert sit up from where he was lying on the floor and then tied Bert to Henry. Jill's fingers curled tighter around my hand.

Henry had his head down. He was mumbling. "HailMaryful-lofgracetheLordis—"

"I SAID SHUT UP!" The white guy kicked him.

They slammed the pantry door and I heard it click as they locked it behind them.

"Blessedartthouamongwomenandblessedisthefruitofthywomb
JesusHolyMarymoth—" Henry's eyes were closed and his lips
were moving but we couldn't hear him too well. "Prayforussin-
nersnowandatthehourofourdeathamenHailMaryfullofgracethe
Lordis—" Henry kept mumbling while the rest of us were quiet.

I looked at the shelves. There were huge jars of catsup and
mayonnaise and five different kinds of salad dressing. Mayonnaise
might be one of the last things in the world I would see. I started
counting the jars.

"Who peed?" Jill hissed.

"It's pickle juice—remember?" I said.

"Prayforussinnersnowandatthehourofourdeath—"

"That pickle juice was cold, Jason," Jill whispered. "This is
warm!"

I felt something warm seeping under my butt. "Oh, yuk—"

"Shh," Bert said. "I hear something—maybe they're back."

"HailMaryfullof—"

"Shh, Henry." Bert kind of shoved him, but Henry kept on
mumbling.

It was quiet—all except for Henry, that is.

Then Jill whispered to me, "It must have been Bert."

I looked at her and nodded. She was right. Bert must have
peed. It had been only pickle juice on the floor before they
brought him in.

"What?" Bert whispered.

"Nothin'." Jill looked at me and rolled her eyes.

All of us—except for Henry—listened. It was real quiet. Then
Bert nudged Henry. "Henry, I don't think you have to pray anymore. I think they're gone."

We all just sat there. We didn't hear a sound. I could hear Bert
and Henry and Jill all breathing. I didn't know people breathed
so loud. I started counting the buns. Not the people's—the hamburger's. Next to the catsup and the mayonnaise and stuff there
were all these huge packages of buns. We waited like that, it
seemed like for hours. Just listening and breathing. I wondered
what everyone else was thinking about. All I was doing was
counting hamburger buns.

Finally Bert said, "I guess there's no reason for them to come back. They got all the money."

"Now what do we do?" Jill asked.

Bert twisted his hands around in the rope. "Let's see if we can get loose from these." We were all wiggling around on the floor, trying to get some slack in the rope, when we thought we heard someone.

"IS ANYBODY BACK THERE?"

We all just looked at each other.

"HEY—IS ANYBODY BACK THERE?"

"I DON'T THINK THERE'S ANYBODY BACK THERE!"

Jill was the one who laughed first, then me, then Henry. Even Bert laughed. We got hysterical, tied up in a heap rolling around the pantry floor in pickle juice, also Bert's pee. I laughed so hard, tears rolled down my face. My side ached.

A lot of people have no idea, I mean zero, zip idea at all, what it's like to go to work at Wendy's every day and have the customers, almost every single customer say "Where's the beef" and other stuff like that from the Wendy's commercials, even though they haven't shown those commercials for years. Each customer thinks it's hilarious.

Bert tried to yell, "We're here . . . we're here!" but he was laughing too hard and you couldn't figure out what he was saying.

"Help! Help!" Jill starts yelling, and then she cracks up.

"Ha ha ha! Help! Help!" I tried to yell too.

The next thing we knew, someone was pounding on the door to the pantry. "If you don't come out—I'm going to McDonald's!"

"We can't come out," Bert said. "We're locked in here."

"We've been robbed," Henry said.

"Yeah, we've been robbed," Jill said.

"Oh. Shall I unlock the door?"

"That would be very nice of you," Bert said.

The pantry door opened and we looked up and saw this lady. She was tall and thin and she had a pointy nose and her hair was pulled up on top of her head in a knot. She had on a brown raincoat and she was holding an umbrella. It was hard to tell how old she was.

"Oh," she said, as she stood there staring at us. "Well, maybe I better go to McDonald's." She turned and started to walk away.

"Lady," Bert called out, "we'd appreciate it if you could help untie us."

"Oh." The lady turned around and looked down at us again. "Yes. Well—I guess so."

Bert was closest to the door, so she untied him first, and as soon as Bert was untied she just left.

Bert untied the rest of us and then went and locked the doors of the restaurant and put the CLOSED sign on the door. Then he went back to the office and called the police.

When Bert got off the phone from talking with the police, he came into the front of the restaurant to talk to us. "I'm sorry you guys, but they want everyone to wait here. They want to talk to each one of us."

"I want to go home, Bert." Jill looked down at her pants. "I want to get out of these stinky clothes." She looked at me. "Don't you want to change too, Jason?"

"Yeah." Besides everything else I'd been sitting in, I still had that salad dressing crap all over my pants.

"I don't know what to tell you—the police just said they wanted to talk to everyone. They should be here any minute."

The four of us just sat there while we waited for the police. Outside it had started to rain. It was a light rain, a hazy drizzle, the kind we get a lot of the time in Seattle. I looked out the window. A car had driven in the parking lot and was heading to the drive-through window. The driver must have noticed the CLOSED sign Bert had put on the window, because in a minute the car headed back out toward the street. While the guy waited to turn into the traffic he looked back and saw the four of us sitting around the table. He gave us the finger and then drove off.

"Crap." Henry had seen the guy too.

"I wish the police would get here." Jill tapped the table with her nails. She had these long red fingernails, and they went clickety-click on the table. "I gotta get outa these clothes—I can't stand it." She looked down at her hands and then held them out in front of her. "My God, I'm still shaking—are you Jason?"

"Yeah." I was too.

Pretty soon a police car with its front headlights shining through the gray drizzle came down Mountainview Avenue and turned in to the Wendy's parking lot. As soon as Bert saw it he jumped up and went over to the side door and unlocked it. He let the policemen in and then locked the door behind them again, still keeping up the CLOSED sign.

The policemen were pretty nice. They took down our names and asked each one of us to tell them exactly what we saw and heard and to each describe the robbers. It took a while for all of us to tell about it. Then they told us that if they caught the suspects they'd be notifying us to come downtown to see if we could identify them. I wanted them to catch the robbers, but I have to admit that the idea of me having to be a person to point them out in a lineup—the idea of me, Jason Kovak having to put the finger, as they say, on a vicious hardened criminal—would not exactly be my idea of a good time.

After the policemen told us that we'd hear from them if they caught the guys, they checked over the forms they had filled out to make sure they had all our names and addresses and our home phones. Then they headed toward the door and Bert unlocked it and let them out. Bert said he'd keep the CLOSED sign on the door until the manager from the downtown Wendy's came, and he told the three of us to go home. We didn't complain about that.

It was weird saying good-bye to Jill and Henry at the bus stop. Henry wanted all of us to march right down the street to McDonald's and ask for jobs—he said they didn't have too many robberies at McDonald's because they had one of those video cameras up over the register. Jill said all she wanted to do was go home and take a bath. That's what I wanted to do, too (not go home with Jill to take a bath, I mean—although come to think of it, that's a fantastic thought, I really could get off on that idea) but I wasn't about to go apply for a job at McDonald's in a Wendy's uni with blue cheese salad dressing splattered all over it, as well as everything else on my pants—which you already know about and its getting old talking about. Forget it. Going down to McDonald's like that was not one of Henry's better ideas. But I knew how he felt—wanting us to stick together and all. At the bus stop we started saying good-bye, but we just kept hanging around. We kept talking about the robbery, just talking about it over and over. About how scared we were and thinking we would be killed and the funny stuff too. Henry said those robbers were the Ebony and Ivory of crime, and we laughed and then cracked up all over again about that lady saying "I don't think there's anybody back there!" We kept talking about what had happened over and over again—no one wanted to leave. War buddies probably feel like that.

When I got home I went straight down to the basement and pulled off my clothes. The first thing I did was get in the shower. The warm water felt good. I hadn't realized how cold I had been, or maybe I was still cold and numb from fright or something. It was strange, because as I started feeling warmer and relaxing, my back started to hurt like hell. I reached around and felt it and there was this big swollen place; some of the skin had broken, and when I looked at my hands there was blood on them. I felt weak all of a sudden. I crumpled up and just sat in the bottom of the shower. I looked at my hands again and there were these red swollen marks where the ropes had cut across my wrists. It was weird. I hadn't even known that stuff was there.

I sat in the bottom of the shower for a while longer and closed my eyes. My head was tilted up toward the shower head and I let the water just run down my face. I thought about the robbery and I could see the way the whole thing should have gone.

The minute I see the guy with the sawed-off shotgun, like lightning I heave the jar of salad dressing. My arm is like a gun, better than Fouts, better than Marino, better than Elway, better than Montana. The salad dressing hits the creep in the face, the glass splatters, it cuts him a little—just a little, on his nose. His gun is covered with blue cheese, but he tries to fire anyway, as his fellow robber comes toward me. But always quick and brave (I am known as Jason, the Quick and the Brave) I start heaving another jar of dressing. WHAP! French dressing gets him in the crotch. BAM! The oil and vinegar knocks his buddy in the kneecaps. SPLAT! Green Goddess to the groin. I jump across the room and tie them up with their own ropes. Then I dump all the lettuce and the vegetables on their heads. "Just a little something to go with the salad dressing, boys," I say in a deep voice. Everyone laughs (except the robbers). Jill and I go home and take a bath.

I stood up and washed my hair. When I got out of the shower, I put a towel around my waist and went to my room, where I got *The Weekly*. I decided to pick up where I had left off this morning reading the personal column. The first ad I read was:

TAKE MY HAND! let's feel the magic. Dark-eyed beauty, classy and sharp, seeks devilish gentle male. Age not important. Box . . .

I read it over and over again—AGE NOT IMPORTANT! I could just see it. I'd answer the ad with this name I always use, "T. Worthington Jones"—I've always thought that sounded a lot better than "Jason Kovak." I would answer the ad of this dark-eyed beauty. We would set up this date. It would be wonderful. There I would be, striding into a dimly lit cocktail lounge with long purposeful strides. I would hesitate a bit by the bar as my eyes scanned the room. In the corner the dark-eyed beauty would lift her eyes to mine. Expectantly she'd cock her head, looking quizzically at me with her deep dark eyes. I would nod to her and cross the room with long purposeful strides. "You must be T. Worthington Jones," she would say.

"Yes, it is I. And you are—?"

"Pamela."

"What a beautiful name, it fits you perfectly," I would say, sitting across from her and meeting her gaze with mine.

"You are so young, T. Worthington."

"Yes, I am."

"I had hoped you would be," she would say, with smoldering eyes. "I have longed for a young man."

"Pamela?"

"Yes, T. Worthington?"

"Let us not waste this precious time with idle chatter—wanna do it?"

"Oh, yes, yes, yes," she says, breathlessly.

I enjoyed daydreaming about Pamela, the dark-eyed beauty. I had a whole lot of delectable fantasies—all in living color. I wished these tantalizing visions had continued forever, but that night I woke up about three in the morning with another kind of dream. Nightmare, that's what it was.

I was all sweaty when I woke up and the covers were a mess. I'd probably been thrashing around, although I didn't remember doing that. But in it, in the dream—nightmare, I mean, because that's what it was—I had been drowning in salad dressing and there were some people with guns shooting lettuce heads, and tomatoes were splattered all over, and it was all red and slimy from the tomatoes, but then it turned into blood. God, it was awful. Then as soon as I was awake, I thought I started hearing things in the house, this creaking noise—noises, noises like someone was breaking in.

"Calm yourself, Jason," I tell myself in this strong voice.

"Oh, shit, I'm scared," I say.

"You just had a bad dream. It's nothing."

"What if it's a robber!"

"Don't be a wimp—it's probably just the furnace or something."

"Or something? Oh, my God."

"Look. Just go upstairs and check it out."

"Yeah. And come face to face with a sawed-off shotgun!"

"Then get a weapon."

"What weapon!"

It went on like this—me talking to myself back and forth like a lunatic while, meanwhile, I am lying there in the messed up covers totally frozen stiff, like I'm dead.

I couldn't move—it seemed like hours. Finally I remembered the set of weights at the end of my bed. I crawled to the end of the bed. Sweat was now pouring off my body and I reached down and grabbed the bar. I went over to the door holding the metal bar in my hand like a club, and I crept out, shaking a lot, and I got as far as the bottom of the basement stairs. I listened there. Everything was real quiet. I just waited, shaking and listening.

"Just go up the goddam stairs," I tell myself.

"Maybe I could run into the bathroom and lock the door and climb out the window."

"Oh, great. And run around the neighborhood in your underpants at three in the morning waving the bar from your weight set."

So I put one foot on the stairs, then another. It was agony. Slowly I climbed them. I listened at each step. And when I didn't hear anything, I'd go up one more step. When I got up to the kitchen, I held the bar over my head with one hand while I switched on the light with the other.

The kitchen was empty. Everything was quiet. So I went from room to room like that. Slowly, through the whole goddam house, putting the lights on in every room. Upstairs, my parents' room was the last room where I had to look. I put one hand on the doorknob and I had the bar over my head. But I froze again.

"Open the door, dummy."

"I'm scared."

"Just do it."

"What if he's in there."

"You would have heard him."

"But he could be in there!"

"Go in and bash him!"

"Oh, crap."

"Do it! You've come this far."

"Oh, what the hell." I held the bar over my head as I whipped open the door and switched on the light.

Empty . . . it was totally empty. For a minute I got real panicky. What had happened to Mom and Dad? But then I remembered that they were out of town.

I saw Dad's golf bag propped up in the corner of the room. So I took the metal bar and I went over to his clubs and just smashed hell out of the bag. I pretended it was a robber or something. BAM! TAKE THAT, YOU DIRTBAG! WHAP!—AND THAT, YOU SCUM!

Then I went back down to the kitchen and got a beer out of the refrigerator and took it down to my room. I left the lights on everywhere in the whole house. It seemed like a good idea—in case there were any robbers out there they'd think there were a whole lot of people home. In my room I sat up in bed and drank the beer. I kind of chugged it. Then I went up to the kitchen and got another one—I chugged it too. I felt kind of sick. I'll bet it was five in the morning before I got back to sleep.

It was the phone ringing next to my bed that finally woke me up. When I picked it up, I saw that the clock on the nightstand said it was one o'clock in the afternoon. I couldn't believe I had slept so late.

"Hello."

"Mr. Jason Kovak?"

"Yes?" I squeaked. Then I cleared my throat and sat up in bed.

"This is Detective Andy Rule—Seattle Police—"

"Uh-huh—"

"I have your name listed as a witness to the robbery yesterday at Wendy's on Mountainview Avenue."

"Uh-huh—"

"We'd like you to come down to headquarters at two thirty today. We have arrested a suspect and we'd like to see if you can make an identification."

"Oh."

"Mr. Kovak?"

"Uh-huh—"

"We haven't been able to locate the other witnesses. No one answers the phone at the numbers we have for them and we've decided to go ahead with you—we'd like to proceed with this as soon as possible."

"Oh."

"We're in the Public Safety Building right downtown on Third, between James and Cherry—can you make that, Mr. Kovak?"

"Oh—uh—"

"We need your help, Mr. Kovak."

"Oh, uh—okay—I guess."

"Take the elevator to the fifth floor, turn left, follow the sign to the phone, then pick it up and let us know you're there."

"Uh-huh."

"See you at two thirty, Mr. Kovak."

When I got off the phone, I thought I was going to throw up. I couldn't believe I had told that man I'd go to police headquarters.

While I took a shower and got dressed, I tried to think of ways to get out of it. Maybe I could call him back and tell him I had suddenly taken sick, that I was deathly ill and wouldn't be able to make it. Actually I did feel sick, but I knew it was because I was deathly afraid to go to police headquarters.

What if that criminal figured out I was the one who put the finger on him and he got out of jail quickly and came after me? I started to sweat just thinking about it. But I was just as scared not to show up—then that detective guy might come after me. I sat around worrying about all of this and then it really hit me. Just yesterday, just a little over twenty-four hours ago, I sat tied up on the floor of the Wendy's pantry looking at large mayonnaise jars, believing I was near death, and what I thought about was not wanting to be a wimp. "Jason," I said to myself, "it's time to keep your promise."

"Right—starting tomorrow."

"Today—quit being a wimp today."

"I said I'd only *try* to quit being a wimp."

"That was a wimpy promise."

"But I'm scared."

"Go there anyway."

I went on like this, just talking to myself back and forth—and I wondered if I was flipping out. I could have just now gone totally nuts from the robbery or something. It's Looney Tunes time at Jason's house, folks.

I kept on talking to myself like that the whole way to the Public Safety Building. When I got to Third and James, I was hoping that maybe I wouldn't be able to find a place to park and then I could just drive around the block forever and the detective would get tired of waiting so he'd decide to cancel the lineup. But I forgot it was Sunday. There were mass parking places everywhere.

I took the elevator to the fifth floor. When I got off, I was in this hallway with tan walls and asphalt tile on the floor. All I saw were a couple of bathrooms and this sign that said CRIMES AGAINST PERSONS and it had an arrow pointing to the left. Just seeing that sign, I got more scared than I already was. I followed the arrow, and at the end of the hall there was a door with a phone on the wall next to it. It wasn't a phone with regular numbers on it, it just had this one button. I picked it up and pushed the button.

"Yes."

"Uh—I'm Jason Ko—"

"Speak up, I can't hear you."

"I'm Jason Kovak, and—"

"Oh, yes. Detective Rule is expecting you. He'll be right with you."

Then I heard a click, so I hung up. I was thinking that it might be a good time to go and get back on the elevator and go home, when the door next to the phone opened. A red-haired guy with a regular shirt and pants on came out and shook hands with me.

"Jason Kovak?"

"Uh-huh."

"I'm Andy Rule—just follow me, son."

We went through the door down another hall and then through some double glass doors. There was a counter with a desk and a typewriter behind it. The detective guy got some forms from out of the desk and explained the lineup to me. He handed me a form. It had eight circles in a row on it and each one was numbered. I was supposed to put an X through the circle which matched the position in the line of the man I thought was the robber. Then I was supposed to check either (1) I'm certain, (2) I can't be sure, or (3) None of the above. He told me he'd ask each man in the lineup to repeat a phrase that had been said during the robbery. Then he told me to wait in that room for a few minutes.

It seemed like hours before he came back, but I suppose it really was only a few minutes.

"We're ready for you, Jason."

"Okay," I squeaked.

"Just follow me."

We went out through the double glass doors and then to a door marked ROOM 529. I followed him in, and it was all dark like an auditorium. It had ten rows with about six seats in each row. Detective Rule and I sat toward the back. I started shaking as soon as these eight men walked in all wearing these one-piece blue coverall-type clothes.

"They can't see you," Detective Rule whispered to me.

"Okay."

As I looked at the lineup, I thought about just checking "None of the above" for all the circles and getting out of there. But I looked over at Detective Rule—he seemed to be trying hard to catch these creeps. So I took a deep breath and decided that I should at least try to calm down and look carefully at each guy.

When I did that, they all looked alike. They all looked rotten. They were all white guys and they all had brownish hair and brown eyes—Detective Rule told me that they had only picked up one suspect and they were hoping to get the other suspect later today.

He made them all stand to the side, and then to the back, and after that he had each one say, "I said shut up." Their voices all sounded equally rotten, but there was one—the third guy from the left—something about him seemed familiar. I looked at his feet and he had on these boots. They looked just like the boots of the guy that had kicked Henry. Remembering Henry getting kicked made me mad. I stared at the guy for a long time—I couldn't be sure about his face but his voice seemed right and so did his boots. I took the pencil Detective Rule had given me and I put an X in the third circle from the left. Then under it I checked where it said "I can't be sure."

"Need any more time, son?"

"No." I handed the form to him and we left the auditorium.

"I'm sorry I couldn't be sure."

"That's okay, Jason. I appreciate your volunteering to come down here and help us out. That takes some guts."

"Yeah?"

"A lot of folks won't do it—don't want to get involved, you know. People are scared."

"Yeah, I guess some people might be." (Ha)

Detective Rule held out his hand and shook hands with me again. He was nice. "Thanks for your time, son."

"Okay."

In the elevator on the way out of the building I thought I

might throw up, but then I started whistling "Macho Macho Man" from one of my old Village People albums. I felt better when I did that and I whistled it all the way home, and when I got home I went down to my room and read the ad from the dark-eyed beauty again.

Then I decided to press a few pounds with my weight set. I got all the way up to 160—I'd never done that much before—and I said to myself, "Jason, today the police station, tomorrow Pamela, the dark-eyed beauty!"

JEAN DAVIES OKIMOTO

Jean Davies Okimoto, originally from Cleveland, Ohio, lives in Seattle with her psychiatrist husband. Between them they have four children and a dog named LaVerne. In addition to being an author, she has been a high school teacher of remedial reading, an assistant to the director of a Youth Services Bureau, and is a psychotherapist in private practice.

Along with those activities, her sense of humor contributes greatly to her novels for young adults. (Her first husband was almost kicked out of the air force because of the satirical articles she wrote for the Officers' Wives Club magazine.) The most notable elements in her novels, however, are the sensitive family relationships.

Her novels for young adults include *My Mother Is Not Married to My Father*, the story of an eleven-year-old girl's anger and confusion about —and eventual acceptance of—her parents' divorce. In its sequel, *It's Just Too Much*, the girl has to deal with her mother's remarriage, two stepbrothers, and the onset of puberty. That book won the Washington Governor's Writers' Award in 1982.

Norman Schnurman, Average Person, her third book, also focuses on family problems, but this time from the point of view of a sixth-grade boy. Norman feels forced by his father to play football when his own greatest interests are video games and garage sales. Norman just can't be what his father wants him to be. Suspense and humor fill *Who Did It, Jenny Lake?* Sixteen-year-old Jenny and her friend solve a murder mystery that disrupts their vacation in Hawaii.

Jean Okimoto's latest novel for young adults is *Jason's Women*, which includes and further develops the story "Jason Kovak, the Quick and the Brave."

Sometimes what you expect is very different from what you get. But Fan didn't think about that when she agreed to go with Richie to the cemetery. . . .

WHAT HAPPENED IN THE CEMETERY

NORMA FOX MAZER

As a child, Fan Steptoe had been firmly convinced that sex happened only at night, in the dark. Of course she wasn't a child anymore, but the notion had persisted: the linking of sex and darkness. Maybe because Fan herself was pretty much in the dark about sex. Well, to be absolutely straight, she didn't know diddley boo about the fascinating subject.

When she was nine or ten she'd had a discussion with her two best friends, Beth Lazev and Jaime Fuller. "Look," Jaime explained, "it's nighttime, see, and the man and the lady are in bed and he's got his thing—stop laughing! I'm telling you something!" Beth and Fan looked at each other and nearly choked. "He's got his thing," Jaime went on, "and she's got—you know!" She swatted herself, causing Fan and Beth to go into convulsions of laughter again. When they quieted down, Jaime went on with her lecture. "And they kiss. And *then*"—she dropped her voice to a whisper.

"Oh, gross!" Beth groaned.

"It's like nature," Jaime said. "He plants a seed." She looked at Fan. "Your parents did it six times."

Fan's face got as hot as fire. "I don't think my parents do that!"

"Six times," Jaime said. She frowned. "Did you have any other brothers and sisters?"

Fan stared at her. Jaime knew she didn't. Tim and Phil were in the navy. Laura was grown up and living in New York City. At home it was her, Martha, and Sue.

"Fan! Did your mother ever have a baby that died?"

Fan shook her head.

"Okay! Then your parents did it six times. And yours"—she turned to Beth—"did it *two* times. And mine, because my mother had a miscarriage besides me and Neil," she said importantly, "did it *three* times. They like doing it," she added.

Fan switched her braids over her shoulder. "They like doing it?" She didn't believe it.

"Yes."

"You telling me they *like* doing that?"

"Yes!" And as a clincher, Jaime said, "My mother told me so." Since Jaime's mother was a teacher, Fan shut up.

Maybe, Fan thought later, it was like cooking. Some people liked cooking. Some didn't. Her mother said she was half and half about cooking. Half of her liked to cook, half of her didn't like to. "If I could cook less, I'd like it more. Any of you guys want to stop eating for a while?" Whenever Fan's mother said that, Fan's father reminded her that once a week he made fish stew and she didn't have to do a thing except clean up the kitchen.

Fan herself liked baking. Even though it was silly, she still sometimes made up stories as she mixed cookie dough or beat the egg whites. "How do you do, I'm Mrs. Flour." "So pleased to meet you, Mrs. Flour. I'm Mr. Sugar. I'm sure we're going to get along." "Mmm, mmm, you're sweet, Mr. Sugar." "Well, thank you, Mrs. Flour. You're cute too." "Tee hee. Let's get mixed up together!"

Was sex like that? Like sugar and flour? Like following a recipe? (Only how did you follow a recipe in the dark?) Or was it more like what her grandmother said when Fan asked her how she made her apricot raisin cookies. "Fan, how do I know? A pinch of this, a pinch of that, and it's done."

Oh. A pinch of this and a pinch of that and it was done—and yummy! But the afternoon she went to the cemetery in Richie Roberts's car, what Fan remembered afterwards was the time she'd followed a recipe for Creamy Vanilla Wonder Cake. It had sounded so special, but when it was done, the cake wasn't either creamy or wonderful. A big disappointment. Fan had slashed an X across the recipe with a red crayon.

Too bad she couldn't red-X Richie the same way, red-X right

through Richie Roberts and that afternoon like a bad recipe. In a way, though, Fan wasn't at all surprised about the cemetery. Why should things have gone well on that afternoon when everything else had been going haywire for so long?

First her sister Martha had moved out of the house. Fan knew she should have been prepared for that. Months before, Martha had graduated from Community College of the Mountains as a dental hygienist and since then she'd been looking for work. Still, when Martha moved down to Schenectady, Fan was shocked. Now, out of the six Steptoe kids, only she and Sue were left at home.

Then her father's heart went bad. Nobody expected it. Kevin Steptoe was a big man, over six feet tall, with round powerful arms. Once, going downtown, Fan had stopped at a work site to watch an old brick building being demolished. The huge round metal ball on the derrick swung through the air. The building groaned. Bricks rained to the ground. Then Fan saw that it was her father operating the derrick, sitting high in the cab. "Daddy!" She waved, but he didn't see her.

After he got too weak to work, he was home all the time.

And right about that same time, a new girl, Cecily Rowder, came to school and got friendly with Beth. Another shock. Jamie had moved away years ago, but Beth and Fan had gone on being best friends. Now suddenly it was Beth and Cecily—and Fan hanging around the edges of their friendship, like a little dog trying to get under a fence.

Fan's father didn't work for almost a year before his open heart surgery. Everything at home had changed. Her mother took a second job. The living room was her father's room—dim, shades down all day, the TV always on, a blue blur. Then, when Fan couldn't imagine anything else happening, Sue went to live with Martha in Schenectady and finish high school there. Fan felt weird, all alone in the upstairs. Her footsteps sounded so loud. The whole house sounded different. It looked different. It even smelled different.

Fan's mother noticed that she didn't bring friends home anymore. "Bring your friends home, Fan," she said. "We don't want to act like this is a sickhouse. You want to be cheerful around your father, act normal, you know what I mean? He's going to get better. It just takes time." She jiggled her keys and glanced at the clock. She was always running.

Fan gulped a glass of milk. "Sure, Mom."

After Fan's father came home from the hospital, there was an article in the newspaper about him. FORMER CONSTRUCTION WORKER HOPEFUL SURGERY WILL RESTORE HIS STRENGTH. And a picture showing Kevin Steptoe sitting up in a chair in the living room in his bathrobe and hardhat.

Every day he walked around the living room and through the dining room and into the kitchen and then out to the hall to look at the steps to the second floor. He couldn't make it up them yet. "But that's okay, you will," Fan's mother said. And Fan's father added, "Now that I'm back from the living dead."

That was how he put it to the friends and relatives who came to visit. "For a year I was near dead. Getting weaker and weaker. I was fading out. I was one of the living dead. Now I'm alive again. It's a miracle."

Fan's mother promised that when her father was well again, they'd all go out to eat pizza and play pool at Grancy's again. Fan nodded, didn't say it would all be different, just the three of them —nothing like old times when their family had been a whole mob scene by itself. Quite some evenings! Her dad, strutting around, smiling, instructing everyone, showing Fan and Sue how to hold the cue stick. The very first time she played pool, Fan, eyes narrowed, had sent a yellow ball flying into a green ball and everybody laughed and screamed as the green ball bounded across the felt and landed smoothly in a pocket. "Hey, champ!" her father had said and he'd given her a big hug.

The afternoon they took their tenth-grade basic-skills test, Fan come home afterwards with Beth and Cecily. She'd lured them with the promise of the fresh Dutch chocolate cake she'd baked the night before. They clattered up on the porch, walked into the living room. The couch was littered with blankets and science fiction magazines, pill bottles, empty glasses, and old tissues. The TV was on, as usual. Racing cars tore around a track and puffs of smoke and dust filled the screen.

"Hello, Daddy," Fan said. "This is Cecily. You know Beth."

"Hello, girls." Sitting in the flowered armchair in his green-and-white striped pajamas, Fan's father smoothed down his thinning blond hair. "Been working hard in school?"

Beth and Cecily knocked against each other. Cecily had red lips, bright red nails. "Cecily's just *gorgeous*!" the girls in school told each other.

Fan shoved Beth and Cecily toward the kitchen. She was afraid her father would start his back-from-the-living-dead speech.

"Sit down," he said. "I don't have much company." His hand went up, then fell down to the arm of the chair, a limp flag of welcome. "Girls, I'm on vacation. Just got operated on. Nice, huh? Just sitting around, letting people wait on me and showing off my scar." With that, Fan's father whipped up his pajama top to show a ladder of violent purple stitches running down the middle of his chest, from throat to navel.

"Let's go in the kitchen," Fan said. Her face and chest burned.

"Nice scar, girls? That's where they sliced me open. I'm supposed to be good as new pretty soon. If not, maybe I'll go into business, charge fifty cents a look at my scar."

Fan ran into the kitchen, banging the door against the wall. "Are you coming?" she yelled. The cake was in its baking pan on the counter, covered with wax paper. She heard Beth and Cecily whispering. "Cake's ready!" In the kitchen Beth and Cecily kept shoving each other and laughing a lot.

"What's the matter with you two?" Fan said. She felt sick. She put milk and glasses on the table.

"Noth-ing," Cecily sang out, crumbling a little piece of cake delicately with her long red nails. "Just noth-ing!" And she and Beth burst out laughing.

"So what's the big joke?" Fan stuffed cake in her mouth. Her heart thumped violently. Maybe she was having a heart attack. She imagined herself with a ladder of purple stitches running between her breasts.

"No joke, just enjoying life," Beth said. This caused another outburst of laughter between her and Cecily.

Cecily was a talker. By tomorrow everyone in school would know about Fan's father showing off his scar.

Beth reached for the cake knife, but Fan stood up and took the pan of cake off the table.

"I want another piece," Beth said. She wasn't shy in Fan's house. She'd been here too many times.

"You can't have any more," Fan said.

"Why not?" She and Cecily looked at each other, suppressing laughter.

"Because I say so."

"What's your problem, Fan?" Beth said. She rolled her eyes at Cecily.

"Oh, you and your stupid giggling. You're the one with a problem."

"Is that so? Well, Fan, for your information, you give me a pain where I definitely don't need a pain."

Beth and Cecily left. Fan sat at the kitchen table, her hand over her heart, listening.

After a while Fan's father stopped showing off his scar and talking about the miracle of being alive. He wasn't getting his strength back. He was alive all right, but not alive the way he wanted to be. The miracle wasn't miraculous enough for Kevin Steptoe, who wanted to be the same old Kevin he'd been before his heart played its dirty trick on him. He wanted to go to work every morning, bring home a big paycheck every Friday, cruise around in his car and play baseball Sunday afternoons in Moneghega Park with the other guys from the job. "Come on, big guy!" his teammates would yell as Kevin threw down the bat and raced around the bases.

"Just don't mention work to him," Fan's mother said. Her father sat in the chair in his striped pajamas and no longer showed off his scar or boasted he'd come back from the living dead.

One day Fan came home and he wasn't in the livingroom. "Dad?" She went into the kitchen. He was there, sitting at the table, crying. A fly threw itself against the window. There was an empty cup in front of him. On the stove the teapot shrilled.

"Dad?"

He didn't move. The living dead. He sat there, looking out the window, his mouth half open, crying silently.

Fan thought her chest might burst apart. "Daddy." He knew she was there. He knew she was watching him cry. Why didn't he rise up, raise his hand, raise his voice, tell her to get the hell out of there, Fan, and leave a man alone?

She put the tea kettle on a cold burner. "Do you want tea?" He didn't answer. "Daddy!" He had to stop crying. The floor surged under her feet like an ocean. The waters were rising and she flung out her arms to save herself. "Daddy, remember that time you threw me in the water? Remember? I couldn't swim. I was afraid of the water and you threw me off the dock."

Everyone was swimming, everyone except her; they were all in the water, paddling away. Sue was floating like a cork. Her father had picked Fan up, hugged her. "Look at your brothers and sisters, kiddo. They're not afraid."

Fan had squeezed her father back. He smelled so good. He smelled like cigarettes and hot sun and burned toast. "I can swim," she said. "If I want to. I don't want to."

"Aw, don't try to fool your old man, Fan. You can't swim."

"I can too."

She shouldn't have said it.

He swung her out over the water. "Okay. Show me how good you can swim." He threw her in. Fan had time for a single moment of shocked disbelief, then she hit the water and went under. I'm going to die, she thought. She thrashed up to the surface. "Swim," she heard her father yell. "Swim, damn it!" She went under again. Her feet scraped bottom mud. She clawed the water, popped through to air. Her father grabbed her arms, pulled her up on the dock. "I didn't see you swim, big mouth."

Her eyes and throat burned. "I can swim," she whispered foolishly, defiantly. Through her blurred lashes, her father, bare hairy legs bent toward her, looked like a giant.

"Hey, Fanfan." He roughed up her wet head. "You can't go around in life saying you can do things you can't do. Otherwise you're going to be knocked around and down and out for the count. You hear me? Pay attention. I'm giving you some good advice. You get knocked down enough times, you won't want to get up, and in this world you always gotta get up."

"I'll get up," Fan said. Her nose dripped and she hated her father.

Hated him and loved him. That's how she felt now, seeing him sitting there at the table, crying. "Stop crying," she said. "Get up. You have to get up."

He paid her no attention. He didn't hear her—maybe he couldn't hear her. He cried silently, in mourning for his life.

Fan walked away in a dull fever whose heat and faint light illuminated dark corners. Just then she seemed to understand everything—why people got buzzed, did drugs, totaled their cars, shoplifted. All of it, all the craziness, for the simple pleasure of not caring, of just—*letting it happen.*

That was why, if there was any one particular reason, she went with Richie Roberts to the cemetery. So that whatever was going to happen would—just *happen.*

She was on her way home, walking as slowly as possible, not wanting to get home, when Richie drove by in his little banged-up red Datsun. Fan thought, If I had a car, I could go someplace. Maybe she said it out loud? Or waved to Richie? She didn't think so, but he stopped, squealing the brakes, and stuck his head out the window. "Want a ride?"

They were in the same math class but had never spoken. Had passed each other in the halls hundreds of times, maybe thousands, and never spoken. Fan stared at him.

"Want a ride?" he said again. And she got in the car. It was something to do.

He pulled away from the curb, drove sedately down the street. Fan glanced at him briefly. He had a hawk nose that ran before his face. He drove with one hand on the wheel, the other hooked on the top of the open window.

"You're Fan Steptoe."

She nodded.

"I'm Richie Roberts."

"I know."

"We're in the same math class."

"Right."

He drove up one street, down another. Both hands were on the wheel now. Looking straight ahead, he said, "So what do you say? You want to go to the cemetery?"

All the tantalizing whispers overheard in halls and locker rooms rushed through Fan's head. *Patti and Vince, Saturday night in the cemetery. . . . Did you hear about Mindy . . . what happened in the cemetery?*

The sum total of Fan's experience: she had kissed a few boys, let them press against her. Once made out for hours at a party at Beth's house with a visiting cousin of Beth's. She'd come home late, tiptoed past her parents' bedroom door.

"Fan?"

"Yes."

"You're late."

"I know. I'm sorry."

Silence. Then, from her father, "I'll talk to you in the morning."

But in the morning it was her mother who took her down for not keeping her curfew. "You know we worry about you. Anything could have happened."

"I was at Beth's."

"Did you want me to call and check up on you?"

"No!"

"All right, then, you see!"

Fan didn't, but she said what she knew she had to say. "Sorry. I'm sorry. It won't happen again."

It hadn't. Not because she'd willed it or wanted it. It was just that nothing had happened to her. Nothing. Nothing. Nothing. She might as well still be nine years old! Ignorant! Yet there were girls who laughed with every word, laughed as if they knew everything Fan didn't know. Everything she wanted to know, everything that would fill the empty spaces created by her father's illness.

"You want to go to the cemetery?" Richie said again.

"Okay," she said.

"Yeah?" Richie sounded amazed. "Okay?" He whipped the car around, almost ran a red light.

"Well, don't get us killed," Fan said.

In the cemetery Richie tucked the car away on a service road overhung with ancient dark trees. "So how's this?"

Fan shivered. The air was greenish, almost black—dank, like the inside of a cave. "It's okay."

Richie twanged his nose, looked delighted. He jumped out of the car.

What now? Fran slid under the wheel. She should really learn to drive. Her father would have taught her by now if he hadn't gotten sick. Her mother could teach her but didn't have the time.

Richie popped back in on the passenger side, holding out a blanket to Fan.

"I'm not cold," Fan said.

"It's not for—it's for, you know—to, uh—"

Fan looked out the window, irritated that she had said something stupid. Given away what a dope ignoramus she was. She looked at him. If he was laughing, she was leaving.

"What's the matter?" Richie said. "You okay?" He moved closer to her, dropped his arm around her shoulder. "We're gonna—you want to, don't you?"

He started kissing her in a brisk manner. Was this how it started? His kisses were noisy. She wished it were more . . . well, *something*. Maybe if he would stop talking. Or maybe if he would talk, but say different things. *Darling, I've dreamed of you for so long* . . . Except that would be a lie. Fan didn't like lies.

Richie pushed her down on the seat and put both hands over her breasts. His delighted face hung over hers, giving her a closeup technicolor view of a pimple on his forehead.

"I never have," she said.

"What?"

"Uh—" She didn't want to repeat it.

"I thought you said—"

"What'd I say? What?"

"Hey, listen, hey, did you ever hear the joke about the boy and the girl playing in the bathtub? The boy says let's play cars, I'll be the driver and you'll be the—"

"I heard that in third grade," Fan said.

Was this it, then? Was this what everyone talked about and everyone wanted? Was this the secret stuff, the good stuff?

Scrunched up in the front seat of a car, with the steering wheel threatening to decapitate her and this boy she hardly knew breathing moistly all over her? Fan shoved at Richie.

"Hey, come on," he said, lifting his head. "Come on. What, are you getting tense or something?"

Fan thought about it. "Or something," she said.

She looked over Richie's shoulder, out the window. A robin flew up in front of the car. Her heart flew up with it. She'd wanted to jolt the world loose, let something happen—or maybe make it happen by giving up, giving in, letting go. A change— that was what she'd wanted, things to be different. Instead, here she was, the worm in Richie's beak.

She pushed him again, then squirmed out from under him, landing on the floor. "Hey, where you going?" he said. She opened the door and slid out of the car, Fan the worm, slithering and sliding, half falling to the ground.

"Home," she said, standing up. She took a few steps. "Where do you think I'm going?"

"Well, don't think I'm driving you," he yelled after her.

Fan hunched her shoulders and kept walking. Not once had he said her name. Even if he had—she started laughing, hard embarrassed giggles mixing with tears. What a fool she must have looked crawling out of the car! And who would he tell? Was everyone going to know?

She wiped her eyes. The sky was blue above the trees. And Fan, at heart an optimist, as her father had once been, and a believer, as her mother still was, thought: Well, what could I do? Had to get out of there some way. And she walked on, lifting her arms to the sky, as if it were her true love.

NORMA FOX MAZER

Norma Mazer's novels explore a variety of topics: the effects of divorce on children *(I, Trissy)*, problems of aging *(A Figure of Speech)*, self-image *(Mrs. Fish, Ape, and Me, the Dump Queen)*, and teenage sexual conflicts *(Up in Seth's Room)*. She has also written about a modern teenage girl in a prehistoric setting *(Saturday, the Twelfth of October)*, the problems two college students face when they move in together *(Someone to Love)*, how the love between two teenagers is affected when the girl discovers that her boyfriend's mother was the driver who accidentally killed her sister a year earlier *(When We First Met)*, and what happens when a divorced father steals his young daughter from her mother *(Taking Terri Mueller)*. That novel won the Edgar Allan Poe Award for Best Juvenile Mystery in 1982 and recently won the California Young Readers' Award.

Critical acclaim has also been bestowed on Mazer's two short-story collections, *Dear Bill, Remember Me? and Other Stories* and *Summer Girls, Love Boys and Other Short Stories,* the first of which was chosen as a *New York Times* Outstanding Book of the Year as well as an American Library Association Best Book for Young Adults.

Norma Fox Mazer grew up in Glens Falls, New York, and now lives in the Pompey Hills with her writer husband, Harry, with whom she wrote *The Solid Gold Kid,* another ALA Best Book for Young Adults. *Downtown,* the story of what happens when a young man's love for a girl forces him to reveal a dark secret about his parents' past, was also listed as an ALA Best Book for Young Adults and a *New York Times* Notable Book.

One of Mazer's recent novels resulted from her being one of three sisters and having three daughters; it is appropriately called *Three Sisters. A, My Name Is Ami* is her most recent novel.

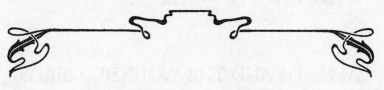

CONFLICTS

Her mother's radio program provides sensitive, helpful advice for emotionally troubled callers. But having a famous psychotherapist for a mother is no comfort to Amanda. . . .

AMANDA AND THE WOUNDED BIRDS

COLBY RODOWSKY

It's not that my mother doesn't understand, because she does. In fact, she understands so well, and so much, and so single-mindedly, that half the time she goes around with a glazed look in her eyes and forgets to get her hair cut, and go to the dentist and that we're almost out of toilet paper or tuna fish.

She makes her living understanding, which may make more sense when I tell you that my mother is Dr. Emma Hart. Now, if that doesn't help, then probably, like me until my consciousness was raised, you've always thought of radio as the place to hear the Top 40 or sometimes the weather report when you're heading for the shore on a summer Friday afternoon. But just try twiddling the dial and you'll find her, way over to the left on the band, next to the country and western station.

Maybe what I should do is go back a little and explain. You see, my mother is a psychotherapist, which means that she counsels people and tries to help them find ways of dealing with their problems. She's also a widow. My father died when I was a baby, and sometimes I try to imagine what it must have been like for her, taking care of a baby alone and trying to establish a practice all at the same time. One thing I'm sure of is that knowing Mom, she handled it gracefully, and stoically, and with that funny way she has of biting her lower lip so that for all her hanging-in-there attitude she still looks like a ten-year-old kid—the kind you want to do something for because she's not always whining or sniffling. I guess you'd have to say that as much as possible my mother is in charge of her own life, which is the way she tries to get the people who call in to her on the radio to be.

The way the radio program got started was that several years ago the producer was looking for something to put on in the late afternoon when people were mostly fixing dinner or driving carpool or just sitting with their feet up. It wasn't exactly prime time. Then he remembered how he'd heard Mom speak at a dinner once and had thought at the time that putting someone like her on radio would be a real public service. Besides, the ratings couldn't be any lower than they had been for the Handy Home Fixit show he'd had on before. Anyway, he tracked her down, arranged for a test, and then Mom was on the air.

I never will forget that first show. I mean, there was my mother's voice coming out of our kitchen radio, sounding slightly frantic and giving those first callers more than they bargained for: I guess she was afraid if she let them off the line there wouldn't *be* any more. That day even the producer called with a question. And the boy in the studio who went for coffee. But Mom hung in there, and calls continued to come in, and then they started backing up, and it wasn't long before people opened by saying, "I didn't think I'd *ever* get through to you." After only a month on the air the Emma Hart show went from one hour to two; and the way I figured it, a lot of people were eating dinner later than they ever had before. Including us.

Mom really cared about the people who telephoned her, and almost right from the beginning she was calling them her "wounded birds." Not on the air, of course, and *never* to anyone but me. I got used to her looking up in the middle of dinner or from watching the late news on TV and saying, "I hope my wounded bird with the abusive husband will get herself into counseling" or "The wounded bird with those children who walk all over her had better learn to assert herself before it's too late." And *I* sure learned not to joke around: once I referred to one of her callers as a fractured canary and almost started World War III.

Not long after this, things really started to happen. First, Mom's show was moved to a better time slot. Then it was syndicated, so that she wasn't just on the air here but in a bunch of other cities, too. The way "Doonesbury" and "Dick Tracy" are in a bunch of newspapers. Now, I have to say that for the most part my mother's pretty cool about things, but the day she found out that the Emma Hart show was being syndicated she just about flipped. She called me from the studio and told me to meet her at the Terrace Garden for dinner, to be sure and get spiffed up because we were going all out.

During dinner Mom spent a lot of time staring into the candlelight and smiling to herself. Finally she said, "Just think of all those people who'll be listening now." And let me tell you, I *was* thinking about them, and it worried me a lot. I mean the way I saw it, there were going to be even more problems: more victims who were downtrodden or misunderstood. More stories about people who had been abused or who had kids on drugs or dropping out, or ne'er-do-well relatives moving in. But when I tried to say that, Mom was suddenly all attention. "Don't be silly, Amanda. It's the same amount of time and the same number of calls—you'll hardly notice any difference. Only now I'll have wounded birds in Phoenix and Pittsburgh and Philadelphia."

In one way she was right: the show sounded pretty much the same. (Except that *I* found out that when your husband/lover/friend walks out on you it hurts as much in Peoria as it does in Perth Amboy.)

In another way she was wrong: she was busier than she had ever been before, what with traveling and lecturing and doing guest shows from other cities. For a while there, it was as if I was spending as much time at my best friend Terri's as I was at my own house. Then eventually Mom decided I could stay at our place when she had to be out of town, as long as Terri stayed there with me, which wasn't as good or as bad as it sounds, because Terri lives right across the street and her mother has X-ray eyes. I mean we can hardly manage to reach for our favorite breakfast of Twinkies and Oreo ice cream with an orange juice chaser before her mother is on the telephone telling us to eat cornflakes instead—and to wash the dishes.

Sometimes I felt that life was nothing but a revolving door: Mom going out while I was coming in. I know there are some kids who would've thought I was lucky, but the thing about my mother is that she's okay. And I wanted to see more of her. Besides that, I needed to talk to her. I don't know why, but all of a sudden it seemed that things were piling up around me. No major crises, you understand. Nothing that would exactly stop traffic.

I'll give you an example.

Take my friend Terri. I have a terrible feeling that she has a secret crush on my boyfriend Josh. If she does, it would be a disaster, because how could we really be friends anymore? But then again how could Terri and I *not* be friends? I'm not sure *why* I think this, unless it's because she gets quiet and acts bored when I talk about him a lot—the way you do when you don't want to let on about liking someone. I mean she couldn't *really* be bored. Could she?

Then there's Miss Spellman, my English teacher, who has this really atrocious breath and is forever leaning into people as she reads poetry in class. Imagine somebody breathing garbage fumes on you as she recites Emily Dickinson. If something doesn't happen soon I may never like poetry again.

Now, maybe these aren't world problems, any more than the incident with the guidance counselor was, but it bugged me all the same. Our school has an obsession about students getting into *good* colleges a.s.a.p. and knowing what they want to do with the rest of their lives (Terri and I call it the life-packaging syndrome). Anyway, this particular day I was coming out of gym on my way to study hall when Mr. Burnside, the guidance counselor, stopped me and started asking me all this stuff, like what my career goals were and had I decided what I wanted to major in in college.

What I said (only politer than it sounds here) was that how did I know what I wanted to major in when I didn't even know where I wanted to *go* to college. Mr. Burnside got a wild look in his eyes and started opening and closing his mouth so that all I could see was a shiny strand of spit running between his top and bottom teeth while he lectured me on how I was going about this whole college thing the wrong way. He said I should come into the guidance office someday and let him feed me into the computer—well, not me exactly, but stuff like my grades, extra curricular activities, and whether or not I needed financial aid.

"And what does your mother say?" he asked as he rooted in his pocket for a late pass to get me into study hall. "You'll certainly have it easier than anybody else in your class, or the school either for that matter—living with Dr. Emma Hart." He laughed that horselaugh of his and slapped me on the back. "She'll get right to the *Hart* of it." Another laugh. "Anybody else'd have to call her on the telephone." His laughter seemed to follow me all the way to study hall. I even heard it bouncing around in my head as I settled down to do my Spanish.

"Anybody else'd have to call her on the telephone," he had said.

Why not? I thought as I was walking home from school.

Why not? I asked myself when Josh and I were eating popcorn and playing Scrabble on the living room floor that night.

And pretty soon *why not?* changed to *when?* The answer to that one was easy though, because spring vacation was only a week and a half away and that would give me the perfect opportunity.

The funny thing was that once I'd decided to do it, I never worried about getting through. Maybe that was because I'd heard Mom say plenty of times that they always liked it when kids called into the show, and I guess I figured that unless everybody on spring vacation decided to call the Dr. Emma Hart Show, I wouldn't have any trouble. Besides, I practiced in the shower making my voice huskier than usual and just a little breathless, hoping that it would sound sincere and make an impression on Jordan, the guy who screens the calls and tries for just the right balance of men, women, and kids, with not too much emphasis on busted romances as opposed to anxiety attacks.

The next funny thing was that once I'd made up my mind to call Dr. Emma Hart, I began to feel like a wounded bird myself, and I was suddenly awfully glad that she cared about them the way she did. I had a little trouble deciding what I wanted to ask her on the show, and even before I could make up my mind I began to think of other things that bothered me too. Not problems, but stuff I'd like to talk over with Mom. Like Vietnam, for example. I'd watched *Apocalypse Now* on TV and there was a lot I didn't understand. And what about the sixties?—was Mom ever involved in sit-ins or walkouts or any of that? I somehow doubted it, but it would be important to know for sure. Finally it came to me: what I wanted to ask Dr. Hart about was not being able to talk to Mom because there she was all wrapped up with her wounded birds. Only the whole thing got confusing, one being the other and all.

Anyway, I did it. I put the call in just before eleven on the Monday morning of spring vacation and almost chickened out when Jordan answered. I had met him a couple of times down at the studio, and I could almost see him now, looking like some kind of an intense juggler who is trying to keep everything going at once. I heard my voice, as if it were coming from somewhere far away, giving my name as Claire (it's my middle name) and outlining my problem. When I got finished, Jordan said that he was putting me on hold and not to go away, that Dr. Hart would be with me shortly.

And all of a sudden she was. I mean, there I was talking to my own mother and telling her how I couldn't talk to my mother, and how the things I wanted to talk to her about weren't actually big deals anyway, but still—.

Dr. Hart let me go on for a while and then she broke in and said that it was important for me to know that my concerns were as real as anybody else's and it sounded as if my mother and I had a pretty good relationship that had just gotten a little off the track and what I had to do was be really up-front with her and let her know how I felt. Then she suggested that I make a date with my mother for lunch so that I could tell her (Mom) exactly what I'd told her (Dr. Emma Hart), and that I should be sure to call back and let her know how it worked out.

After that I said, "Okay," and "Thank you." Then I hung up.

The only trouble was that as soon as Mom got home that day I knew it wasn't going to work.

She was sort of coming unglued. It had been a bad day, she told me. One of her private patients was in the midst of a crisis; the producer of the show was having a fight with his wife and wanted to tell Mom all about it. She had a dinner speech to give Saturday night and didn't have a thought about what to say, and my uncle Alex had called from Scranton to ask Mom to try to talk some sense into his teenage son, who was driving them all crazy.

Then she looked at me and said, "Thank heavens you've got it all together."

Talk about guilt. Right away I knew I was going to break rule number one: I wasn't going to be able to be up-front.

The thing was, I knew I couldn't take what was already one rotten week for Mom and dump all my problems (which seemed to be getting bigger by the minute) on her. Even though I felt like I was going to explode.

By Friday I knew I needed another talk with Dr. Hart. After all, she'd said to call back, hadn't she?

Getting through Jordan was even easier the second time. All I had to say was that I'd spoken to Dr. Hart earlier in the week and that she'd said to let her know what happened.

"Oh, good, a success story," Jordan said right away, jumping to conclusions. I guess he knew what kind of a week it had been too. "Hold on; Dr. Hart will be with you soon," he said.

And there was Dr. Emma Hart again. And suddenly there *I* was, unloading about how what she had suggested wasn't going to work.

"Why not?" she wanted to know. "Did you try?"

"Yes—no," I said. Then I was going on again, all about Bad-Breath Spellman, the guidance counselor, and how maybe my best friend had a thing for my boyfriend. She kept steering me back to the subject of my mother and why I hadn't arranged to have lunch with her.

I said that my mother had had a bad week. That she was swamped, preoccupied, distracted, and running behind. And then it happened. I mean, I heard the words sliding off my lips and couldn't stop them. I said, "The thing about my mother is that she has all these wounded birds who have really important problems and they take all the time she has."

A silence ballooned up between us and was so loud I couldn't hear anything else—and if you know anything about radio, you know that the worst thing that can happen is silence. It lasted forever, and while it was going on I gave serious thought to running away from home, or at least hanging up.

When Mom finally spoke, her voice sounded choked, as if she had swallowed a gumball.

"We've been talking to Claire this morning, who is really Amanda," she said. "And one of the things we talk a lot about on this show is saying what you have to say—even if that's not always easy. Are you still there, Amanda?"

"Yes," I squeaked.

"If I know Amanda," my mother went on, "she would rather have run away, or hung up, but instead she did something harder. She hung on."

I gulped.

"Amanda is my daughter, and it seems we have some things to talk about, so what I'm going to do is to ask my assistant to make a reservation for lunch at the Terrace Garden." Then it sounded as though Mom had moved in closer to the microphone and was speaking just to me. "If you hurry, Amanda, I'll meet you at 1:30. So we can talk."

And we did: about Bad-breath Spellman, and Terri, and how it's okay not to know now what I want to do with the rest of my life.

We talked about saving the whales, and our two weeks at the shore this summer, and how some day we're going to Ireland. About books and movies and the time in fourth grade when I got the chicken pox and Mom caught them from me.

And we talked about how we had missed talking to each other and what we could do about it.

We ate lunch slowly, and took ages deciding on dessert, and ages more eating it.

We sat there all afternoon, until the light streaking in the windows changed from yellow to a deep, burning gold and the busboys started setting the tables for dinner.

COLBY RODOWSKY

The children and young adults in the books of Colby Rodowsky are perceptive and sensitive characters who find themselves in difficult situations. For example, there is fifteen-year-old Dorrie, who learns to come to terms with her embarrassment and resentment about her younger brother, a victim of Down's syndrome. Then there is fourteen-year-old Thad (in *A Summer's Worth of Shame*), whose father is put into prison for embezzlement, causing Thad all kinds of embarrassment and understandable anger.

P.S. Write Soon follows the development of Tanner, a twelve-year-old girl who copes with her heavy leg brace by pretending to her pen pal that she leads an active, exciting life—until her pen pal comes to visit her. And in *H. My Name Is Henley*, a twelve-year-old girl, grown weary and frustrated over her irresponsible mother's need to move frequently, one day refuses to accompany her mother, finding security eventually in the home of an "aunt" and an old woman.

Rodowsky's most unusual character is nine-year-old Mudge (in *The Gathering Room*), who lives in the gatehouse of a historic cemetery with his parents, who are the caretakers. In the gathering room (the mourners' waiting room), the lonely and isolated Mudge imagines the inhabitants of the cemetery as his playmates. This book was named a Notable Book for Children by the American Library Association in 1981.

Colby Rodowsky is also the author of *Evy-Ivy-Over*, *Keeping Time*, and most recently, *Julie's Daughter*. She was born in Baltimore, lived in New York and Washington, D.C., taught third grade and then special education, and returned to Baltimore, where she now lives with her husband, who is a judge on the Maryland Court of Appeals. They have five daughters and a son.

Running away seems to be the only alternative to Josh. He's tired of his parents' nagging. His best friend is moving to California as soon as the semester is over. There is nothing to keep him here any longer. . . .

PLAYING GOD

OUIDA SEBESTYEN

He was almost to the river, walking fast, when he saw Laurel on her bicycle, racing to catch him. In a space between the gusts of raw March wind she yelled, "Josh, wait up, or I'll break your legs."

So he wasn't going to get away without saying good-bye after all.

Laurel came puffing up, fierce and wind-whipped. He braced himself as she stared at the duffel bag he'd taken from his folks' closet and stuffed with all the clothes and things he thought he'd need.

"You're doing it," she said. The pain that came into her eyes hurt him, too. "Why? Without telling me? I thought we were friends! If I hadn't seen you sneaking through the alley—"

We *are* friends, he wanted to assure her. Best friends. The best. But he said, walking on, "So? One more thing I didn't do right today." Suddenly it came pouring out. "At breakfast they jumped down my throat about my grades. Then they got started on why can't I grow up and shape up and do my part now with him out of work. Boy. I didn't get him laid off."

"But it's a hard time for them, Josh."

"Not for her. She's tickled pink. All this schooling's going to get her back into that *career* she gave up when I came along." It seemed vital to stay cold and angry. Even with Laurel. Especially with Laurel, because she knew what he really was. "So I figured I've been enough trouble—I might as well get on out there and do something with my life." He stared at the distant river waiting to be crossed.

"It's dumb," Laurel said, with the directness they had never been afraid to use with each other. "They'll just haul you back. Parents aren't perfect. You're feeling sorry for yourself." She stopped in the road, trying to make him turn around, rethink. But he kept walking. "Please, Josh," she said behind him. "Don't do it."

"*You're* leaving," he said.

"But not until school's out. And I wouldn't be, if we didn't have to move out to the Coast."

"But you are," he said. It wasn't her fault, he knew. She couldn't make her own choices. But he could. "Maybe I'll see you in sunny Cal."

"How'll you live, without money?" she asked into the wind. "Josh? How'll you eat? It scares me."

He turned around. She was outlined against the far-off knob of land called Throne of Kings, where they had sat one day in dusty autumn grass, growing quieter and quieter until their faces turned and their mouths touched in a kiss as intent and sunstruck as the silent hawks gliding over them.

His feet kept moving him backward. "Hey, just don't worry about me," he called. "Nobody else does. Okay?" She didn't answer, but her eyelids blinked fast. He relented. "Would you come as far as the bridge with me?"

She shook her head. "I have to get back to the library. I'm supposed to be helping with the party right now."

Hearing her say she should be getting punch and cookies ready for some stumpy old lady who wrote bad poetry, at the moment he was running away, gave him the new rush of anger he needed to turn around and march out of her life.

The river sprawled ahead of him, more sand than water. There was an eeriness in what he was doing: leaving someone he cared so much about without ending it right. He wished she'd run after him. But what could she say?

When he got to the bridge he looked back, expecting to see her pedaling away, but she stood in the road, her hair blowing across her funny freckled face.

The long bridge turned his footsteps hollow as he started across. He had planned to wait for the bus at the crossroad a mile or so farther on. Between wind gusts he found himself straining to hear the hum of traffic. But the only sound was closer, a small lonesome squeak like a bird he didn't recognize, or something grating under the bridge.

When would they notice he'd left home? he wondered. Maybe they wouldn't even miss him.

Near the end of the bridge the sound got louder. He scanned the sky and the flat brown horizon. Then he leaned over the bridge rail and looked down into a cardboard box on the sand at the water's edge. A jumble of yips and squeals came from something dark squirming inside it.

He felt his muscles clamp into knots. He had to catch a bus. He was this far. He had to straighten up and walk on past whatever was down there crying for help. But he couldn't.

He glanced at Laurel. She hadn't moved. He went to the far end of the bridge and climbed down through the weeds. The box twitched as he bent warily and looked in.

Puppies. Five of them, no bigger than fuzzy mittens, crawling in their prison.

Josh drew a weary sigh and squatted to touch them. They went silent, rooting hungrily against his hands. He lifted up a soft black puppy with eyes that melted a hole in his heart, and dropped it back into the pile. "No," he warned them. "I can't do anything, you guys. No."

Their little claws grated on the high sides of the box as they struggled to reach him. He saw Laurel hanging over the bridge rail. "What's down there, Josh?" she called.

"Five puppies," he called back.

She came scrambling down. Her eyes were blazing. "What kind of gutless wonder would throw them into the river! Oh, look at them." She gathered two against her cheeks.

"Maybe somebody couldn't take care of them," he said, trying to be fair. But it wasn't fair. He flicked his hands angrily, staying aloof. "Didn't want to be bothered. So, plop, off the bridge."

"But it's cruel," she said. "It's sad. Like back in early times, in the book Miss Rainey gave you, remember? When people left the defective babies on a mountain so if the gods wanted them saved they could do a miracle." Suddenly she handed him a puppy. "And guess what—along came good old Josh."

"No," he said. "Dang—I've got a bus to catch!" He dropped the puppy into the heap, as trapped as it was. "Why me? What'll I do with the dumb things?"

"You said you've always wanted a dog. You just got five of your wishes." She looked at his eyes and stopped trying to make him smile. "Take them back into town and find them homes. There'll be another bus. If you still . . ."

He followed her gaze down the road he should be striding along, and turned helplessly to the box. "Want a nice puppy?"

"Oh, I do. But my mom's deathly allergic. And when we move I couldn't take it—we'll be renting till we find a house." She nudged him up onto the bridge. "Stand in front of the supermarket, Josh. Won't you? Somebody'll take them. Look, I've got to get back, or I'll get canned."

She went to her bike, but her worried eyes kept studying him. He could feel the box pressing against the folded lump of bus-ticket money in his pocket. What did she want? Why should he be the one to care, when nobody else did?

"Do you think they'd fall out of my basket if I tried to carry them?" she asked.

"You just worry about getting on back," he said. Her face fell. It touched him to see how hard she was trying to keep this from being good-bye. He shrugged, defeated. "They're not all that heavy. But you could carry the duffel."

Most of the shoppers glanced into his box and went on past to buy their groceries. A few paused. The children stopped and stayed, cuddling puppies until they were dragged away by their parents.

He felt stupid. He resented what those helpless crawling blobs in the box had done to his plans, and was still angry at the person who had left them by the edge of the river. And at himself because he hadn't.

Several times, during the hour he stood in front of the store, he saw a shadowy movement at one of the high library windows down the block. Laurel. Checking to see what luck he was having. Or if he had left.

He felt exposed, there in full view of everyone on the street. He knew that his mother was thirty miles away, in one of those nifty workshops that was going to expand her options. But his dad might drive past any minute, checking out a job prospect, and see him and the duffel. He couldn't take a public quarrel, not after leaving that morning feeling so righteous and ready.

A little girl forced her mother to stop at the box.

"Could I have one?" she begged, entranced.

"They'd make great pets. Or watchdogs, or whatever," Josh said quickly, trying to cover every possibility.

The woman smiled. "How much?"

"Oh, free," Josh exclaimed. "Free. And they don't eat much at all."

The woman squeezed the little girl, almost laughing. "Which one do you like?"

The little girl picked up each puppy in turn, studying it nose to nose. The last one stretched to give her a lick. "This one," she breathed, dazzled. "He likes me already!" She turned suddenly to Josh. "We'll love it good."

"We will," the woman agreed. "Thank you."

He felt an unexpected emptiness as they walked away huddled over their treasure. He guessed it was for the puppy leaving the warmth of its brothers and sisters forever, with its little head jiggling trustfully. Or maybe it was because the woman hugged the little girl the way his father hugged him in his fantasies.

A man came out of the store. Proud of his change of luck, Josh had opened his mouth to say, "How about a beautiful puppy?" when he noticed that the tag on the man's jacket said MANAGER.

He gathered up his duffel and his dogs, and mushed.

As he passed the library, Laurel leaped out onto the top step and beckoned. "Josh! I saved some cookies for you."

He climbed up, weary. "A lady took a puppy."

Her glad smile faded. "You've only given away *one?*"

"Miss Rainey won't like me bringing them into the library, either," he said. "Have you started the party for old lady Snap Crackle Pop?"

Laurel nodded. "Grace Whipple Cox," she corrected him. "She's sitting there, waiting to autograph a stack of books taller than she is, that nobody wants to buy."

He went in, trying to be invisible behind Laurel. A tiny, round powder keg of a lady in a velvet hat sat talking to a few matronly types holding punch cups and paper napkins. He could see now why Laurel called her the Gnome de Plume, although at first she'd had to explain the pun to him. He was curious about anybody who could write poetry. He'd tried it himself. Nobody knew, except Laurel, unless Miss Rainey had guessed.

Laurel led him to a little room full of magazines and gave him four pink cookies. "What'll you do now?" she asked. "Oh, Josh, they're hungry. When they're this young they need food every few hours. Could I give them some coffee-creamer stuff, do you think?"

"I don't know. Maybe not." Yips began to come from the box. He put his jacket over it. "I've got to give them *away*. This is crazy."

"Let's try Miss Rainey," Laurel said. "I know she has cats, but maybe—" She winced as the yapping rose in a needle-sharp chorus.

He started through the door with his box and almost bulldozed Miss Rainey off her feet as she started in.

"What on earth!" She flipped through her memory card index for his name. "Josh. What have you got?" She looked in. Her face softened. "Well bless their little deafening hearts."

"Somebody left them under the bridge," Laurel said.

Miss Rainey breathed an angry sigh.

"I found a home for one already." Josh tilted the box so Miss Rainey would see yearning eyes and smell warm puppy. "Laurel thought maybe you'd like one."

"Oh, listen, Josh, they're already trying to zone my house as a zoo. I just couldn't. I'm gone all day. Cats and chameleons and macaws can manage. But a puppy—nope." She turned away. Then she gestured him close again, and muttered, "Try the literary ladies. It's a long shot, but try."

She was leading them out through rows of shelves, when she stopped abruptly. Every face they saw was staring at a long table of refreshments. Another of Miss Rainey's assistants, a little older than Laurel, sat at a punch bowl with her mouth ajar. Her startled eyes were riveted on a scruffy man with no socks who was helping himself to punch and cookies. His hand, the size of a baseball mitt, was already stacked with sand tarts and brownies and macaroons and six of those pink cartwheels Josh had wolfed down in the little room. The man drained his paper cup, smiled at the hypnotized girl, and refilled it. He studied his hand, and added another brownie.

Miss Rainey came alive. "Good lord—he's cleaning us out! Where did he come from?" She headed toward the man so vigorously that Josh thought she was going to grab his cookies. But she drew herself tall and said, "Sir, have you met our distinguished guest, or read her previous books of poetry?"

The scraggy man froze in his tracks. "I can't say I have," he admitted, still chewing. "But I did literally cut my teeth on poetry, ma'am. The complete unexpurgated works of Rudyard Kipling, if I remember rightly." He gave her a big shameless smile, then studied the puppies in Josh's box. "Part shepherd, wouldn't you say—the ears and head shape?"

He left Miss Rainey speechless and walked into the reference section to finish his meal in peace. The girl at the punch bowl exclaimed in a whisper, "I didn't know what to *do*, Miss Rainey! When he started loading up—"

Miss Rainey patted her shoulder mechanically. "It's all right." Her face had softened as it had when she saw the puppies. "He's hungry."

Laurel elbowed Josh toward the autographing table. A boy from high school was interviewing the Gnome de Plume, scribbling frantically at half the speed of her rushing words. Josh stopped at a distance, not wanting to interrupt but eager to get the women's attention when he could. Somebody had to take another puppy.

"Could you explain why you entitled your newest book *The Second Highest Point in Beymer County?*" the boy asked.

"To make a statement," the Gnome de Plume snapped, from behind the stack of unsold books. "Everybody knows that Crown Hill is the highest point—it's on the maps, it's written about. We act as if second-best is second-rate. I wanted to say that there can be only one topmost *anything*—all the rest of this glorious fascinating world is second. Or third, or tenth. Empty words. Hogwash. Everything has worth, for its own reasons." She knocked the mountain of books askew. "I'm not even a tenth-rate poet, although you don't have to quote me on that. I'm just a funny old lady. But why shouldn't I write a *ton* of poetry if I want to? God doesn't label blades of grass Grade A and Grade B. He creates. For the fun of it! Because he's a creator!"

The boy had lost her, back at Crown Hill. Josh watched him write down GRADE A and take a bite of his pencil.

Two of the literary ladies, equally startled, peeped into Josh's box. Miss Rainey said, "Listen, we need homes for these abandoned little things. Someone dropped them in the river without having the decency, or the heart, to finish the job."

The ladies shook their heads sadly. One said, "A ten-to-fifteen-year commitment is too much for me. Besides, they need children to play with. A farm or something." They turned away from the box, unobtrusively putting distance also between themselves and the old lady glaring around her mountain of books.

"What's the second highest point in Beymer County?" Josh whispered.

A pink flush crossed Laurel's face. "Throne of Kings," she whispered back.

He felt his own cheeks go warm. There would never be a spot on earth higher than the Throne of Kings on an autumn day, enchanted by hawks. *Why do you have to leave me?* he wanted to beg her through the ache in his throat.

But he was leaving first. You do it to them before they do it to you. You don't just stand there on the reject pile, smiling like it doesn't hurt.

The grungy guy tapped him on the shoulder. "You say you're giving pups away?" His cookies were gone, except for the frosting on his beard.

Josh nodded, surprised.

"I'll take one," the man said.

Everyone looked at Josh. The man put his paper cup on the stack of books. It looked like a lighthouse.

"Oh," Miss Rainey said. "I don't think—" She stopped, flustered.

"I don't know," Josh said carefully. "I mean—I don't know you." He hadn't known the woman with the little girl, either, he remembered. "Aren't you just—on the road? I mean, if you don't have a job or anything, how could you feed it, and all?"

"I live here," the man said. "Hey, I wouldn't take it if I couldn't come up with the goods. I take care of *me*, don't I? What's your name? I look like I can manage to take care of a pup, don't I?"

"Josh," he told him, nodding in spite of his doubts.

"Joshua fit the battle of Jericho," the man said, as if he had the habit of telling himself things. "Well, Josh, you trust me or you don't. It's a risk."

"I don't know," Josh said in desperation. How could he tell? What kind of life would a puppy have with a man like that?

But what did it take to beat dying in a box by the river?

Suddenly the man grubbed in the pocket of his ragged pea jacket and brought out a pencil in a handful of lint and crumbs. "I'll tell you what, Josh, my friend, I'll give you my address. You come check on me. Check on your pup—see if I don't do a commendable job on it." He handed Josh a napkin with a street number on it. There were no houses there, Josh knew from his paper route days. A warehouse. So? Guard dogs stayed in warehouses okay. The man gave him a half glance with wary watery eyes. He's begging, Josh thought. It's rough by yourself.

He held out the box. "Which one do you want?"

The man said softly, "The runt." He lifted out the smallest puppy, smoothing its fuzzy head with his thumb. He said, "You keep that address. You come out and check."

"I will," Josh warned him. "You better be telling me the truth."

The man tucked the puppy inside his jacket. "I'll be gentle with it, Josh, my friend. I had a belt taken to me too many times to ever lift my hand to another creature."

He bowed to the ladies, smiling, and went out.

The Gnome de Plume thrust a book into Laurel's hand. "Run

catch him," she ordered. Her squinty old eyes glinted with what looked to Josh like pleasure.

Laurel darted out. Josh felt a spurt of happiness. Two pups down—three to go. The rest of March, April, May before Laurel left. They'd go to the Throne of Kings again, and this time he would be able to say, *I'm glad we knew each other and liked and loved each other. Even if it can't be the way I wanted it to be.*

The Gnome de Plume brought a box from under the table and began to fill it with her books. The ladies gathered to help.

Josh was folding the napkin into his pocket when his hand froze. What was he doing? He wasn't going to be here to check on anybody's address. He was going to be out there on a bus. Finding his own warehouse to sleep in. There wouldn't be another day on the Throne of Kings. Never another day. He slung his head, blinking as if he'd run into a door in the dark.

He went out blindly and stood on the sidewalk, breathing hard. The box of puppies, lighter now, bulged and bumped in his hands. Laurel came back and stood beside him. They watched the cars go by in the long afternoon shadows.

"Were you just saying that?" she asked, with a pinched, anxious smile. "When you told him you'd check on the puppy?"

A car like his dad's came toward them. He went tight. It passed, driven by a boy in a baseball cap. Josh let out his breath. His voice, sounding far away, said, "Just once, if my folks would just look up and notice I was there. That's all it would take."

Laurel nodded. She always nodded, understanding, and he always went on explaining and defending himself, like some kind of neglected machine grinding itself to pieces.

"I mean, they talk to me—sure—but they're doing other things while they're yelling at me. Like I was some emergency they wished they weren't having."

Grace Whipple Cox came out the door with a load of books. Miss Rainey followed with another box and the last of the cookies under plastic on a wobbly paper plate.

"Let me carry that," Laurel said, taking the Gnome's load. Josh set the puppies down and took the books and plate from Miss Rainey. They followed the Gnome down the chilly street to her beat-up car and put the boxes in the back.

"Not much of an afternoon, dollar-wise," she said. He didn't understand why she followed them back to the library. She looked down at the puppies. "I wish I was sure I *had* ten-to-fifteen years to commit," she said, and laughed. "But so what? We can't wait for life to be perfect, can we?" She lifted up two puppies.

He heard Laurel draw a soft breath.

The Gnome de Plume said, "I can't take all three—I'm tempting fate as it is. But fate has sent them a guardian angel once already." She smiled at Josh. "Fate can do it again, if I don't last long enough. And they'll have each other." She bent closer. "Would you like one of my books?"

He gulped. "Yes," he told her, taking it. "I would."

The Gnome smiled at Laurel and handed her the puppies. "Come, young lady. I'll drive you home."

Laurel turned to Josh. Her anxious eyes tried to read his. "Your duffel is in the little room."

"I know," he said. He didn't move.

Slowly she started after the Gnome. "Josh?" she entreated, looking back.

"It won't work," he said. "I go home—they're madder than ever—we start yelling—"

"Part of that's up to you, isn't it?" she asked.

Her soft words let him down with a thump. Dang—*help* me, he wanted to yell. Don't just pile it back on me.

"Josh, can't you try? We have to get through things the best we can." Her voice was shaking. "I'll listen and listen, if it'll help, but it's up to you, finally."

He turned away. Inside the library he stared through the window as the Gnome's car, and then others, and then others, passed in the dusk.

His dad was watching the news. He asked, "Where've you been?" without turning from the TV.

Josh felt the eeriness start again, matching the jumpy light of the screen that lit the room. He took the puppy out of his jacket. It seemed like fate, really, because the one that had been left was the one whose tender eyes had grabbed his heart beside the river.

"What's that?" his dad said, when he noticed. "You can't keep a dog. Your mother's got too much to do already."

"She won't have to take care of it," Josh said, keeping his voice even and slow. "I will. Feeding and housebreaking and shots and tags and spaying and everything."

His dad looked at him a long time. "Talk is cheap," he said.

"I guess you're going to have to risk it," Josh said, braced against the gaze.

His dad turned back to the news. "She can't do everything. The house, her schooling. She's got big dreams for herself. Give her a chance."

The puppy tried to crawl inside Josh's collar. He had to feed it. He had to buy a bag of something. "I live here too," he said. He felt for his ticket money. Maybe if he called Laurel she'd walk to the store with him and carry the pup while he lugged home a bag of dog chow. And they could talk. "Give me a chance too. Okay?"

His dad switched channels uneasily, testing, rejecting. He doesn't know how to answer me, Josh thought. He doesn't know what to say to any of this—to not having a job, or to her getting ahead of him, or to being my father.

A commercial came on. His dad said, watching it, "When I went into the army my folks kept my dog for me. They said he got lost. Ran away. But I was never sure." His face slowly warped in the shifting light. "Maybe he tried to find me. Or maybe he got killed and they hated to tell me. So I never could be sure, you know? For a long time I used to listen to the dogs barking, off in town. For years, I guess. Hoping I'd hear him."

Josh stopped halfway to the door. Hesitantly he came back, and sat on the arm of the couch, stroking the hungry puppy with his thumb. He stared at the television like his dad, not seeing it. Even with the sound turned high, he caught himself trying to hear other things. The far-off whine of buses. The almost inaudible cries and urgings and answers coming from everywhere.

OUIDA SEBESTYEN

Ouida Sebestyen always "wanted intensely to write fiction that celebrated life, love, growing, and the human family—stories that showed people overcoming and triumphing." Her four novels for young people do just that. *Words by Heart,* named one of the year's Ten Best by *Learning Magazine* and one of the Best Books of 1979 by both *The New York Times* and the American Library Association, deals with the hope as well as the agony of being a young black girl in 1910 Texas. *Words by Heart* also received the 1982 American Book Award for best children's fiction in paperback and was made into a television movie which received two Emmy nominations.

Like *Words by Heart,* much of Sebestyen's writing reflects her southern heritage and early life in the small Texas town of Vernon. She now lives in Boulder, Colorado.

The success of *Words by Heart* came after more than twenty frustrating years of writing and not selling dozens of stories, four novels, and a play. Once started, however, Sebestyen's success continued with *Far from Home,* the touching story of a thirteen-year-old boy's struggle to care for his great-grandmother after his mother dies. It was named an ALA Best Book for Young Adults in 1980.

IOU's is also about love and caring within a splintered family. Thirteen-year-old Stowe Garrett and his mother work to make a life together after Stowe's grandfather has disowned them and his father has deserted them. In addition to being named one of the ALA Best Books of the Year in 1982, *IOU's* received the Zilveren Griffel (Silver Pencil) Award from Holland as the best translated children's book of 1984.

Unwilling to allow the questions raised at the end of *Words by Heart* to go unexplored, Ouida Sebestyen follows the Haney family in *On Fire* as they try to escape the consequences of Tater Haney's violent act. Tater and his brother, Sammy, through whose eyes the story is told, become involved in a strike by Colorado miners and in the violence that accompanies it.

*Selling brushes door to door after school is no easy job for Donald.
It is difficult to deal with the rejections, to handle the disappoint-
ments. But it is so much harder for him to face his mother. . . .*

THE FULLER BRUSH MAN

GLORIA D. MIKLOWITZ

Donald leaned into the car trunk to find the box holding the
giveaways. He had to pay for each letter opener, shoehorn, and
vegetable brush, money out of his own commission, but it was
worth it. Why else would people listen to his sales spiel if it
wasn't because they felt indebted the second they reached for a
sample?

What a mess, he thought, getting grease on his hand. Ever
since Mom stopped driving. Ever since she . . . Well, there was
no use dwelling on that. When he had time he'd try to get rid of
some of the junk. He dropped a dozen plastic shoehorns into his
sample case, snapped the lock, and glanced at his watch.

Man, he was hungry. He'd been working steadily since right
after school, four hours. All he'd eaten was a doughnut left in the
breadbox at home, running out the door with Ava calling after
him to get a glass of milk first.

He'd sold enough brushes to call it quits for the day, but
maybe he'd work another hour. If he went home now, even
though it would mean a real meal, not McDonald's, Ava would
be there. Their newest housekeeper, she'd sit there at the kitchen
table, arms folded, watching him, and she'd go into her usual
song and dance.

"Go in to your mother. Just for a minute. Say hello. Say *something*."

"Later."

"*Now*. She'll be asleep later."

"Why? She can't talk. She probably doesn't even know who I
am. What difference does it make?"

"Donnie, Donnie. You love her. I know you do. Do it for you, if not for her."

"Leave me alone."

He'd get this picture in his head of Mom, the way she had become lately. Bloated face, dull eyes that followed him without seeming to see, a stomach as if she was pregnant. And her arms skinny, all bones. *Why? How could she do that to him, to them?*

No. He'd just get a bite nearby and go home later. He could maybe make five more sales. More money for the college fund. And with what Dad was putting out in medical bills and nursing care, every cent counted.

He crossed the street and was nearly knocked down by a kid on a two-wheeler, shooting out of a driveway, wobbling his way down the road. When had *he* learned to ride a bike? Eight, nine years ago? Yes. In the Apperson Street schoolyard, late afternoons. He could hear the crickets chirping even now, and for a second he felt the same surge of fear and exultation he'd felt then gripping the handlebars.

"I can't! I can't! I'm falling! Mom, Mom! Help me!"

"You can! You can! Keep going! That's right! You're doing it!"

Running alongside, face sweating and flushed, red hair flying about her eyes and cheeks, she was laughing with joy. And when he finally managed to stop she threw her arms around him and cried, "See? You did it! I knew you could!"

He swallowed a lump in his throat and marched briskly up the walk to the door of a small, wooden house. He rang the bell and waited, peering through the screen door into a living room with a worn couch, a TV flickering against one wall, and a small child sitting in front of it.

"If you don't behave, you'll have to watch TV," his mother would say when he was that age, as if watching TV was punishment. Maybe that's why he hardly watched even now.

When *he* was little, this was the time of day he loved most. Right after supper and before bedtime. He'd climb up on the couch to sit beside Mom. Bonnie would take her place on Mom's other side and for a half hour it was "weed books" time.

He felt an overwhelming hunger for those times, for Mom's

arm around him and her warm voice reading. He wiped a hand across his eyes as a woman, holding a baby, came to the door.

"Fuller brush man! Good evening, missus. Would you like a sample?" Donald held out a brush, a letter opener, and a shoe-horn. With but a second's hesitation the woman unlatched the door and stepped forward, eyeing the samples greedily. She took the brush.

"Good choice," Donald said. "They're great for scrubbing vegetables. Now, would you like to see our specials?" He held the catalog open to the specials page, but the light was fading.

"I don't need any . . ."

"Then maybe you'd like to try our new tile-cleaning foam. See?" He plucked a can from his case and showed her the cap with its stiff bristles for the "hard-to-clean places between the tiles."

"I have Formica."

"Sally? Sally? Who the devil is that?"

"Just a brush salesman, honey!"

"Well, tell him you don't need any!"

The woman gave him a sheepish grin, backed away, and said, "Sorry." She closed the screen door and latched it again.

He used to take rejection hard, getting a pain in his stomach that grew with each door shut in his face, each disgusted "Don't bother me." He still withdrew inside when people turned him away, although he wouldn't show it now, keeping his voice pleasant and a smile on his face. If anyone asked, he'd say he hated the job even though he was learning a lot about human nature and keeping books, and it did pay well.

"Sell door to door?" his mother had asked when he first proposed the idea. "Absolutely not!"

"Why not? I could save what I make for college!"

"No!"

"Why? That's not fair!"

"Because." He watched her struggle to find words for what she hadn't thought out. "Because it's not safe, knocking on strange people's doors. The world is full of crazies. Because I don't want you to have to get doors slammed in your face. Because it will be summer soon and too hot to work outdoors. If you want a job, find one where it's air-conditioned."

"Let him try," Dad said. "One day of it and he'll quit."

"*Please*, Mom?"

"Oh, all right," she conceded, but only because that morning he'd accused her of still treating him like a baby. "But only to try it. *One* day!"

It was three months now. She must have been sick even then, because after that first day when he'd come home triumphant with having made fifty-four dollars in only six hours, he didn't hear anything more about quitting. It was about then that she went into the hospital for the first time and his whole life began to change.

When he finished another block, he circled back to the car, a dog barking at his heels. One of the hazards of selling things in strange neighborhoods was the dogs. He carried Mace but hated using it. He found that if he stood his ground and shouted "No," most dogs would go through their ferocious act and run off when they figured they'd done their duty.

In the dim light of the car he looked over his orders and decided to drive down to the boulevard for something to eat. Maybe he'd phone Shannon afterwards, drop by for a few minutes before going home. He started the engine, turned on the headlights, and drove down the hill.

"How's your Mom?" Shannon asked when he reached her from the phone in the parking lot. There was so much traffic noise he had to press the receiver tight against his ear.

"What are you doing?" he asked in response. "I can be by in ten minutes. We could go for a walk."

"When are you going to talk about it?" Shannon asked. "Bonnie says she's worse. It's awful how you're acting. It's not her fault."

For a second he considered not answering at all, but finally he said, "Stop bugging me. Everyone's after me about it. It's *my* mom. It's my business. If that's all you want to talk about, forget it."

"But, Donnie! You can't put it off much longer."

He hung up without answering and ran back to the car.

Slamming the door, he slumped in the driver's seat and stared out at the ribbon of lights on the freeway. If he let himself think about what Shannon said, he'd just start blubbering like a baby. Better to work. He'd get at the orders for the week. They were due to be toted up and recorded on the big order sheet by tomorrow. Usually he'd work on it at home, spreading the papers out on his desk and marking how many of this or that he'd sold that week. But if he went home now, they'd *all* be there: Dad, Bonnie, and Ava. All accusing. Bonnie with her *Please, Donnie*'s. Ava with her *Why don't you*'s. And Dad with his sad silence, worse than words.

But worst of all was knowing that Mom lay in the next room wasting away, dying, not even fighting anymore. He felt that if he was forced to go in there, all he'd do is scream at her. "Don't you care? Try! You always told us never to give up! You're not trying!" And he'd want to strike out at her. Well, maybe not at her, but at something!

There wasn't a moment in the day that he didn't think about her. It was as if they were joined by an invisible wire and he felt everything she did. And he felt now that she was slipping away. He couldn't stop it. He couldn't do a thing about it. There was nothing to say, nothing! Everything he thought of saying sounded false or stupid.

Well, all right! If that's what he had to do, he'd do it. He'd go home. He'd go into her room. He'd look at that woman who was and wasn't his mother anymore and he'd say *something*. Whatever came into his head, no matter how mean or dumb. *All right!* If that's what they all wanted, that's what he'd do.

He turned the key in the ignition and gunned the car out of the parking lot and into the street. He drove above the speed limit, mouth clenched in a tight line, totally intent on the road, mind empty except for the determination to get home fast.

He parked the car in the drive and ran into the house. Suddenly he was terribly afraid. What if it was too late? He almost felt in his gut that he'd waited too long.

"Donnie?" Dad called from the family room. "That you?"

He made some kind of guttural response and ran past the room, not even nodding. He had a fleeting sense that Dad was there reading the paper, that Bonnie was doing homework. His heart hammered loudly in his ears. An electrical pulse ran down his arms to his legs as he reached his mother's bedroom door and put a hand on the knob.

And then he stopped. For a long moment he stood waiting for his legs to quit trembling, for his heart to slow down. And then he closed his eyes, took a deep breath, and straightened his shoulders. Fixing a smile on his face, he knocked. "Fuller brush man!" he called, lightly opening the door.

GLORIA D. MIKLOWITZ

Gloria Miklowitz is the author of over thirty-five books for children and young adults. She has written about divorce *(A Time to Hurt, A Time to Heal)*, teenage pregnancy *(Unwed Mother)*, runaways *(Runaway)*, and rape *(Did You Hear What Happened to Andrea?).* That book won the Australian Young Reader's Trophy in 1984 and was made into an ABC-TV Afterschool Special under the title "Andrea's Story, a Hitchhiking Tragedy," which earned five Emmy awards.

In her novels, she says, "I try to offer or suggest alternatives to destructive behavior." In *The Love Bombers,* she examines the influence of religious cults on teenagers and the right to make one's own decisions. In *Close to the Edge,* a suicidal teenager gains strength through her work with senior citizens and by befriending another student who has tried to kill herself. *After the Bomb* urges teenagers to become informed about nuclear issues by examining the effects of an accidentally dropped nuclear bomb from a teenage boy's point of view. It's sequel, *After the Bomb—Week One* deals with the question of retaliation and the aftereffects of nuclear destruction.

Teenage marriage is at issue in *The Day the Senior Class Got Married.* Because of their economics class marriage unit, Lori and Garrick are forced to deal with the difficulties of married life before they follow through on their wedding plans. High school is also the setting for *The War Between the Classes,* the story of a classroom experiment called the Color Game, in which students are judged, in unexpected ways, by skin color and economic status. The CBS-TV film of this novel won an Emmy for Best Children's Special.

Miklowitz's most recent books are *Love Story, Take Three,* about a teenage TV actress on the brink of fame who longs for a normal life; *Secrets Not Meant to Be Kept,* an account of a teenager's investigation of child abuse in a nursery school; and a book about AIDS called *Goodbye Tomorrow.*

She teaches writing at Pasadena City College and lives nearby with her husband in LaCanada, California.

*Mary Louise has a secret—a terrible secret—that her father has told
her never to reveal. Then she meets Patty-Warren, who also has a
secret—a terrible secret. . . .*

THE GOOD GIRLS

FRAN ARRICK

Mary Louise opened her bedroom door a crack and peeked
through to the living room. There he was, on the couch, looking
as though he were asleep, but she knew he wasn't. He was only
completely passed out when his mouth hung open and you could
hear his raspy breathing clear through to the back of the house.
She couldn't hear it yet, so she stayed in her room, not daring to
cross to the front door until she was sure he was sleeping soundly.

She tapped her foot impatiently. He was almost always out by
late afternoon, leaving her free to her comings and goings. And
when he wasn't on the couch, he could be found in The Road-
house at the edge of town, right on the border between Armenia
and Braverlee. But here he was, still partly awake and right in her
way.

It was early spring and beginning to be hot, but Mary Louise
still wore her dancer's gear of tights and protective legwarmers
and had begun to sweat through them. She knew she'd be soaked
through before she even got to the Center to start work. She
rubbed the end of her ash-blond pigtail across her lips, stared
hard at the couch, and willed her father to slip into oblivion.

Her heart sank as he sat up.

"Hey!" he called. His eyes were still closed and she prayed that
he was talking in his sleep.

But "Hey!" he said again, and rolled over, facing her door. His
knee knocked an ashtray from the pine coffee table. *"Frances?"*
he called.

Mary Louise's mother. Frances. She'd run off when Mary Louise was eleven. She'd been gone five years.

"Hey, Frances!" her father yelled. "Where you at?" He lurched into a sitting position and bellowed again. "Get yourself over here, I said!"

Mary Louise decided to chance running for the door. Even if he hadn't passed out yet, he looked too sodden to stop her if she was quick. And by the time she got back, he'd be dead to the world.

Her father sank back down. He was breathing heavily, but only from the effort of having sat up.

I won't be late, Mary Louise said to herself. I just won't be late for this class. Miss Dorothy had fought for her to have this job. Miss Dorothy knew that, at only sixteen, Mary Louise was the best instructor for the little ones the Center could have. She'd only taught three weeks, but it was going so well and she loved it so much!

I'm leaving, Mary Louise said to herself. I'm just going to go.

She was wearing her soft ballet slippers. She wouldn't make a sound crossing the room, if only he'd just keep his eyes closed. But the door—the sound of that door opening and closing—

She took a breath and held it, opened her door wider, and slipped through, taking one tiny trial step into the bigger room. Her father lay with one arm thrown over his forehead, not moving.

Watching him as a cat watches when it's stalking, she propelled her dancer's body across the floor. Only thirteen steps, but it felt like miles, and trickles of perspiration rolled down both her sides.

Her fingers touched the doorknob. Oh, please, she prayed softly. Please.

"Where you goin', Mary Louise?"

She froze.

"I said, where you think you goin'?"

"To work, Daddy." Her voice came out in a whisper and he didn't seem to hear her.

"I ast you where you think you're goin', girl!" he roared at the ceiling.

Mary Louise stood with her hand on the doorknob and her

foot on the sill. She cleared her throat. "To work, Daddy," she repeated. "I'm going to work now."

"Not till I say so, you ain't!"

"Go to sleep now, Daddy," she said. "I'll be—"

"You tellin' me what to do? It's the other way round, girl!"

Mary Louise managed a soothing voice. "Now, don't you worry, Daddy. I'll be back to fix your supper, 'bout an hour or two." Eyes on him till she slipped through the door onto the porch. She didn't think he'd moved, thank the Lord. He'd forgotten her already. Still, she closed the door as quietly as she could behind her before scurrying down the wooden steps and through the back lot—the shortcut to the Center downtown.

Downtown Armenia, Georgia, was eight stores including a Fast-Way supermarket, a Baptist and a Methodist church diagonally across the road from each other, and a new wood structure near a green, built by both churches to be used as a teen center, a dancing school, a meetinghouse, a lecture hall, and anything else someone might want to rent it out for.

Miss Dorothy Teaman had one of its rooms three days a week —Monday, Wednesday, and Friday—for her École Pour la Dance, and it had turned out to be a big success. Girls from five to fourteen applied in droves, coming all the way from Brittany, Spencer, and Ravenswood, because it was the only school of its kind and because Miss Dorothy's advertisement proclaimed she had actually danced with the famous Rockettes on the stage of the Radio City Music Hall. So the girls dreamed that if they were really good, maybe some of them could someday kick their legs on that big stage and be as far as they could get from Armenia or Brittany or Spencer or Ravenswood.

Mary Louise was one of the dreamers. With money she'd saved from baby-sitting and cleaning houses, she'd joined the Wednesday afternoon jazz class and had progressed so rapidly that Miss Dorothy had managed to convince suspicious parents that Mary Louise Wattles was not too young or too inexperienced to start their own little ones on the road to fame and fortune. She taught Friday afternoons and got to take two other classes from Miss Dorothy herself, free.

Drenched and panting, Mary Louise raced down the long inner hall that led to the big room at the back, where Miss Dorothy had put up a huge mirror on one wall and a barre along the opposite one. Mary Louise could hear the music. They had begun without her.

Eleven five- and six-year-olds were grouped in rows and bent over at the waist, dangling their arms loosely in front of them. Miss Dorothy, her back to the mirror, looked up.

"Here you are, Mary Louise," she said, and smiled.

"I'm so sorry I'm late."

"No problem, we've just begun. You're awfully out of breath. Want to sit and rest for a minute?"

"Oh, no, ma'am, I'm ready," Mary Louise insisted. "And I won't be late again."

"Now, don't worry about it." Miss Dorothy gave her a long look. "Are you all right, Mary Louise?"

"Oh, yes, I'm fine."

"Well, good, then. They're all yours. And I've brought your record in too. It's right next to the machine. I'll be in the office." She smiled again and left.

Mary Louise stepped to the front, filled now with confidence and relief.

"Listen up, now, girls," she said cheerfully. "I want to see those flat backs now. Everybody. Come on now, Lizbeth. You, too, Patty-Warren. One, two, three, four, five, six, seven, *eight!* All right, now, hit the floor—on your backs—" She did it with them, and the sweat she felt now was a good one, a clean one, one she didn't mind at all.

"Feet flexed in the air," she called, "Now, sit up and touch your toes eight times . . . five, six, seven, *eight!* Ro-o-ll-ll down, chest in, lie down on count of eight. Patty-Warren, why you sittin' up, honey?" She looked over at a small girl, trying to hide behind a bigger one in the front row.

"Patty-Warren?" Mary Louise repeated. The child was new in town, the only daughter of an architect and his wife, here from Atlanta for the planning of a modern shopping mall. It was the talk of the town.

"She don't have to move," a little girl called out. "She'll just git someone to carry her!"

There was some giggling.

Plain mean, Mary Louise thought. They just repeat what the bigger folks say out of jealousy. "Stop that, Sally," she said to the girl who'd called out. "And you other girls, is that any way to treat someone new? Y'all know better. Now, on your feet and let's do this one. Plié . . . heels up . . . down. Plié . . . heels up . . . down. Ready?"

Out of the corner of her eye she saw Patty-Warren blink her eyes tightly with each count. She was working, but something was wrong.

"You okay, Patty-Warren?" she asked.

"She always slows us up," another girl complained. "Why we have to slow ourselves just 'cause Patty-Warren can't keep up?"

"Now, Marcia, she does keep up. She must be sick today or something, isn't that right, Patty-Warren? Now, let's do those pliés again. Ready?"

Maybe she's just not coordinated too well, Mary Louise thought as she watched the little ones plié, stretch, arch, and bend. There was always one who stood out that way. In her own class it was Dale McMellin, and all the girls called her Dale the Whale, Destined to Fail. Once Dale McMellin had cried, right there in front of everyone, which made it all worse, but little Patty-Warren, ten years younger than Dale and Mary Louise, wasn't crying at all. Her thin little face was pinched in determination and she looked as if she hadn't even heard the others discussing her.

When the warm-up exercises were finished, Mary Louise put on the jazz record that Miss Dorothy had let her pick out, and the girls began the little routine Mary Louise had choreographed for them. This was the part they all loved, because it made them feel like the teenagers they watched in television commercials or at their big sisters' and brothers' parties on Saturday nights. When Miss Dorothy looked in, they were gyrating wildly and grinning from ear to ear. Even little Patty-Warren had closed her eyes and was smiling to herself.

At the end of the class the little girls filed out into the hall, where their mothers waited. Their cheeks were red and their hair damp and curling on their foreheads.

"They looked good doing that routine, Mary Louise," Miss Dorothy said. "You know, I thought at first their parents might object to their doing that sophisticated stuff, but they seem pretty proud of them."

"Yes, ma'am! Marcia Willis said her mama wakes her up sometimes to show off for company!"

"Well, I certainly did the right thing by getting you to teach them. You have real talent, Mary Louise."

The next class, a group of eight-year-olds, had begun to move into the room, some whirling with each other in their own version of *Swan Lake.*

"Come on, let's go into the office for a minute," Miss Dorothy said, taking Mary Louise's arm. "Girls, form a circle with Alice in the middle. And, Alice, you start the warm-ups with the neck exercises—all right, dear?"

She steered Mary Louise into the little room that was supposed to be the church's office but which Miss Dorothy had appropriated for herself, decorating it with her own green leather couch and pictures of herself and all the Rockettes kicking in various costumes and routines.

"Sit down, Mary Louise," she said, pushing some papers off the green leather couch and onto the floor.

Mary Louise sat, but she was nervous, so she began to rub the tip of her pigtail across her lips.

"Honey . . . I don't want to pry. But I want to help if I can."

"I don't need help, Miss Dorothy. Besides, you'll never believe how much you've helped me already, with—"

"I know you're a dancer. I wish you'd been able to start at the age your class is now. But you're awfully good and you'll get better. There are all kinds of things you'll be able to do with it. But no, that's not what I mean. This is a small town—"

"Don't I know it!"

"Well, yes. But— Now look, I don't want to embarrass you. But you hear things, Mary Louise. I know your mother has been gone awhile now, and your father's had a hard time, hasn't he?"

He had a hard time long before she left, Mary Louise thought, but all she said was, "Well, we manage all right, Miss Dorothy."

"All I want, Mary Louise, is for you to know that you have

someone to help you if you ever need it. That's all, Mary Louise. Just for you to know that. Do you understand?"

She was putting tap water in the kettle to boil for instant coffee when the blow came, knocking the kettle out of her hand as she fell, her ballet shoe skidding in the spilled water. She only cried out once, with surprise more than pain, but she whimpered and held her arms over her head as he loomed over her, his arm raised again.

She went through her mental routine. Don't cry, don't fight. You fight, he'll hurt you. Don't cry, don't scream, neighbors'll know, people will hear, people will know. Guilty and ashamed and protective of her body, she pressed her lips tight together, so that no one would know that Roy Wattles was not only a loud town drunk. No one would know what life was like in that bungalow in Armenia, Georgia, for Roy Wattles and his daughter, Mary Louise. So she crouched and cringed and willed herself to faint so she wouldn't feel him pick her up and drag her across the floor.

"A-*round* and a-*round* and a-*round* and a-*round*. . . . Good! Feel those neck muscles relax now? What about you, Bonnie? Y'all feeling those muscles loosen now?"

"Yes, Miss Mary Louise," they chorused.

"Then o-ver and *down* and o-ver and *down*, a-*gain*—" She glanced around as she bent with them. Patty-Warren was bent over but she wasn't bobbing like the others. She seemed frozen, like one of those rubber dolls that can be bent into any position. Mary Louise was about to say something but stopped herself. The others might tease the girl. Maybe she is lazy, Mary Louise thought. If she were sick, her mother surely wouldn't have let her come. She went on with the class.

When it was over, Patty-Warren was one of the last of the children to retrieve her dance bag and leave. Mary Louise noticed that Patty-Warren's bag was of soft chamois, while all the others were made of nylon or canvas.

"You seemed kinda stiff today, Patty-Warren," Mary Louise said.

Patty-Warren looked up and Mary Louise caught her breath. It was such a strange look, such a haunted one. Not at all the look of a child of six. Still she didn't speak.

Mary Louise went to her and knelt down on one knee.

"Patty-Warren, you like to dance?" she asked softly.

And then the face changed. Patty-Warren was suddenly a delighted, beautiful little girl. "I love to," she said softly.

One of the children had stopped in the doorway and stood unabashedly listening to the exchange. Now that there was whispering, she moved in closer.

Mary Louise turned. "Go on home, Natalie," she said. "You go on, now. Your mama's waiting." Only when the child had reluctantly plodded out did Mary Louise turn again to Patty-Warren, who was neatly placing her folded legwarmers in her dance bag.

"If you love to dance, then you're starting out at the best age," Mary Louise continued as the child patted her belongings in the bag. "That's what Miss Dorothy says. But you have to work hard on your—"

"Patty-Warren Stokely! My goodness, I've been standing out there in the hall forever!" The voice came from the doorway and made both girls jump. "Seems every other child is long gone!"

"I'm coming, Mama," Patty-Warren answered, and brushing quickly past Mary Louise, she headed toward the door, swinging her dance bag over her shoulder.

When Mary Louise arrived for her own Monday class, she heard angry voices coming from the office and she recognized one of them.

". . . can't imagine what you're talking about!" (Miss Dorothy)

"I'll just bet you can't! I just want to hear what some of the other mothers have to say!" (Someone Else)

"Now, please, all you have to do is watch—" (Miss Dorothy)

"I'm going to talk to my husband about taking you to court!" The door opened and the Someone Else, who turned out to be Mrs. Stokely, Patty-Warren's mother, stormed out, leaving the door open.

Mary Louise went in.

"What on earth was that all about?" she asked.

Miss Dorothy leaned heavily against a big oak desk, the only thing in the room that belonged to the churches. "That woman's got to be crazy," she said, shaking her head back and forth. "She barged in here and accused us of 'working' the children too hard. Said it was practically forced labor! Can you believe it? She said her daughter, Patty, was just exhausted, achy, bruised—all but fainting Friday night."

"Patty-Warren barely does the warm-ups," Mary Louise said. "Honestly, I can't get her to move!"

"Well, what is the matter with that woman? Did you hear her mention *court?* Really, Mary Louise, you know the Stokelys have only been here a few months, but they do carry weight in town. Everyone knows who they are. If she spreads word that we're hurting the children— Oh, she makes me so mad! I tried to get her to watch a class, but you saw! She just stormed out!"

"I saw," Mary Louise said. She was picturing the two faces of Patty-Warren Stokely: one, odd, haunted; the other . . . *Do you like to dance, Patty-Warren? I love to.*

"Well, I'll tell you something, Mary Louise," Miss Dorothy was saying. "She won't hurt us. Believe me. There isn't a thing she can do, because she's just plain wrong! And I'll fight her and anybody else for what we've got going here—because it's right!"

Mary Louise glowed. Miss Dorothy had said "we," and Mary Louise knew she was being included. She studied the dance teacher. No one would ever guess her age, whatever it was, with her lean dancer's body, that chestnut hair pulled tight into a ponytail. She would fight, she'd fight anybody—all by herself if she had to—and here was someone you'd want to have on your side.

"Yes, *ma'am,*" Mary Louise said with a nod.

On Friday, Patty-Warren was absent from jazz class and so were Marcia Willis, Sally Munro, and Natalie Laroquette. Miss Dorothy looked in on the class briefly, shook her head, rolled her eyes, and ducked out again.

Mary Louise, on the floor bicycling with the remaining students, thought: I have to see that child again. I have to see that child again.

There isn't much mystery to most six-year-olds, Mary Louise thought. They haven't lived that long. Yet here was one. A pretty mama with pretty clothes, a rich daddy, a big house—that old Bishop place they did over—yet she doesn't seem spoiled rotten. She doesn't run the group—even gets teased by them. She doesn't do warm-up exercises, but her mama says she's worked like a donkey. Doesn't figure up. And those two faces. Especially that first one, that odd one—where have I seen it before? . . . I have to see that child again.

After class, Mary Louise hurriedly pulled on her jeans over her tights and whipped off the sweatband from under her curly bangs.

"Where are you off to in such a hurry?" Miss Dorothy asked.

"Nowhere special," Mary Louise grunted.

"Uh-huh, and you're just fine, right?"

"Right."

"And everything's fine at home, right?"

"That's right."

"And you aren't going anywhere special."

"Right again."

"Mary Louise, I told you I don't pry . . ."

"Yes, ma'am."

"But I told you that when you need help you've got it, didn't I?"

"Yes, ma'am."

"Just remember that."

Mary Louise looked up at Miss Dorothy and caught a glimpse of herself in the big mirror on the far wall of the dance room. It was her own face, her own, still wearing the expression it had shown to Miss Dorothy, but suddenly Mary Louise couldn't breathe. She recognized the face, and the pain she felt was actually physical. She knelt quickly and pretended to fiddle with her shoe to hide what she was feeling from Miss Dorothy.

"Here come the girls," Miss Dorothy said, turning away. "See you Monday, Mary Louise."

"I don't want her to see you," Mrs. Stokely said. "She's in bed. Poor little thing—still in pain from last week's dance class. You people are going to regret this, I promise you. My husband and I are going to take this further!"

"Please, Mrs. Stokely," Mary Louise begged. She stood shivering in the doorway of the old Bishop house, even though the evening was warm and she had tights on under her jeans. "All's I want is to talk to Patty-Warren, just for a few minutes. Just cheer her up a little if she's feeling bad. I got to care for her, Mrs. Stokely, even though I haven't known her that long. Please, Mrs. Stokely, *please!*" It didn't matter to her if Mrs. Stokely refused her. Mary Louise would see that child if it meant climbing up the vines on the side of the house in the middle of the night. She would see her if it meant hiding in the bushes till winter! If it meant waiting on the grounds of this house forever and ever, Mary Louise knew she couldn't go anywhere, do anything, until she had some time alone with Patty-Warren Stokely, aged six.

But Mrs. Stokely was tired. She wasn't in the mood for fighting with this small-town teenager. She wasn't much in the mood for anything. She sighed, backed away, and let Mary Louise in.

Patty-Warren's room was the size of Mary Louise's whole bungalow. It was all pink, green, and white and filled with lace and eyelet and chintz and ruffles and stuffed animals and dolls.

In the middle of a pink, green, and white quilted canopied bed, Patty-Warren sat, hunched over a clown doll. She glanced up, and Mary Louise touched her chest with her fingers. On the child's face was the look she had seen on her own face in the mirror not fifteen minutes ago. The same look.

A sixteen-year-old, a six-year-old. One dirt poor, the other rich by all standards. One with an absentee mother and a crazed drunk for a father, the other with doting parents. But their faces —their eyes—were the same. And Mary Louise knew it at once.

"Hello, there, Patty-Warren," she said, moving slowly toward the child on the bed. "Honey, this is just about the prettiest room I ever did see!" Patty-Warren only stared at her. "Could I sit here? On your bed with you? Only if you say it's okay, though." Mary Louise turned her head. There was no one in the doorway.

"Could I sit, Patty-Warren? *May* I? Isn't that what they're always tellin' us? Say *may* I, not *can* I or *could* I? Doesn't your mama say that?" She glanced again toward the door.

Patty-Warren nodded. The corners of her mouth were turned down. She glanced toward the edge of her bed and Mary Louise understood without words that it was all right if she sat down.

"That's a cute doll, Patty-Warren," Mary Louise said, and smiled at the clown in the child's lap. She felt as though her heart would pound right through her chest, but she was more than adept at hiding fear, and outwardly she was calm and quiet. Just like the child.

"Patty-Warren, your mama says you're home here because you hurt yourself in dance class last week."

The child clutched the doll tightly and looked at her knees.

Mary Louise dropped her voice to almost a whisper. "But it doesn't hurt you to dance, does it? You love to dance, don't you, Patty-Warren?"

"Yessss," the child breathed.

"I know it," Mary Louise said. "I know it. Me, too. I used to dance all by myself before Miss Dorothy came to town. It was my own secret. Used to do it out in the back lot near our house, where the trees and bushgrowth hid me from the road. Never loved anything more—you know what I mean, Patty-Warren?"

The child only looked at her, but Mary Louise knew she knew.

"Used to think I could make my body float right away from the ground. Made my body move like a swaying flower, like a thing without any bones at all. But . . . the thing of it is . . ." She picked up the scalloped edge of Patty-Warren's pink sheet and began to twirl it with her fingers. "The thing of it is, I found out if I fight my daddy, then he hurts me. Hurts my body. And if he does that, Patty-Warren . . . if he hurts me . . . then . . . I can't dance. Hurts to bend, you know? Hurts to move . . ."

It seemed to Mary Louise that Patty-Warren wasn't breathing.

"So anyway," she went on, "what I learned to do, I learned not to fight." She said it with a shrug, in a matter-of-fact voice. "And then, no matter how much I hate what my daddy's doin', well . . . I still get to dance. If I don't fight."

Patty-Warren hadn't moved except for her fingers, which were now grasping the arm of her toy clown.

"My mama never knew about it, either, just like yours," Mary Louise continued. " 'Course it was different with me. My mama just left 'cause my daddy drank and beat on her, not 'cause of what was goin' on with me. He told me never to tell. Just like your daddy told you, right?"

Patty-Warren swallowed.

"It hurts more when you're little, I know," Mary Louise said. "So you fight and that makes it worse." She took the little girl's chin and tilted it upward. "You never told on your daddy, did you, Patty-Warren? Just like he told you. You were a good girl, just like me. Neither one of us ever told, we were good girls, Patty-Warren, isn't that right."

Without warning, Patty-Warren broke, flung her body, skinny little arms outstretched, and hugged Mary Louise's neck for all she was worth, weeping hot tears into the collar of the older girl's shirt.

After a while Mary Louise took the little face in her two hands. "Patty-Warren, we're still good girls, you and me. Here's how we can do it so's it'll be all right: I'll be the one to tell for you. I'll do it. And the only thing you have to do is say, 'Yes, ma'am, that's right,' when I'm done. That's not telling—*I'll* do the telling. You see?"

Mary Louise walked out of the big house, walked slowly back toward town, toward the lights of the Armenia Town Center where they were getting ready for a jukebox party for the junior high . . . where the last of the tap and jazz and ballet classes would have just finished . . . and where Miss Dorothy would be sprawled on the green leather couch in the office, sipping a Coke, wiggling her toes, listening to a record. And she'd be almost but not quite ready to head for home.

Mary Louise still felt Patty-Warren's arms around her neck, and her collar was damp from the child's tears. But what she remembered—what she would always remember—was the child's answer as they hugged each other: "And then . . . Miss Mary Louise . . . do I tell for you?"

FRAN ARRICK

Fran Arrick's highly praised novels all deal with the harsher aspects of teenage lives. Her first novel, *Steffie Can't Come Out to Play*, tells the story of a runaway teenager who is led into prostitution in New York City. It was named an Outstanding Book for Young Adults by the American Library Association in 1978 and was followed by *Tunnel Vision*, which was listed among ALA's "Best of the Best" books in 1983. In *Tunnel Vision*, several characters—teenagers as well as adults—examine their past relationship with Anthony, a bright, well-liked fifteen-year-old who has committed suicide.

In *Chernowitz!*, a teenager in a small community has to confront anti-Semitism spread by a vicious bully in his school. Religious extremism is the subject of *God's Radar*, another ALA Best Book for Young Adults. Fran Arrick's most recent novel, *Nice Girl from Good Home*, explores the destructive reactions of a girl whose father has lost his job and whose mother cannot cope with the loss of their comfortable existence.

Arrick is well known among younger readers as Judie Angell. This former elementary school teacher, editor for *TV Guide*, and continuity writer for Channel 13, New York City's educational television station, is the author of *In Summertime It's Tuffy; Tina Gogo; Ronnie and Rosey; A Word from Our Sponsor, or My Friend Alfred; Secret Selves; Dear Lola, or How to Build Your Own Family; What's Best for You; The Buffalo Nickel Blues Band; Suds; First the Good News;* and *A Home Is to Share . . . And Share . . . And Share.* Angell's most recent publication is *One Way to Ansonia*, a novel that takes place from 1891 to 1899 and is based on her immigrant grandmother's life on the lower east side of New York City when she first came to America.

The author lives with her musician husband and two sons in South Salem, New York.

CHOICES

Adam is one tough kid. And Seth wants to be just like him, right down to his sleeveless denim jacket and the way he flicks his cigarette away. Pretty cool. . . .

ON THE BRIDGE

TODD STRASSER

"I beat the crap out of this guy at the mall yesterday," Adam Lockwood said. He was leaning on the stone wall of the bridge, smoking a cigarette and watching the cars speed by on the highway beneath him. His black hair fell down into his eyes.

"How come?" Seth Dawson asked, leaning on the stone wall next to him.

Adam shrugged. The turned-up collar of his leather jacket rose and fell along his neck. "He just bugged me, that's all. He was bigger, probably a senior. I guess he thought he could take me 'cause I was smaller. But I don't let anyone push me around."

"What'd you do to him?" Seth asked. He too was smoking a cigarette. It was his first ever, and he wasn't really inhaling. Just holding the smoke in his mouth for a while and then blowing it out.

"I'm pretty sure I broke his nose," Adam said. "I couldn't hang around to find out because the guy in the pizza place called the cops. I'm already in enough trouble with them."

"What for?" Seth asked. He noticed that when Adam took a drag, he seemed to hold the smoke in his mouth and then blow it out his nose. But it was probably just a different way of inhaling. Adam definitely inhaled.

"They just don't like me," Adam said. "You know how it is."

Seth nodded. Actually, he didn't know how it was. But there was no way he'd admit that. It was just pretty cool to think that the cops didn't like you. Seth was pretty sure the cops didn't even know who he was.

The two boys looked back down at the highway. It was a warm

spring afternoon, and instead of taking the bus home after school, they'd decided to walk to the diner. There Adam had instructed Seth on how to feed quarters into the cigarette machine and get a pack of Marlboros. Seth had been really nervous about getting caught, but Adam told him it was no sweat. If the owner came out, you'd just tell him you were picking them up for your mother.

Now the pack of Marlboros was sticking out of the breast pocket of Seth's new denim jacket. It wasn't supposed to look new because he'd ripped the sleeves off and had washed it in the washing machine a hundred times to make it look old and worn. But somehow it had come out looking new and worn. Seth had decided to wear it anyway, but he felt like a fraud. Like a kid trying to imitate someone truly cool. On the other hand, Adam's leather jacket looked authentically old and worn. The right sleeve was ripped and the leather was creased and pliant. It looked like he'd been in a hundred fights with it. Seth had never been in a fight in his life. Not a serious punching fight, at least.

The other thing about Adam was, he wore the leather jacket to school every day. Adam wasn't one of these kids who kept their cool clothes in their lockers and only wore them in school because their parents wouldn't let them wear them at home. Seth had parents like that. His mother would have had a fit if she ever saw him wearing his sleeveless denim jacket, so he had to hide it in the garage every day before he went into the house. Then in the morning when he left for school he'd go through the garage and pick it up.

Seth leaned forward and felt the smooth cold granite of the bridge with his fingers. The bridge was old and made of large granite blocks. Its heavy stone abutments stood close to the cars that sped past on the highway beneath it. Newer bridges were made of steel. Their spans were longer and the abutments were farther from the road.

On the highway, a red Fiat convertible approached with two girls riding in the front seat. Adam waved, and one of the girls waved back. A second later the car shot under the bridge and disappeared. He turned to Seth and grinned. "Maybe they'll get off on the exit ramp and come back," he said.

"You think?" Seth asked. Actually, the thought made him nervous. "They must be old enough at least to drive."

"So?" Adam asked. "I go out with older girls all the time."

"Really?" Seth asked.

"Sure," Adam said. He took another drag off his cigarette and blew the smoke out of his nose. Seth wanted to try that, but he was afraid he'd start to cough or do something else equally uncool.

"What do you do with them?" Seth asked.

Adam glanced at him with a sly smile. "What do you think I do with them?"

"I mean, do you go out?"

"Sure, if they want to take me out, we go out. Otherwise sometimes we just hang around and make out."

Seth was awestruck. At a party once he'd played spin the bottle and pass the orange and had kissed a few girls in the process. But he'd never seriously made out.

In the distance a big semitrailer appeared on the highway. Adam raised his arm in the air and pumped his fist up and down. The driver responded with three loud blasts of his air horns. A moment later the semi rumbled under them and disappeared.

"Let me try that," Seth said. Another truck was coming and he leaned over the stone ledge and jerked his arm up and down. But the trucker ignored him.

Adam laughed.

"How come it didn't work?" Seth asked.

"You gotta do it a special way," Adam told him.

"Show me," Seth said.

"Can't, man," Adam said. "You just have to have the right touch. It's something you're born with."

Seth smirked. It figured. It was just his luck to be born without the touch that made truckers blow their horns.

The traffic was gradually getting thicker as the afternoon rush hour approached. Many of the drivers and passengers in the cars seemed unaware of the two boys on the overpass. But a few others stared up through their windshields at them.

"Bet they're wondering if we're gonna drop something on them," Adam said. He lifted his hand in the air as if he was holding an imaginery rock. On the highway more of the people in the cars were watching now. Suddenly Adam threw his arm forward. Even though there was nothing in his hand, a woman driving a blue Toyota put her hands up in fear. Her car swirved momentarily out of its lane.

Seth felt his jaw drop. He couldn't believe Adam had done that. If the car had been going faster it might have gone out of control and crashed into the stone abutment next to the highway.

Meanwhile Adam grinned at him. "Scared the crap out of her."

"Maybe we ought to go," Seth said, suddenly worried that they were going to get into trouble. What if a cop had seen them? Or what if the woman was really mad?

"Why?" Adam asked.

"She could get off and come back here."

Adam shrugged. "Let her," he said. "The last person in the world I'd be afraid of is some old lady." He took a drag off his cigarette and turned away to watch the cars again.

Seth kept glancing toward the exit ramp to see if the woman in the blue Toyota had gotten off. He was really tempted to leave, but he stayed because he liked being with Adam. It made him feel good that a cool guy like Adam let him hang around.

A few minutes passed and the blue Toyota still did not appear on the exit ramp. Seth relaxed a little. He had smoked his Marlboro almost all the way down to the filter and his mouth tasted awful. Smoke kept getting in his eyes and making them water. He dropped the cigarette to the sidewalk and crushed it under his sneaker, relieved to be finished with it.

"Here's the way to do it," Adam said. He took the butt of his cigarette between his thumb and middle finger and flicked it over the side of the bridge and down into the traffic. With a burst of red sparks it hit the windshield of a black Camaro passing below. Adam turned and grinned. Seth smiled back uncomfortably. He was beginning to wonder just how far Adam would go.

Neither of them saw the black Camaro pull off onto the exit ramp and come up behind them on the bridge. Seth didn't notice it until he heard a door slam. He turned and saw three big guys getting out of the car. They were all wearing nylon sweatsuits, and they looked strong. Seth suddenly decided that it was time to go, but he quickly realized that the three guys had spread out, cutting off any way to escape. He and Adam were surrounded.

"Uh, Adam." Seth nudged him with his elbow.

"Wha—?" Adam turned around and looked shocked. In the meantime the three big guys were coming closer. Seth and Adam backed against the bridge wall. Seth felt his stomach tighten. His heart began to beat like a machine gun. Adam looked pretty scared too. Was it Seth's imagination, or was his friend trembling?

"Which one of you twerps flicked that butt on my car?" The question came from the husky guy with a black moustache and long black hair that curled behind his ears.

Seth and Adam glanced at each other. Seth was determined not to tell. He didn't believe in squealing on his friends. But suddenly he noticed that all three guys were staring at him. He quickly looked at Adam and saw why. Adam was pointing at him.

Before Seth could say anything, the husky guy reached forward and lifted him off the ground by the collar of his jacket. His feet kicked in the air uselessly for a second and then he was thrown against the front fender of the Camaro. He hit with a thud and lost his breath. Before he had a chance to recover, the guy grabbed him by the hair and forced his face toward the windshield.

"Lick it off," he grumbled.

Seth didn't know what he was talking about. He tried to raise his head, but the husky guy pushed his face closer to the windshield. God, he was strong.

"I said, lick it."

Lick what? Seth wanted to shout. Then he looked down at the glass and saw the little spot of gray ash where Adam's cigarette had hit. Oh, no. He stiffened. The thought made him sick. He tried to twist his head around, but the guy leaned his weight against Seth and pushed his face down again.

"Till it's clean," the guy said, pressing Seth's face down until it was only an inch from the smooth tinted glass. Seth stared at the little spot of ash. With the husky guy's weight on him, he could hardly breathe. The car's fender was digging into his ribs. Where was Adam?

The husky guy leaned harder against him, squeezing Seth painfully against the car. He pushed Seth's face down until it actually pressed against the cool glass. Seth could feel a spasm in his chest as his lungs cried for air. But he clamped his mouth closed. He wasn't going to give the guy the satisfaction of seeing him lick that spot.

The husky guy must have known it. Suddenly he pulled Seth's head up, then slammed it back down against the windshield. *Wham!* Seth reeled backwards, his hands covering his nose and mouth. Everything felt numb, and he was certain his nose and some teeth were broken. He slipped and landed in a sitting position, bending forward, his throbbing face buried in his hands.

A second passed and he heard someone laugh. Looking up he saw the three guys get back into the Camaro. The car lurched away, leaving rubber.

"You're bleeding." Adam was standing over him. Seth took his hand away from his mouth and saw that it was covered with bright red blood. It was dripping down from his nose and chin onto his denim jacket, leaving red spots. He tilted his head back, trying to stop the bleeding. At the same time he squeezed the bridge of his nose. It hurt, but somehow he knew it was not broken after all. He touched his front teeth with his tongue. They were all still there, and none felt loose.

"You want a hand?" Adam asked.

Seth nodded and Adam helped pull him up slowly. He was shaky on his feet and worried that his nose was going to start bleeding again. He looked down and saw that his denim jacket was covered with blood.

"I tried to help you," Adam said, "but one of them held a knife on me."

Seth glanced at him.

"It was a small knife," Adam said. "I guess he didn't want anyone to see it."

Seth felt his nose again. It was swollen and throbbed painfully. "Why'd you point at me?" he asked.

"I figured I could jump them if they made a move at you," Adam said. "How could I know they had knives?"

Seth shook his head. He didn't believe Adam. He started to walk toward home.

"You gonna make it okay?" Adam asked.

Seth nodded. He just wanted to be alone.

"I'll get those guys for you, man," Adam said. "I think I once saw one of them at the diner. I'm gonna go back there and see. Okay?"

Seth nodded again. He didn't even turn to watch Adam go.

On the way to his house, Seth stopped near some garbage cans a neighbor had put on the curb for collection. He looked down at his denim jacket. The spots of blood had turned dark. If he took it home and washed it now, the stains would probably make it look pretty cool. Like a jacket that had been worn in tons of fights. Seth smirked. He took it off and threw it in the garbage can.

TODD STRASSER

In spite of being a terrible speller and not a very good writer in high school, Todd Strasser went on to become a newspaper reporter and an advertising copywriter before turning to fiction. His first novel, *Angel Dust Blues*, earned the respect of both teenagers and critics for its examination of teenage drug dealing and its consequences. His second novel, *Friends Till the End*—the story of a high school athlete's friendship with a dying classmate—was named a Best Book for Young Adults by the American Library Association.

In a lighter vein, Strasser's *Rock 'n' Roll Nights* and *Turn It Up!* follow Gary Specter and his band as they struggle from playing in small, noisy clubs to eventually appearing before thousands of fans at Madison Square Garden. *Rock 'n' Roll Nights* was named a Best Book for Young Adults by the ALA.

Workin' for Peanuts deals with the conflict that occurs when a vendor at a baseball stadium becomes involved with the daughter of the family that runs the consessions. That book was made into a film for television, as was *A Very Touchy Subject*, which focuses on the temptations and frustrations of a high school senior who can think of little else besides girls and sex, and his next-door neighbor, a troubled girl with a "bad" reputation.

Mr. Strasser is also the author of *The Complete Computer Popularity Program*, a humorous novel about a seventh-grade boy who uses a computer program to make friends, and *The Wave*, the novelization of a television movie about a teacher who sets up a Nazi-like organization in his high school social studies classroom. That book was published under Strasser's pseudonym, Morton Rhue.

When he is not writing, visiting high schools, and speaking at conferences around the country, Todd Strasser manages a fortune cookie company in New York City.

Having the two most brilliant, most athletic, most handsome boys in the class fighting to take you to the dance might sound exciting to some girls. But while Jeff and Steve are fighting over Annie, no one has invited her best friend Brenda to the Valentine's Day dance. . . .

GREAT MOVES

SANDY ASHER

I sat cross-legged on Annie's tufted pink bedspread, chin to fist, elbow to knee, as she reviewed her problem. Some people would pay good money for a crack at Annie's problems, I thought. Me, for instance. This one is worth its weight in platinum.

Annie was perched on a plush pink stool at her white dressing table, her back to me, her sneakered feet spread for balance, Levi jeans tight as she leaned toward the oval mirror, applying mascara. "I just can't believe those two, can you?" she asked, squinting past her own reflection toward mine. "I mean, right there in the cafeteria, in front of *everybody,* they come charging up, practically knocking over half the line, and ask me to the dance. *Together.* I don't understand it. What could they have been thinking of?"

"Of asking you to the dance," I observed drily. I shifted from right to left elbow on knee, right to left fist under chin. I felt weary, barely able to hold up my head, let alone my end of this conversation.

Annie spun the stool around to face me, accidentally streaking a black mascara smudge across her nose. She paused to rub it off with a handful of tissues before responding. "Well, I know that much," she began. "What I mean is . . ."

She stopped short, having caught the look in my eyes. Best friends can do that, read your mind through your eyeballs. At least mine can.

"Oh, Tigger, I'm sorry," she said, dropping the mascara and tissue to shift onto the bed beside me. She's the only person in the world allowed to call me Tigger. It started way back in elementary school. She named me Tigger because I was always the bouncy type, and I began calling her Pooh, for her teddy bear shape and other qualities. But this past summer, while she was at her father's house in St. Louis, she grew two inches and slimmed down a lot. She came home just before school started, and the minute I saw her, I felt weird about calling her Pooh, so I went back to "Annie."

"I know what you're thinking," she went on, "and you've got to stop worrying about it. Somebody'll ask you to the dance. Who could resist a bouncy little redhead like you?"

Apparently everybody, I thought, but didn't mention it. Anyway, I wasn't feeling all that bouncy lately.

Annie continued: "Or you could ask somebody yourself, you know. Or go stag. Lots of people are."

"What's the point of going stag to a Valentine's dance?" I wondered aloud.

"To have *fun*," Annie replied, reasonably enough.

But I was in no mood to be reasonable. Besides, it was easy for her to say. She had the two best guys in the freshman class ready to duel over her. How could I show up stag knowing *that?*

"Don't worry about me," I told Annie, unlocking my chin from my knuckles and swinging myself off the edge of the bed to avoid her sympathy.

I knew she'd go right on worrying, though. That's the kind of person she is, teddy bear sweet to the core. It makes it very difficult for me to hate her, and believe me, ever since we hit Ulysses S. Grant Senior High in the fall, I've had reason to try: her with her perfect little figure (same poundage as before the summer, only arranged better), her terrific mane of blond hair (out of braids and just born to be feathered), and her big blue eyes (in full focus now, thanks to new contact lenses). It used to be such an easy job, being Annie's best friend: a couple of giggles now and then, a glass of lemonade to share . . . I gave a moment's fantasy to reenrolling in elementary school, where you don't need a date to play jacks.

"So who are you going with?" I asked. "Have you made up your mind?" I took over Annie's position at the dressing table and played with her makeup, dabbing blush, flicking liner, ever so nonchalant.

"No," she admitted. "First of all, I was so shocked, I couldn't even speak. I stood there going ubuh-dubuh-dubuh while the whole lunch line cracked up."

"Ubuh-dubuh-dubuh?" I asked, gagging on a giggle.

"It's not funny, Brenda," she began, then collapsed backward onto the bedspread, howling. It took us five minutes of fits and starts to stop laughing.

"Oh, nuts," Annie said finally, sitting up as we gasped for breath, "now I have to take out my lenses. They get these little white deposits on them when my eyes tear up. It's disgusting."

While she loped down the hall and into the bathroom, I chose two tones of blush and tried a sophisticated contoured cheekbone on my better side, my left, but my freckles kept getting in the way. Then the phone on Annie's night table rang.

(Yes, Annie Pooh Macauley has her own phone, with her own private number, no less. When her parents got divorced last spring, the phone was her father's way of proving he still cared. My parents are together, and together they agreed—when I asked about a phone for me—that saying no is another way of proving you care. A week later, Annie's mother gave her a TV. I didn't bother mentioning it to Mom and Dad.)

"Get it, please, Tigger!" Annie yelled from the bathroom.

I picked up the pink princess receiver. "Hello?"

"Um—um—is Anne Macauley there?" a low male voice asked. It seemed to be trying to whisper.

"Yes, she is. Just a—"

Suddenly there was an awful banging at the other end of the line and shouts of "Gimme that!" and "Hey, leggo!" Annie appeared in the doorway. Squinting, she picked up on my astonishment, then gingerly raised the receiver to her ear. After a moment's puzzled listening, she replaced it in its cradle. "They hung up," she announced, frowning.

"They?"

"The dynamic duo. From what I could make out, they were at

Steve's house and Jeff tried to call me on his phone." She sat down on the bed slowly, the furrow deepening between her brows.

"Still battling it out, huh?" I observed, feeling my depression take a sudden dip. A boy calling—*two* boys—two *great* boys—but not for me! The stuff sad songs are made of.

"It's been like that since they asked me," Annie said. "The minute I try to talk to one, the other shows up and won't let me. How am I supposed to choose when I never get a minute alone with either of them?" She put away her lens case, dug her wire-rims out of the night table drawer, and almost looked like my old Pooh again. Still frowning, she yanked her history book off the bottom shelf, flipped a handful of pages, then let it slide off her lap onto the bed. "I don't know what to do," she said. "I don't want to hurt either one of them. They're nice guys. But they sure are making this hard on me."

Jeff Brayburn and Steve Drew are more than nice guys: they are the local heroes of Thermopylae, Missouri. As starting guards on the jv basketball team, they've had their great moves written up almost weekly in the school and town papers. They're also president and vice president of the freshman class, and winner and runner-up for Joe Freshman, the guys' answer to Homecoming Queen. I have honors English with Jeff and honors math with Steve; believe me, I can attest to their brilliance. They came from Lee Junior High on the other side of town, so Annie and I had never met them until Grant, but we'd heard about them. Who hadn't? They were legends by eighth grade: in school, in sports, in scouting—you name it—they were first and second, second and first.

"They couldn't have spoken exactly in unison," I pointed out to Annie. "Which one asked you first?"

"I can't remember," Annie moaned. "It happened so quickly, and it was so unexpected. And now Jeff insists he was first, and Steve insists *he* was first, and they're both pressuring me to decide, but neither one will let me. Whoever I pick, the other one's going to be sore. I lose either way."

"You also win either way."

"I guess," Annie said, with a sigh.

For the personal choice of the personal choices of the entire female freshman class of Ulysses S. Grant Senior High, she did not look happy. I couldn't imagine why not. I would have traded places with her gladly, but that wasn't an option. We decided not to decide for a while. Between us and the dance, there loomed a history exam over the major battles of World War I. "The war to end war" held us captive until I had to leave for dinner.

I was reviewing the Marne before first-hour English the next morning when I became aware of someone breathing over my shoulder. I snapped the book shut and whirled around, realizing, with a gasp, that it was Jeff Brayburn, hunched up over the desk behind me.

"I'd like to talk to you about Anne Macauley," he said in the hushed tone I'd heard on Annie's princess. "You're her buddy, right?"

"Right," I said, not failing to note the green of his eyes, the tan of his cheek, the muscle of his shoulders under the blue basketball jersey.

"You've got to tell her to go to the dance with me," he blurted out. From the alarm in his eyes, he seemed to have surprised himself as much as me.

"I do? Why?" I asked him.

A blush crept in under the tan. He lowered incredibly long black lashes. "Because," he mumbled, "it's important to me."

I hesitated, searching for words, touched by his shyness, his sincerity. His gorgeousness. "Well, gee, I don't know," I said, hitting a new low for clever comebacks.

His lashes lifted; his eyes, filled with longing, sent emerald shivers through my life-support system. "Please?" he said.

"I'll see what I can do," I offered hoarsely.

"You will? Honest? Hey, you're all right, Brenda!"

Blushing three shades deeper than my freckles, I realized I'd just fallen madly in love with Jeff Brayburn.

After the history exam, I reported to Annie—not everything, just Jeff's message. She sighed deeply and trudged away toward fourth-period lunch, noting that she had both of them to face there, without me. I felt guilty, but for an entirely different reason.

Honors math brought Steve Drew to my side. What surprised me this time was that I was somehow not totally surprised.

"You're Anne Macauley's friend, aren't you?" he asked, plopping down on the next desk, sandy-haired and grinning over the familiar blue jersey. There was a game that night, I remembered. The team and cheerleaders were wearing their uniforms to generate excitement. It was working. Brown eyes this time, big and twinkling. I couldn't deny it. I was Anne's friend, Anne's best friend, the one with the traitorous heart.

"Well, listen, friend," Steve said, leaning toward me confidentially, "I've got a very special favor to ask you. I'd really like Anne to go to the dance with me, you know? And I was thinking maybe a word from you would be just the thing to swing it my way. What do you think?"

He winked, drawing me in on his side, sealing his little secret plot between us. Suspicion, moving faster than a shooting star, zipped across my brain: A *plot?* Against *whom?* The questions disintegrated, sinking into warm murky mush as dimples deepened around Steve's smile.

"I'll do what I can," I told him, my own smile rising in response.

"Hey, Brenda, you're okay," he said, and brushed one finger across the back of my hand as he left. The spot he'd touched tingled long after. I was *also* in love with Steve Drew!

As soon as the last bell rang, I charged to my locker, grabbed my stuff, delivered Steve's message to Annie, and hurried home alone, pleading a sudden dental emergency. (It wasn't a total lie: love-struck and guilt-ridden as I was, I couldn't trust my mouth around Annie.) So, instead of the pink-and-white cloud of her bedroom, where I've spent a lifetime of pleasant afternoons, I doomed myself to the racket of my kid brother Tony and his best friend Lou galloping through the house, doing their daily horse imitations.

"Something wrong?" Dad asked, poking his head in at my door to find me in bed, barricaded behind a fifteen-year collection of stuffed animals. Behind him, I could hear the front door crash open, followed by the clatter of clumsy hooves: da-da-dum, da-da-dum, da-da-dum-dum-dum. A series of shrill whinnies split the air as stallions collided in our living room.

"Can't you stop them?" I snapped. Might as well blame this day's gloom on Tony; I'd saddled him with plenty of others.

"They're just playing wild horses," Dad explained, as if I didn't know. (Tony doesn't want to be a cowboy when he grows up. He wants to be a horse.)

"The herd needs thinning," I told Dad. "Shoot a couple."

Dad rolled his eyes and disappeared, closing the door behind him. Faintly, from the kitchen, I heard the phone ring and Mom calling my name. In spite of my depression, I bounced out of bed, scattering animals everywhere, and hightailed it into the hall. Force of habit. Mom was holding the receiver and smiling at me weirdly.

"Brenda Prescott?" I heard as I took the phone from her. My stomach quaked. The voice was very familiar. "Brenda, this is Steve Drew. From your math class. Remember me?"

Who could forget? But before I'd mustered up an answer, I heard sounds of a struggle, a thud, an "Oof!" and some muffled words, followed by a loud click. The line went dead. Dial tone.

As I hung up, I couldn't help but notice Mom's face falling. What *is* it with her that she can't stop hoping I'll turn out to be the belle of the ball? I mean, she talks a blue streak about Gloria Steinem and liberation and how *not* making Homecoming Queen helps a girl develop character, but whenever she spots a boy on the horizon, she forgets all that and goes wimpy with yearning. She never says anything, exactly, but I can practically hear her prayers: "Take my daughter, somebody, *anybody*. Don't let her be a wallflower. *Please!*"

I guess I knew what she was thinking because I was thinking the exact same thing. At that moment I would gladly have laid down my character, my brother, my own best friend, for just *one* Jeff Brayburn or *one* Steve Drew. Somewhere at the top of the heap, women were on the move, striving for justice, equality, and world peace. Down here, we were still stuck scrambling for boys. When were we going to make a great move of our own?

Mom furrowed her brow. I could see the questions forming.

"They hung up," I explained quickly, as if that were really an explanation. I didn't have the heart to tell her it was just the latest episode in the struggle over Annie.

I escaped back to my room.

Just after dawn I called Annie with a story about needing to get to school early, so I wouldn't have to walk with her. It was Valentine's Day, I had no date, I was in love with both of hers. No way could I face her. I hid in the girls' room till the first bell rang, kept my nose in my textbook all through history, and stayed behind in the art room well after last hour until I thought Annie and everyone else had left for home. But I failed to figure on the dance decorating committee.

The minute I hit my locker, Jeff and Steve were beside me, elbowing each other out of the way.

"Brenda—(Beat it, Brayburn)—"

"Brenda—(I was here first, Drew)—"

"You wanna—(Oh, yeah? Says who?)—"

"You wanna—(Says me, that's who. Bug off!)—"

"Go to—(Who's gonna make me?)—"

"Go to—(Me, that's who!)—"

"The dance—(You and what army?)—"

"The dance—(Me and one swift kick!)—"

"With me tonight?" ("Try it, sucker, and buy a sling for your lip!") they asked. Or threatened? In unison.

"Ubuh-dubuh-dubuh," I replied, then quickly pulled myself together. "Wait a minute! I thought you wanted to take Annie."

"She won't choose," Jeff whined—or was it Steve? They'd become a two-headed octopus, maneuvering for position in front of me, all limbs and facial contortions. "The dance is tonight, so I figured I'd better go ahead and ask you."

"*You* figured?" Steve—or was it Jeff?—shot back. "You heard that *I* was figuring, so you figured on figuring first. You do it every time."

"*I* do it? *You're* the one! It's always you. Ever since third grade—"

While they carried on in that vein, I had time to consider recent developments. First, I was thrilled down to my socks. The two objects of my affection were fighting over me, engaged in actual hand-to-hand combat! I had Annie's problem, the one I'd've traded platinum for!

Yelping like puppies, the guys tripped each other up and collapsed into a writhing heap on the floor. Curious onlookers began to gather. I felt the rising heat of a blush crawling out of my collar and took a giant step backward to get out of the guys' way. Fists continued to fly, met by grunts and groans—and a few cheers from the sidelines. Experimentally, I took another step back. And one more, for good measure. My hunch was right: the guys never noticed.

They're not fighting *for me*, I realized; they're fighting *against each other*.

Suddenly, Annie stepped up beside me. Judging from the look on her face, she'd been there long enough to know what was up. She was hurt. She was trying to hide it, but I could tell. I'd seen that look before. My brain flashed back to the end of summer, then to her father and the pink princess, and it suddenly dawned on me that not all of Annie's problems were worth platinum. Divorce is a kick in the head, even with your own TV and phone. Being the spoils of a small-time war isn't all that great, either. And having your best friend turn cool green with envy is the very last thing you need.

The guys had worn themselves out by now and were sitting up against opposite lockers, rubbing their heads. The onlookers drifted away.

"I'm sorry, Pooh," I said. "It's not that they want to go with me instead of you. It's that they want to beat each other out, and you weren't letting them because you couldn't hurt one and choose the other. We're another two points to them, that's all, or one more office to run for."

Annie swallowed hard.

"Don't cry!" I begged her. "It's not our problem; it's *theirs*. Besides, you'll have to take out your lenses."

A giggle broke through; one of mine rushed out to meet it. Then we turned and began to walk away, matching our strides as always.

"Hey!" one of the guys yelled after us. "The dance is *tonight!* Aren't you going to make up your mind?"

The two of us paused, and took our time about turning around. We sucked in deep breaths, reading each other's faces. It was too late for any of us to ask anyone else to the dance. We'd all end up going stag—or not at all. This is it, I thought, my chance to develop some character, to make my great move. Annie raised an eyebrow. I gave the nod.

"Choose!" the boys demanded.

"No," we said, standing our ground.

In an instant, we found ourselves surrounded.

"You *have* to choose!" Steve insisted, brown eyes flashing indignantly.

"We've got to know who wins," Jeff added, green eyes pleading.

"No winners this time," Annie announced, linking her arm through mine.

"But look on the bright side," I continued. "No losers, either."

At first the guys seemed confused, and then angry. But finally, because there was simply no way under it, no way over it, and no way around it, peace broke out in Thermopylae.

SANDY ASHER

By the time she published her first novel for young adults, Sandy Asher had written over fifty short stories, dozens of poems, numerous articles, and seven children's plays. She also had been an actress on a Mississippi River showboat, a ballerina dancer, an advertising copywriter, a frozen-custard salesperson, and a teacher of creative writing.

From the beginning she was determined not to write teenage "problem novels" that were "deadly serious." Instead, she has chosen to write about more ordinary teenagers in "sometimes humorous, sometimes unpleasant" situations. In *Summer Begins,* a quiet eighth grader suddenly finds herself the topic of discussion after she writes what turns out to be a controversial article for the school newspaper. Asher combines elements of school, family, and self-image in *Just Like Jenny,* where Stephanie learns how competent she is while competing for a spot in the ballet troupe. In *Daughters of the Law,* an anti-Semitic incident forces a shy teenager to face painful realizations about her parents' past in a concentration camp as she simultaneously prepares for her bat mitzvah.

School, friendships, family, and teenage pressures are also topics in *Things Are Seldom What They Seem.* In Debbie's life, one thing that is not what it seems is the relationship the drama teacher has with some female students in his high school plays, and one of those girls is Debbie's sister. Fortunately, Debbie's new friend Murray lightens the story through his humorous and offbeat approach to life.

In *Missing Pieces,* sophomore Heather Connelly learns to come to terms with her own and her mother's grief after her father dies. She is aided by Nicky Simpson, her first romantic companion.

Asher's most recent book for young adults is *Everything Is Not Enough;* for children she has published *Teddy Teabury's Fabulous Fact.* In addition, as Sandra Fenichel Asher, she received a National Endowment for the Arts Fellowship grant in playwriting. Many of her plays for children and adults have been published and produced and have won awards. She and her family live in Springfield, Missouri.

Finding money on the street is cause for celebration. The larger the find, the greater the joy. Spending it wisely, however, sometimes isn't any fun. . . .

A HUNDRED BUCKS OF HAPPY

SUSAN BETH PFEFFER

I found it on the corner of Maple and Grove streets. That isn't the way I usually walk home from school, but that day I had gotten lost in thought and forgotten to turn at Oak, which saves me a half block. Which only goes to prove that daydreaming can be cost-effective.

Anyway, there it was, not exactly glistening in the sunlight, because dollar bills don't glisten. I knew it was a bill of some sort, because it had that well-used green look to it, but I assumed that it was a five, or maybe if my luck were extraordinary, a ten. Whatever it was, I was going to be happy to have it, so I bent down fast, to make sure I got it before anybody else walking down Grove or Maple could find it. It's a well-walked intersection.

I bent down, scooped the money up, and started walking away fast, with that heartbeating sensation of having done something exciting and wrong, even though as far as I know, there's no crime in finding money on the street. I've read about people who do that for a hobby, jog with their heads down, collecting the nickels and dimes they find as they run. Whatever this was, it wasn't a dime, and I didn't feel like taking any chances. So I bent, swooped, and increased my pace until by the time I reached Elm I was half running. Not that anybody cared. The rest of the world kept on walking toward whatever their lives were propelling them to. The money was as much mine as if it had been left to me by some munificent great aunt.

I was three doors away from my house before I took the bill out of my jacket pocket, to check its denomination. As I did, I noticed there was a hole in my pocket and the money had slipped into the lining. It took a bit of searching before I found it, but eventually my fingers made contact, and I found what I was looking for.

It was a hundred-dollar bill. I had never seen one before, so I wouldn't have recognized it, but it was clearly labeled. Ben Franklin stared at me—and I swear he winked—as I turned his bill over and over, not believing it could be real, not believing my luck.

Once I knew what I had, I ran like the devil the three houses to mine. My fingers shook as I searched for the front-door key, and I dropped my schoolbooks all over the front stoop, I was clutching onto the money so hard.

I got everything together, using what little strength I had left in me, and let myself into the house. Mom was at work, and Danny, my kid brother, was sitting in front of the TV, watching Dance Dynomite and finishing up a bag of potato chips I suspected he'd started not that long ago.

Things hadn't always been like this. For starters, it wasn't until this year that Danny had given up superheroes in exchange for girls dancing on TV. And it used to be that Mom stayed at home, making wholesome and nutritious snacks for us to eat when we got back from school, instead of letting us shove potato chips into our mouths. Or at least into Danny's. He ate them so fast, there were never any left by the time I got home.

Those golden days of nutritious snacks ended when Dad moved out. I have an MIA father. You know the sort. He sends a few bucks every Christmas with a note to Mom telling her to buy herself and the kids something nice, and the rest of the year he's missing in action. He's not one for halfway measures, though. When he finally did leave, after threatening to often enough, he moved six hundred miles away. His address is a post office box, and if for some reason you have to call him, his machine answers for him and swears he'll call right back. Don't hold your breath waiting.

So Mom, not wanting us to starve, got a job and became a statistic. They do studies about people like her. They call it the feminization of poverty, but I've got to tell you Mom looked a lot more feminine before she got poor. Danny looked better in those days too, but maybe the fat and the pimples would have come anyway, once he became aware of girls, and have nothing to do with his potato chip diet.

I went up to my room, thinking about how many bags of potato chips a hundred dollars could buy, threw my books down, and stared at the money a while longer. Ben Franklin had the nicest face. He looked great in green.

We ate frozen for dinner that night, each of us picking our own dinner, which Mom then threw into the oven at 350. She cooks everything at 350 these days, for half an hour, regardless of what the box says to do. As far as I can tell, it doesn't make a difference, so she's probably right going with a single system for everything frozen.

"So," she said, as we each took our trays out of the oven and spread them on the kitchen table. "Anything interesting happen at school today?"

You have to give her points for trying. Nothing interesting has happened in school for the past seven years, but she asks regularly anyway. Seven years ago the goat got loose in the cafeteria, but that's a whole other story.

"I got an 83 in science," Danny announced. "And Michelle Crain got sick in English and practically puked all over everybody."

"No puking talk over dinner," Mom said automatically. She's ended a lot of really neat conversations with that rule. "Chris? What's new with you?"

It was the moment I'd dreaded. I mean, you can hardly deny that finding a hundred-dollar bill is newsworthy, even if, technically speaking, it didn't happen in school and therefore wasn't covered by her original question.

I would have kept the news to myself, except there was no way I could come home from having spent the hundred dollars without Mom noticing. And I didn't want her to think I'd entered into a life of crime. Mom watches a lot of sitcoms, so she worries about things like shoplifting and bank robberies.

"I found some money on the corner of Maple and Grove," I said, trying to sound real casual about it.

I shouldn't have bothered. Mom's eyes lit right away, and even Danny stopped inhaling his frozen dinner.

"How much?" they both asked. It was eerie how fast they got the words out.

There are people in this world who can lie. I'm not one of them. "A hundred dollars," I said. "I found a hundred-dollar bill."

"A hundred bucks!" Danny breathed. "Wow!"

"A hundred dollars," Mom said. "Well you certainly can't keep it."

"Why not?" I asked.

"It isn't yours," she replied. "You have to find its owner."

"How am I supposed to do that?" I asked. Actually, it was a question I'd been asking myself ever since I checked the denomination. "Advertise in the paper? Ask its owner to describe what the money looks like? Does Ben Franklin wear glasses, or does he have his contacts in? Is he wearing a wedding ring? Mom, there's no way to find out who lost it."

"What if it belonged to some poor person?" she asked, but I could see she was weakening.

"Poor people don't carry hundred-dollar bills," I replied.

"I bet it's mob money," Danny said. "And when the mob finds out it's missing, they'll hire a hit man to shoot Chris. Terrific!"

"No one's going to shoot me," I told him. "Besides, I intend to spend the money so fast, there won't be anything for the mob to collect. I thought I'd go to the mall tomorrow and pick some stuff up."

"You can't do that," Mom said. "You have to give me the money."

"How do you figure that?" I asked.

"We need it," she said.

"I sure need it," Danny said. "I want my share."

"I'm not sharing," I told him.

"Fine," Mom said. "So you can give it to me."

I swear they must send mothers to school somewhere, when they're in an embryonic mother state, kind of like the pods in *Invasion of the Body Snatchers*, before they become fully formed humans. At mother school, they're taught how to ignore the obvious to go after what they want.

"If I'm not sharing, I'm not giving," I said. "The money is mine. I found it. There's a lot of stuff I need, and I intend to get myself some of it."

Mom snorted. "Wait until you see how long a hundred dollars lasts," she said.

"I look forward to finding out," I said, trying to sound dignified.

The rest of supper was kind of a drag, with Danny whining and Mom sulking and me thinking about the money sitting on my bed, waiting for the world to come and snatch it. As soon as I could, I went back to my room and shoved the bill into the toe of my boot. Then I hid both boots under my bed. No point taking any chances.

It was positively painful sitting through school the next day. Of course having a hundred-dollar bill shoved inside my boot didn't make things any more comfortable. I kept wiggling my toe around to make sure the money was still there, until my foot started cramping. It's not easy being rich.

When school finally ended, I limped my way over to the mall. I hadn't figured out just how I was going to get the money out of the boot when I started buying stuff, but I figured I could always just take the boot off, whip the money out, and become a local legend.

We have a pretty good mall, with a lot of places where you could spend a hundred dollars. I started by trying on a leather jacket. It fit perfectly, and it made me feel great. I also liked the idea of buying just one perfect thing with the money. After all, if I bought a lot of little stuff, I could buy any one of those things on my own, and it would just be a case of quantity, not quality. But I'd have to save for years to buy a leather jacket, until by the time I could afford it I probably wouldn't want it anyway.

The jacket was on sale too. It had been $120, but it was marked down to $98. I took it over to the sales register, where the woman looked me over real carefully and asked if it was cash or charge.

"Cash," I told her, feeling for the thousandth time the money in the toe.

She rang the numbers up and said "That will be a hundred and four dollars and three cents."

"No," I said. "It's ninety eight dollars. See." I showed her the price tag.

She looked at me like I had just emerged from the primordial swamp. "Sales tax," she said. "A hundred and four dollars and three cents."

I didn't have a hundred and four dollars and three cents. I had two dollars and thirty-five cents, and a hundred dollars stuffed in my boot. Add the two together, and you do not come up with a hundred and four and three cents. Believe me, I tried five different ways of adding the numbers together, and none of them worked.

"I can't afford it," I muttered.

"Kids," the saleslady said.

I nearly took my boot off to throw at her, but then I decided I didn't want to buy anything that cost more than the hundred dollars anyway. It would have been cheating, somehow. So I left the store and looked for something that cost just a few dollars less. I didn't mind having a couple of bucks change left, just as long as I didn't go over my original total. It was kind of like game show rules.

I must have walked through that mall a half-dozen times, upstairs and down, trying to find just the right thing to buy. Most of the stuff I looked at I would have killed to own ordinarily, but somehow nothing was special enough to spend my hundred on. And things didn't cost what I thought they did. I finally decided to buy a Walkman, so I went into one of the department stores to price them. Only they had one on sale, AM/FM radio and cassette player for $29.95. That seemed awfully cheap to me, only there was no point spending more than that for another brand just because it wasn't on sale. So I didn't buy one, and I didn't get any cassettes either. And all the books I used to dream about owning looked like crap, and suddenly I realized there was nothing at the mall I really wanted.

I sat down then, by the fountain, to collect my thoughts.

There was no water in the fountain area, because of the water shortage, and its tile floor was littered with pennies and nickels. I couldn't get over how people had just tossed their money away like that, when I couldn't even make myself take my boot off.

It occurred to me then that I could buy a car for a hundred dollars. Maybe not a great car, but a car, nonetheless. I had this entire fantasy about being behind the wheel of my very own car, driving my friends around, parking in the high school lot, going to drive-ins, moving around the way you could if you owned a car. It was a pretty picture, and I was just about ready to spend part of my $2.35 on a newspaper so I could see what cars were available for a hundred bucks, until common sense made me stop.

The problem wasn't the money for the car, or even the sales tax. I figured I could always argue the owner down the extra couple of bucks. The problem was car insurance. Somehow I didn't think I could count on finding the insurance money on the corner of Maple and Grove every six months. No insurance, no car. No car, no freedom. I still had my money, but the fun was fast going out of it.

Just to show myself that I could, I went into Woolworth's and bought some chewing gum. They were out of my brand, but I bought a package of some other brand, and broke one of my singles. The change jingled as I walked away from the mall, chewing my gum, and limping.

I found myself walking a half block out of my way, to return to the corner of Maple and Grove, but a scary thing happened once I got there. I realized I hadn't gone back to see if there was any more money there but to leave the hundred-dollar bill smack where I'd found it.

You know, I actually wanted the person whose money it was to show up, demanding that I give it back. I looked around for penniless orphans, or Mafia dons, or anybody who looked like they might be searching for a missing Ben Franklin, but the only people on Grove and Maple were the sorts of people who were always on Grove and Maple. I know, because I stood there for close to ten minutes, waiting for someone who looked a hundred dollars poorer than they had the day before.

It was then that I knew what I had to do. So I limped over to the bank. It was Friday, and they were open until five. I walked in, like it was the most ordinary thing in the world for me to be in a bank, and sat down in the section where they keep you waiting if you want to start a new account. For some reason, banks like to keep people waiting before they take their money.

I got comfortable and took my boot off. People looked at me, but there wasn't anything I could do about it. I took out the hundred-dollar bill, and a couple of people actually laughed. I grinned, but it was mostly from relief at getting my toes unjammed.

I straightened the bill out, put my boot back on, and got on line. It took a while, but eventually I got to a teller.

"I'd like a hundred singles," I said, handing her the hundred-dollar bill.

She looked at it like it must be hot, and she called some guy over to check it out. They held it to the light and crinkled it and read the serial numbers and practically asked me for its pedigree before they finally decided the money was legit. I had a bunch of lies available about how it was I happened to have a hundred-dollar bill, but they didn't ask me and I didn't volunteer. Instead the teller counted out a hundred singles, and then I counted them with her, and she gave me an envelope to put the dollars in. The envelope was pretty thick once they were all in, but the bank is only a couple of blocks from my house, and there was no way I was going to shove the money back in my boot. Instead I held on to it carefully and walked home, trying to appear inconspicuous. I probably did too.

At supper that night I handed thirty-three dollars to my mother, and thirty-three dollars to Danny. I kept thirty-three for myself, and the remaining dollar I sent to my father's post office box. I figured he could buy a Hallmark card with it, to send to himself for Father's Day.

After supper Mom drove Danny and me to the mall, and we all went shopping. I bought the Walkman with my thirty-three. Good thing it was on sale.

SUSAN BETH PFEFFER

Born in New York City and graduated from New York University, Susan Beth Pfeffer lives in Middletown, New York. She is a free-lance writer of reviews, articles, and juvenile books, including *Better Than All Right; Just Between Us; What Do You Do When Your Mouth Won't Open?; Courage, Dana!;* and *Rewind to Yesterday.*

Ms. Pfeffer first attracted the attention of teenage readers with *Marly the Kid,* the story of a teenager who runs away from her mother to live with her father and understanding stepmother, then gets into trouble in school by challenging her sexist teacher. That was followed by *Beauty Queen* and *Starring Peter and Leigh.*

Defying school authorities is again an issue in *A Matter of Principle,* where the principal censors the student newspaper and then expels a group of students when they publish an underground newspaper.

About David, a novel for older teenagers, concerns the suicide of a teenage boy and the reactions of his closest friend, who tries to find out why he did it and what she might have done to prevent it. The American Library Association identified *About David* as a Best Book for Young Adults.

Recently, Susan Beth Pfeffer has developed a series called *Make Me a Star,* about a group of young actors in a TV show called *Hard Time High.* It starts with *Prime Time* and is followed by *Take Two and . . . Rolling!, Wanting It All, On the Move,* and *Love Scenes.*

Her latest novel is *Getting Even,* which follows the adventures of Annie Powell, who served as a summer intern for a glamorous New York City magazine—described in *Fantasy Summer*—and who has just been rejected as feature editor of her high school newspaper.

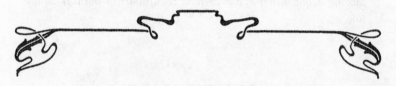

ILLUMINATIONS

JOAN AIKEN

Late at night, in the little bungalow beside the railroad tracks, beneath a towering electric pylon, Fern thinks she hears somebody moving about upstairs. But there is no upstairs in the tiny bungalow. . . .

COUSIN ALICE

JOAN AIKEN

When Fern Robson went to stay with her mother's sister, her aunt Twyla, it was out of acute need, not for any pleasant reason.

"She's an awkward one, Twyla Deane," sighed Mr. Robson. "There's no denying that. But where else to send you, I just do not know."

Mrs. Robson, Fern's mother, had been very badly injured in a coach accident, on a day's outing to Paigle Bay, and it was not even certain yet whether she would recover. She was in intensive care, in a deep coma. And her husband Sam, with a broken leg, was hobbling about in a nearby ward, not allowed out of hospital, though he was well enough to make arrangements about his daughter.

"You'll just have to go to Twyla, dearie. I'm right sorry about it, but there it is."

Fern was sorry too. Apart from the dreadful nonstop pain and fear about her mother, she hated leaving home, because the month was May, and the sweet peas were coming up in her garden patch, and the lilacs in front of the cottage, and the bluebells in Slype Wood down the lane. Who'd want to go and stay on the edge of a growing town, in a house by the railway?

"Who'll feed Smokey while I'm away?"

"The neighbors. He'll manage. You be a good girl now and don't argue."

So Fern miserably packed a bag, and Tom Harman, one of the neighbors, drove her thirty miles to Haleswick and left her at Aunt Twyla's house.

Crossing Cottage the place was called, because of the level crossing nearby. It was not a cottage, really, but a bungalow, built of ugly raw red brick with a slate roof. The garden was flat and bare, not a tree in it, only some empty-looking flowerbeds alternating with concrete paths and poor-looking grass. There wasn't a tree to be seen *anywhere*, in fact; close by lay timber yards and goods yards and factory sheds, a bit of wasteland with junk cars and nettles, the railway, of course, and right on the other side of Aunt Twyla's garden fence, an enormous electric pylon, towering over the squat little house, its four legs planted so far apart that the square of ground between them seemed bigger than the garden itself. There were half a dozen notices fixed on the pylon: DANGER, Keep Away, HIGH VOLTAGE, Beware, Property of the Electricity Board, Trespassers Will Be Prosecuted.

Since almost the first thing Aunt Twyla told Fern was that she would be frizzled up like a thread in a flame if she ever touched the pylon, Trespassers Will Be Prosecuted hardly seemed necessary, Fern thought. There wouldn't be much left of them to prosecute.

The pylon hummed to itself, now and then, a feverish mosquito sound that Fern didn't care for at all. While the hum went on, she found it hard to concentrate on her schoolwork, hard to fall asleep at night, hard to do anything but worry about how Mother was getting on.

The other children at the Haleswick school were standoffish at first.

"Your aunt, Mrs. Deane, is a queer one," they told Fern. "That's why her old man goes to sea; he goes to sea because he can't stand her."

"He goes to sea because he's a merchant seaman," said Fern reasonably. "He comes back every six months."

"He don't stay home long. She quarrels with folk, your aunt does. Where she lived before, she quarreled with the neighbors so bad, she had to move."

This was true, Fern discovered; or partly true. For years the Deanes had lived in the High Street, in a small ancient gabled house, next to a greengrocer's shop. But there had been trouble. What sort of trouble, Fern could not make out, but anyway, while Uncle Frank was off at sea, Aunt Twyla had left the house in which her husband had been born, and moved to Crossing Cottage.

"No neighbors to fret me here," she said tersely. "It's better."

Aunt Twyla was a terse woman, silent, thin, and angry-faced, only uttering when she had to; twelve hours a day she wore an apron, and her hair was scraped back as if she didn't care what it looked like.

It was a pity about the house in the High Street, Fern thought. It had bow windows, was built of stone, and looked solid and comfortable; next door to it the greengrocer's always had beautiful high-piled fragrant masses of pinks and roses and lilies of the valley, besides lettuce and onions and cauliflower and fruit. Flowers and vegetables next door would be much more comfortable than the pylon and the railway; all through each night, trains clanked and shunted and whimpered and flung electric flashes over Fern's bedroom ceiling. Aunt Twyla's curtains were thin cotton; the light flashed through.

"Don't the trains ever keep you awake?" Fern asked, but Aunt Twyla said, "I never do sleep much."

"Mother doesn't either."

"I know," said Twyla. Then she added slowly, "Maybe she's making up for that now."

Fern remembered her mother saying once, "Twyla and I used to have the same dreams. At breakfast we used to check with each other about the bits we couldn't remember. I wonder if we still dream the same things."

What was Mother dreaming now? Fern wondered; and then, looking at Aunt Twyla, thought, Is that what she is wondering too?

The bungalow was small and bare and flimsy; even with only two people there, it was hard to get off and be alone, because every corner seemed visible from every other corner. Unless you went into the bathroom. There were no books or pictures, and the floor was bare polished lino.

No photographs. Fern had wondered if there would be one of Alice, but there was not. Nor of Uncle Frank.

"Whatever you do, don't mention Alice," Father had warned, and Fern had promised she would not.

Alice was her cousin, Aunt Twyla's daughter, who had died in an accident ten years ago. Fern had been only three when Alice died, the same age as her cousin. Of course there wouldn't be any clothes or toys left—Aunt Twyla would have got rid of them long ago. It was all over. It had all happened a long time ago, when the Deanes were living in the other house, the one in the High Street.

Fern used to pass it every day as she went to and from school. She used to look up at the windows and wonder which one had been Alice's room.

Living in a house without any upstairs was queer, and not comfortable. Fern often found herself, in Crossing Cottage, absentmindedly listening for the sound of footsteps overhead, and almost sure that she heard them. Or footsteps coming down the stairs. She never could get used to the fact that there weren't any stairs.

Nobody lived in the High Street house now; it had been turned into estate agents' offices. There were no lights in the window at night.

Coming home late sometimes, from Guides or a school film show, Fern would look up at the dark windows and think: Suppose Alice is still there? Not very nice for her, all alone in a dark empty house full of photographs of houses. And she sent a thought through the black empty glass of the windows: Cousin Alice? Are you there? I'm sorry we never met. It wouldn't be so miserable staying in Crossing Cottage, if *you* were there too.

June the first was Mother's birthday. Fern sent a greetings telegram to the hospital: THINKING ABOUT YOU ALL THE TIME LOVE FERN. And Aunt Twyla rang up Father, who was still in hospital too—his leg wasn't mending as fast as it should. He said there was no change in Mother's condition. Still in a coma.

Fern went to school as usual, feeling as if lead weights were tied on her feet. Coming home, at teatime, past Coney's vegetable and flower shop, she was reminded by the colorful, fragrant display that if it was Mother's birthday it must be Aunt Twyla's birthday too, since they were twins, so she stopped and bought a bunch of pinks. They were pink and white and frilly, and smelt powerfully sweet, of clove and vanilla.

"You are Mrs. Deane's niece, aren't you?" said Mrs. Coney, plump and gray-haired, wrapping a twist of tissue paper round the pinks. "Wasn't your mother in an accident? How is she getting on?"

The concern and kindness in her voice nearly undid Fern, who had managed all through the schoolday to wear a crust of calm. Her lip began to quiver, she muttered, "N-not too well," and almost bolted out of the shop.

She didn't stop, as usual, to send a thought up to Cousin Alice next door, but hurried homewards, out of the cheerful High Street, into Gasworks Road, along Brewery Way, through Salt Passage, and so to Railway Approach and the flimsy iron gate of Crossing Cottage.

There had been rain during the afternoon, and the cracked unmade-up footway of Railway Approach was muddy and puddly. Aunt Twyla detested wet feet making marks in the clean lino floor, and even through her fog of misery about Mother, Fern managed to remember that; she took pains to avoid the puddles and reached the garden gate with dry feet. The sloping concrete path to the front door had already dried off, but as Fern walked up it, she noticed a line of wet footprints ahead of her. Some other person evidently had *not* troubled to avoid the puddles. Some other person had feet about the same size as Fern's own. Who could it be?

Nobody—and specially not children—ever came calling at Crossing Cottage. Twyla's only visitors were men coming to read the meter and ladies selling flags in aid of cancer research.

Fern opened the door and nearly fell over her aunt, who was ironing pillow slips. There wasn't room to do more than one thing at a time in the bungalow—with the ironing board unfolded you had to squeeze along the wall.

Fern put down her schoolbag and looked round the room, which was bare and tidy. No visitor, nothing unusual.

"Is anyone here?" she couldn't help asking.

"*I'm* here. Nobody else," snapped her aunt. "Why?"

Fern was embarrassed. She was afraid Aunt Twyla might think she had expected to find a birthday party in process—which she certainly had not.

"It's just—I thought I saw—" she mumbled, and turned to look through the open front door behind her. But the line of wet footprints had dried off the path. There was nothing to be seen.

"Shut that door, such a perishing draft it makes when the back door's open," said Aunt Twyla sharply. The front and back doors were directly opposite each other, with the scullery, front room, and a bit of passage between; if all the doors happened to be open, in whatever direction the wind was blowing, it seemed to veer round and sweep clean through the house.

"I bought these for you, Aunt Twyla," said Fern. "Happy birthday!" and she handed her aunt the bunch of pinks.

Aunt Twyla's eyes sparked, as she turned back the tissue. "Where did you get these?" she demanded.

"Coneys, in the High Street."

"I don't want you getting things there, ever. D'you hear?"

"Why, Aunt Twyla?"

"Because I say so. I don't want you having anything to do with those Coneys. Just remember that."

Aunt Twyla walked quickly away with the pinks. She certainly did not put them into a vase. After tea, wondering what had happened to them, Fern went out into the glum little back garden, with its rotary clothes dryer, ash heap, dustbin, and empty rabbit hutch left over from the previous owner. On the other side of the fence the pylon hummed menacingly. At first Fern couldn't see the pinks, on the ash heap or anywhere about the garden; but then she noticed them lying under the pylon, midway between its four massive steel feet. Aunt Twyla must have flung them there, over the fence; they were light, she must have flung them with all her strength.

That evening, unusually, Twyla went out and left Fern alone in the bungalow. Where had Aunt Twyla gone? Was she walking fast, angrily, through the draggled fields, past the gasworks and the sewage farm? Fern lay shivering in bed, listening to the hum of the pylon and the howl of passing trains.

Next day at school, Sue Coney, who was fat and curlyheaded

and good-natured, and had, up to now, been rather a friend of Fern's, wrote her a note that said, "After what your aunt did, I don't want to be friends anymore."

Fern hated mysteries. She went up to Sue Coney at break time —Sue was in the class below hers—and said, "What is this about? I don't understand. What did my aunt do?"

"She knocked over our posy tubs," said Sue Coney.

On each side of the greengrocer's shop there were two big ornamental tubs, standing out on the pavement, filled with growing flowers, tulips or marigolds or lobelias, whatever was in season.

Fern had noticed, on the way to school, that the tubs had been pushed over; earth and dying plants lay scattered all over the footway. Perhaps a car had skidded and upset the tubs, Fern thought at the time.

But Sue said, "Your aunt did it."

"How do you know?"

"Dad says so."

"I don't believe it. Why should she do a thing like that?"

"Dad says it must have been her."

"Why?"

"Because of what she did before." And Sue went off to the other side of the playground.

Another girl, Tessa Leigh, explained. "There used to be a lot of trouble between your aunt and the Coneys. That was why she moved to Crossing Cottage. There was always bad feeling, over one thing or another. She complained they made too much noise —their dog bit her cat, or t'other way round—Oz Coney chopped some branches off a tree in the hedge between the gardens that Mrs. Deane said was her tree—there was a row about repairs to an inside wall—they couldn't ever be friendly about anything. Of course, really, it all went back to little Alice."

"*What* about little Alice?" asked Fern, wondering why she found it so hard to breathe.

"That was the kid that died. Mrs. Deane's little girl. She was out playing one day in the back garden—they have nice big gardens behind those houses in the High Street—she scrambled through a gap in the hedge and went into the Coneys' garden."

"Well?"

"That was it. They had a well, a deep one. It's all filled in now, they turned it into a little garden pond, with plants and goldfish. There's a spring, you see. But in those times it was eighty feet deep, with a bucket and winding handle. Folk said it was a wishing well. They still do, as a matter of fact."

"What happened?"

"The kid fell down the well. Wasn't found till it was too late."

"How awful! Oh, how awful!"

"Your aunt blamed the Coneys. Said the well should have been covered over. Said other things too." Tessa stopped short.

How could she bear it? thought Fern. No wonder she had never been on friendly terms with the Coney family since. Though they weren't really to blame.

But still—to upset their tubs and throw the flowers in the road! *Could* Aunt Twyla really have done a spiteful thing like that?

"I don't believe Aunt Twyla did it," Fern said to Sue Coney after school, and Sue said, "Well, Dad thinks she did. He's furious. He's going to arrange the railway walk. He said, if it weren't for that, he wouldn't have bothered, he was going to have let it lapse this year. But now he's going to make sure they do it."

"What on earth is the railway walk?"

"Your aunt bought that bungalow in a hurry from old Fred Stoppard. He was the one who built it. When he built it, he didn't know, and he didn't tell your aunt when he sold it to her, that there's a right of way clean through the house."

"What does that mean?" asked Fern.

"It's like a public footpath going right through. Any person has the right to walk in at your aunt's front door and out at the back, and on through that gate in the right-hand fence, along the path that goes in a tunnel under the railway and out to the river and the sewage farm. I've heard that your uncle nearly had a fit when he came back from the sea and found what she'd got, instead of his old house in the High Street."

"But," said Fern, puzzled, "nobody *does* walk through my aunt's house."

"No, they don't, because people are a bit scared of her. Some of them even think she's a witch. Anyway, there's plenty of other ways to get to the sewage farm. But if there's a right of way, you're supposed to make sure it's walked along, at least once a year, and that's what Sue's dad's always done. He's on the Town Council in charge of footpaths, you see. Your aunt gets riled when they come and do it, but they're allowed; she can't stop them. The councilors bring their wives and people from the Haleswick Historical and any ratepayers who want to come. They're going to do it the day after tomorrow, Sunday."

"Well, *I* think it's hateful," burst out Fern. "Specially—"

Specially when Mother's so ill, perhaps dying, she thought, but she could see that was beside the point.

"Your aunt shouldn't have knocked over those tubs of flowers."

"Nobody saw her. No one can prove she did. And anyway, I'm sure she didn't."

When Fern got home that evening, Aunt Twyla was very pale, even more silent than usual, and her mouth was set in a bitter line. A letter headed Haleswick Urban District Council stood on the mantelpiece; she did not say anything about it to Fern, who had her own matter for silent thought; the line of wet footprints had been there again, ahead of her on the path as she walked up to the house. She had seen them appearing, one by one, all the way to the door.

Who had stepped through the doorway just ahead of her?

Later, as she sat trying to do her homework on the kitchen table, when the hum of the pylon died down, she felt certain that she could hear somebody moving about upstairs—opening a drawer, maybe, taking a book off a shelf or a toy from a cupboard.

But there wasn't any upstairs in the bungalow.

On Sunday morning, Fern, feeling rather sick, said, "I think I'll go out for a walk." But Aunt Twyla said, "No. You stay right here." So Fern stayed. Her mouth was dry; it was like the first day at school, only much worse.

At eleven they all arrived, quite a large group of people, wearing dark respectable clothes as if they were going to a funeral or a court case. A few carried umbrellas, because it was raining a bit. They didn't knock at the door or ring the doorbell, but walked straight in, led by Mr. Coney, a tall man with light-gray fluffy hair and very blue eyes like his daughter. Some of the people looked embarrassed, but he didn't; he was just very serious.

"Come for the right-of-way walk, Mrs. Deane," he said.

Aunt Twyla made no answer. She was ironing curtains and had arranged her board across the room so that there was only just enough space to edge round it.

Mr. Coney made as if to lift the ironing board. Then Aunt Twyla did speak.

"You better not touch that!" she said. "Or I'll have the law on you!"

So Mr. Coney and his twenty-nine companions had to edge carefully round the back of the ironing board, step gingerly over the cord of the iron, and so through the passage, the scullery, the backdoor, and across the garden to the side gate that led into the lane.

"Thank you, Mrs. Deane," each person said politely as he or she left.

Twyla waited until the last was out, Doctor Leigh; then she went into the garden. The group were still in the lane, writing on their clipboards. Aunt Twyla said—and the words seemed to come out of her like water under fierce pressure—

"You have left filthy footprints all over my clean lino. You know what I think of you? I think you are *vermin*. You deserve every bit of bad luck that will come to you. And it can't be worse than I wish it."

Then she turned on her heel and went back into the house.

Next day at school, Fern came in for a good many cold looks. She felt this was rather hard; she was not responsible for the feud between Aunt Twyla and the Coneys, or for any part of what had happened; except, true, that she had bought that unlucky bunch of pinks.

Matters were made worse because Sue Coney, that very day, had suddenly come down with what Doctor Leigh called a particularly tricky kind of virus pneumonia, and her parents were worried to death about her. No one spoke out directly, or said this was a result of Aunt Twyla's ill-wishing, but some people really thought it, and things were muttered behind hands, specially among the children at school.

Fat Ozzie Coney, Sue's retarded elder brother, who was eighteen, and worked in the brick factory, lurched threateningly up to Fern after school, and growled at her, "You better tell your aunt to take that thing off."

"What thing?" said Fern, puzzled.

"That thing she laid on our Sue! Else we'll make this place too hot to hold her."

And Ozzie giggled suddenly, as he was liable to do in the middle of any conversation, whether funny or not, and rolled his eyes sideways at Fern, and shambled away.

"Don't take too much notice of him," said Tessa. "He's always been like that."

In the evening, when Fern went home, she found Aunt Twyla grimly sticking elastic plaster over several holes in the front windows where stones had been thrown. A policeman was there, inspecting the damage. He shook his head, said it was no doubt boys at their pranks, unfortunately the police force was short-staffed, and couldn't possibly keep an eye on Crossing Cottage at all hours of the day or night, but of course they'd do their best.

He did not sound as if he himself intended to do his best.

Next day, though, there was a sudden, unexpected change. People at school were friendly again, and Mrs. Coney, outside her shop arranging bunches of radishes, made a point of stopping Fern, as she walked home with Tessa, to say they were all very sorry for misjudging her aunt over those flower tubs, but mistakes did get made sometimes, and she hoped Mrs. Deane wouldn't have any hard feelings, and how was Fern's mother? She asked as if she really wanted to know, but Fern could only reply that her mother was still much the same.

"Oh, dear, that's too bad." Mrs. Coney sounded honestly sorry.

"Father says we need a miracle," Fern muttered. "What about Sue, Mrs. Coney?"

Mrs. Coney's good-natured face looked suddenly haggard.

"She's poorly. She's very poorly. If miracles are being given out, we could use one too." And she walked slowly inside, past the boxes of oranges.

"You'd think," said Tessa Leigh, "that she'd wish on her wishing well."

"Wishing well? Oh! In the garden. But it doesn't really work, does it?"

"Of course it works!" said Tessa, rather indignantly. "I've wished for lots of things, when I went to tea with Sue, and always got them. A pair of green sandals—and a fine day on my birthday —and to come top in math—"

"You can't prove—"

"Can't prove? Who needs to? I know!"

Perhaps you need to believe in it, Fern thought, and Mrs. Coney doesn't. But I would. Oh, I think I'd believe.

She turned back and went into the shop.

"Mrs. Coney—might I have a wish on your wishing well?"

Mrs. Coney was serving a customer with four pounds of potatoes, a melon, and some rhubarb. She said absently, "Of course, love. Help yourself. Down the path at the side and through the green gate."

She was wrapping up the rhubarb in newspaper. Fern read the headline on it: BOYS OWN UP TO HIGH STREET VANDALISM.

"Shocking, isn't it, the things those young tearaways get up to? Lucky Sergeant Ferson caught them at it," the customer said.

Fern ran down the little snicket path beside the Coneys' house, through the green gate, and made her way to the end of the narrow, quiet garden. There was a pear tree, and a quince tree, a patch of bright green mossy lawn, and a forsythia, just shedding its yellow petals and beginning to put out new green leaves. The pool was under the pear tree, ringed by spears of iris, and with drifted white pearblossom floating on its dark green water.

Fern knelt on the brick paving at the edge and looked in. She could see her own reflection, sliced neatly in two by a goldfish who swam across. The reflection looked much younger than she felt.

She put her hand in the cold water. I ought to drop something in, she thought. I haven't any money. What do I have in my schoolbag that would do? She remembered the ivory penknife that Granny Sands had given her. It had been Granny's and

Great-granny's, it had a large blade and a small, and she loved it dearly.

In it went.

"Mother," whispered Fern. "Oh, *Mother* . . . Sue . . ." And then, for some reason, she was hardly sure why, she whispered, "Alice . . . Cousin Alice," and went on crouching in silence for a while, staring down into the murky water, until a fish jumped for a fly, with a sudden plop, and startled her.

She was late home, and Aunt Twyla was cross.

"Wondering where you'd got to," she snapped. "That Oz Coney's been around, mumbling and muttering and acting peculiar. I don't like his looks. Never have." She bit off something she might have been going to say and slapped a pair of plates down on the table.

"That's strange," said Fern, and gave Aunt Twyla Mrs. Coney's apologetic message. But Twyla sniffed.

"No more than she ought. They caught the two boys who upset Coneys' tubs—cops found 'em kicking over litterbins, brought them in to the station for questioning, and one of them blew the gaff on the other. Nasty little scum—I hope they get sent to preventive."

"Oh, I'm glad," said Fern. "Then—" She was beginning to say, "Then no one can go on thinking you did it," but changed her mind and said instead, "Perhaps they were the ones that broke your windows."

"*Perhaps,*" said Aunt Twyla sourly.

After supper she remarked, "It's odd—I keep thinking I can hear somebody upstairs. I must be going daft in my old age."

"Maybe it's the pylon humming," said Fern uneasily. For no particular reason, she added, "When does Uncle Frank next come home?"

"Not for another six weeks. . . . I think I'll go to the callbox on the corner and ring up to ask after your mother. You'd best go to bed."

"I'll wait up till you come back," said Fern. She felt very reluctant to get undressed and lie under the covers in the dark, in her tiny boxy bedroom with its window looking toward the pylon and the railway.

She locked herself in the bathroom, ran the tap to drown the hum of the pylon, brushed her teeth for a very long time, washed her face over and over, then came out, hoping that Aunt Twyla would be home already, that she would have better news.

The lights were off in the front room, but the passage one, still on, threw some light in each direction. Fern felt a draft and, over the smell of soap and toothpaste, caught another smell—sharp, strong, choking. She walked into the front room and a dark, bulky figure suddenly unbent from something it had been doing low down, knocked against the corner of the table, and let out a hoarse, frightened cry. Fern heard a mighty whoosh! like the bark of an enormous dog, a sheet of flame swept across the room, and tablecloth, chaircovers, curtains all caught fire together.

Fern, not far from the back door, ran for it, then spun around, thinking crazily, "Alice! I must get Cousin Alice out!"

But the front room was already a dazzling cave of gold and scarlet flame; nobody was going to come out of there. Fern ran into the pitch-dark garden and cannoned into somebody—a man; she let out a yelp as he grabbed her, demanding, "Is that the girl? Are you all right? Thank God! Oh, thank God! But your aunt— where is she?"

"She went to phone—she'll be at the front—"

It was Mr. Coney. What in the world was he doing here?

Before they could get round to the front they saw something terrible—a flaming creature that raced across the garden, howling, flung itself through the rickety fence, and collapsed on the ground between the pylon's huge legs, rolling and moaning, "Help me! Help me!"

"Ozzie!" screamed Mr. Coney.

Another figure ran after the first carrying a bundle of something dark and thick which it flung over the burning, rolling creature—then knelt and thumped, beat, thumped again, pressing out the flames. Mr. Coney ran to help, ducking under the pylon, taking no notice of the DANGER signs.

"Is that you—Mrs. Deane?" Fern heard him gasp. And heard

Aunt Twyla's dour reply, "Who did you expect? Cinderella? Take a hand with this groundsheet, Bob Coney."

Fire engines had arrived at the front of the house—which by now was burning so hard that there seemed no possible chance of saving it; all the firemen could do was play their hoses around and stop the fire from spreading to the timber yard or the pylon.

An ambulance carried away Ozzie Coney, who was severely burned. His clothes reeked of petrol, and an empty petrol can was found at the starting point of the fire. A police officer traveled with Ozzie in the ambulance.

"If it hadn't been for Mrs. Deane and her groundsheet, your son would be dead," he told Mr. Coney, who looked terrible, Fern observed—shocked, wretched, suddenly an old man.

"I don't know what to say," he muttered to Aunt Twyla. "You saved him—how can I thank you? I—I only hope you don't think Mary and I egged him on to do this awful thing—?"

"Well, I don't," said Aunt Twyla, roundly and surprisingly. "I've thought plenty hard things of you in the past, Bob Coney, but I never thought you'd take a hand in *arson*."

"He was bumbling away after tea, talking to himself, something about Crossing Cottage and then the fuel for the mower—it was only later I suddenly put two and two together, guessed what he might have in mind, and came hell-for-leather after him. The poor daft boy got a notion in his head you'd had a hand in our Sue's illness."

Aunt Twyla laughed shortly as she turned to watch her house burning.

"If I'd got the powers some folks credit me with, I'd be able to stop this, eh?"

They stood in silence for a moment or two, looking at the roaring flames. Behind them the pylon shone like a scarlet brooch against the black sky.

"I'd best be away to the hospital," said Mr. Coney at length. "See to my poor stupid boy. But Mary said, Mrs. Deane—if anything happened—would you and your niece come and put up at our house, we've beds for you both."

"Oh," she said, "but you've a sick young one—"

"No, Sue's made the turn, Leigh says, just this evening. She's out of danger; that's why I feel so terrible, what that sick boy did. *Please*, Mrs. Deane—Mary wouldn't take no for an answer."

"Then we'll say thank you, and kindly. Come along, Fern. One thing," said Aunt Twyla with rare cheerfulness, "we've naught to carry but ourselves." And indeed she walked along Brewery Way and Gasworks Road as lightly as if she had tossed aside a whole lifetime's load of heavy luggage.

Fern had something to carry; she had picked it up off the front path as they left—something that shone in the firelight and caught her eye.

"What do you think this is, Aunt Twyla?" she asked, as they reached the brighter lights of the High Street.

"That? Let's see. Why—no! *I don't believe it!*" whispered Twyla.

She stared at the thing in Fern's hand as if her eyes were still dazzled by the fire, stung by the smoke, and could hardly see what lay in front of them. It was a small mother-of-pearl fish, with an ivory-and-silver ring attached to it, and a white satin ribbon tied to the ring.

"It belonged to Alice," whispered Twyla. "It was her teething ring."

Alice.

For the first time since the fire, Fern fetched up the courage to ask, "Aunt Twyla? Did you get through to the hospital? Is there—?"

"They said she'll be all right," said Twyla slowly. "Just this evening she opened her eyes, quite sensible, and asked for a cup of tea."

Mrs. Coney welcomed them in, couldn't make enough of them. She gave them hot drinks laced with sherry, lent them nightwear, put hot-water bottles in two beds, side by side in her spare bedroom. Sue, she said, was getting perkier all the time; and Bob had phoned from Haleswick Hospital to say that although Ozzie's burns were very bad—he'd been taken off to a special burn center—he would probably pull through.

"I don't know how to tell you how bad I feel about your house, Mrs. Deane. Our poor backward boy—I'm bound to say—I do

blame ourselves too—he grew up among people thinking hard
thoughts, hearing hard words spoken. We'll try to put that right
now."

"There's been fault on both sides," said Aunt Twyla.

"One thing Bob did say—did you know the house next door is
coming up for sale?"

"Let's hope the insurance money will stretch to cover it," said
Aunt Twyla. And she did a thing she had not done, perhaps for
years, thought Fern: she smiled. "We'd best get to bed. Thank
you, Mary; it's been a long day."

Safe in bed, sandwiched with hot-water bottles, Fern mur-
mured, "Good night, Aunt Twyla." And wondered if Twyla and
her mother would be sharing dreams tonight.

"Sleep well, Fern." After a moment, Twyla said, "My daughter
Alice's little room was just the other side of this wall."

Cousin Alice, thought Fern. Good night, Cousin Alice. Sleep
well.

You'll be glad to be back in your own home again. You'll rest
better there.

JOAN AIKEN

Born in Rye, England, the daughter of famous American poet Conrad Aiken, Joan Aiken is the author of more than sixty books for children and adults as well as for teenagers. Before devoting her full time to writing novels, stories, poems, and plays, Ms. Aiken worked for the British Broadcasting System, then in the London office of the United Nations as a librarian. After marrying and raising two children, she became a features editor for *Argosy* magazine, then a copywriter for a large London advertising agency. She now lives alternately in Sussex, England, and in New York City.

She is probably best known among American children as the author of *The Wolves of Willoughby Chase*, for which she won the Guardian Award for children's literature in 1969, and the Dido Twite novels, the most recent of which is *Dido and Pa*. For *Nightfall* she received the Mystery Writers of America Edgar Allan Poe Award. Among her many stories of fantasy and horror are *Not What You Expected, A Bundle of Nerves, Go Saddle the Sea, The Shadow Guests*, and *A Whisper in the Night*.

For adults her most recent novel is *Mansfield Revisited*, a sequel to Jane Austen's *Mansfield Park*. For younger readers her most recent books are *Up the Chimney Down*, a collection of fantastic stories, *Mortimer Says Nothing*, more adventures of Mortimer the raven, and *Midnight Is a Place*, a Dickens-like story about an orphaned boy, a French-speaking heroine, murdering villains, and the exploitation of child labor in mid-nineteenth-century England.

On the day she becomes a woman, Late Blossoming Flower is sent away to the far hills to seek "The Word That Changes"—the word that will transform her into a woman of power. . . .

WORDS OF POWER

JANE YOLEN

Late Blossoming Flower, the only child of her mother's old age, stared sulkily into the fire. A homely child, with a nose that threatened to turn into a beak and a mouth that seldom smiled, she was nonetheless cherished by her mother and the clan. Her loneness, the striking rise of her nose, the five strands of white hair that streaked through her shiny black hair, were all seen as the early signs of great power, the power her mother had given up when she had chosen to bear a child.

"I would never have made such a choice," Late Blossoming Flower told her mother. "I would never give up *my* power."

Her mother, who had the same fierce nose, the white streak of hair, and the bitter smile but was a striking beauty, replied gently, "You do not have that power yet. And if I had not given up mine, you would not be here now to make such a statement and to chide me for my choice." She shook her head. "Nor would you now be scolded for forgetting to do those things which are yours by duty."

Late Blossoming Flower bit back the reply that was no reply but merely angry words. She rose from the fireside and went out of the cliff house to feed the milk beast. As she climbed down the withy ladder to the valley below, she rehearsed that conversation with her mother as she had done so often before. Always her mother remained calm, her voice never rising into anger. It infuriated Flower, and she nursed that sore like all the others, counting them up as carefully as if she were toting them on a notch stick. The tally by now was long indeed.

But soon, she reminded herself, soon she would herself be a

woman of power, though she was late coming to it. All the signs but one were on her. Under the chamois shirt her breasts had finally begun to bud. There was hair curling in the secret places of her body. Her waist and hips were changing to create a place for the Herb Belt to sit comfortably, instead of chafing her as it did now. And when at last the moon called to her and her first blood flowed, cleansing her body of man's sin, she would be allowed at last to go on her search for her own word of power and be free of her hated, ordinary chores. Boys could not go on such a search, for they were never able to rid themselves of the dirty blood-sin. But she took no great comfort in that, for not all girls who sought found. Still, Late Blossoming Flower knew she was the daughter of a woman of power, a woman so blessed that even though she had had a child and lost the use of the Shaping Hands she still retained the Word That Changes. Late Blossoming Flower never doubted that when she went on her journey she would find what it was she sought.

The unfed milk beast lowed longingly as her feet touched the ground. She bent and gathered up bits of earth, cupped the fragments in her hand, said the few phrases of the *Ke-waha*, the prayer to the land, then stood.

"I'm not *that* late," she said sharply to the agitated beast, and went to the wooden manger for maize.

It was the first day after the rising of the second moon, and the florets of the night-blooming panomom tree were open wide. The sickly sweet smell of the tiny clustered blossoms filled the valley, and all the women of the valley dreamed dreams.

The women of power dreamed in levels. Late Blossoming Flower's mother passed from one level to another with the ease of long practice, but her daughter's dream quester had difficulty going through. She wandered too long on the dreamscape paths, searching for a ladder or a rope or some other familiar token of passage.

When Late Blossoming Flower had awakened, her mother scolded her for her restless sleep.

"If you are to be a true woman of power, you must force yourself to lie down in the dream and fall asleep. Sleep within sleep, dream within dream. Only then will you wake at the next level." Her head had nodded gently every few words and she spoke softly, braiding her hair with quick and supple hands. "You must be like a gardener forcing an early bud to bring out the precious juices."

"Words. Just words," said Late Blossoming Flower. "And none of *those* words has power." She had risen from her pallet, shaking her own hair free of the loose night braiding, brushing it fiercely before plaiting it up again. She could not bear to listen to her mother's advice any longer and had let her thoughts drift instead to the reed hut on the edge of the valley, where old Sand Walker lived. A renegade healer, he lived apart from the others and, as a man, was little thought of. But Late Blossoming Flower liked to go and sit with him and listen to his stories of the time before time, when power had been so active in the world it could be plucked out of the air as easily as fruit from a tree. He said that dreams eventually explained themselves and that to discipline the dream figure was to bind its power. To Late Blossoming Flower that made more sense than all her mother's constant harping on the Forcing Way.

So intent was she on visiting the old man that day, she had raced through her chores, scanting the milk beast and the birds who squatted on hidden nests. She had collected only a few eggs and left them in the basket at the bottom of the cliff. Then, without a backward glance at the withy ladders spanning the levels or the people moving busily against the cliff face, she raced down the path toward Sand Walker's home.

As a girl child she had that freedom, given leave for part of each day to walk the many trails through the valley. On these walks she was supposed to learn the ways of the growing flowers, to watch the gentler creatures at their play, to come to a careful understanding of the way of predator and prey. It was time for her to know the outer landscape of her world as thoroughly as she would, one day, know the inner dream trails. But Late Blossoming Flower was a hurrying child. As if to make up for her late birth and the crushing burden of early power laid on her, she refused to take the time.

"My daughter," her mother often cautioned her, "a woman of

true power must be in love with silence. You must learn all the outward sounds in order to approach the silence that lies within."

But Flower wanted no inner silence. She delighted in tuneless singing and loud sounds: the sharp hoarse cry of the night herons sailing across the marsh; the crisp howl of the jackals calling under the moon; even the scream of the rabbit in the teeth of the wolf. She sought to imitate *those* sounds, make them louder, sing them again in her own mouth. What was silence compared to sound?

And when she was with old Sand Walker in his hut, he sang with her. And told stories, joking stories, about the old women and their silences.

"Soon enough," Sand Walker said, "soon enough it will be silent and dark. In the grave. Those old *bawenahs*"—he used the word that meant the unclean female vulture—"those old *bawenahs* would make us rehearse for our coming deaths with their binding dreams. Laugh *now*, child. Sing out. Silence is for the dead ones, though they call themselves alive and walk the trails. But you and I, ho"—he poked her in the stomach lightly with his stick—"we know the value of noise. It blocks out thinking, and thinking means pain. Cry out for me, child. Loud. Louder."

And as if a trained dog, Late Blossoming Flower always dropped to her knees at this request and howled, scratching at the dirt and wagging her bottom. Then she would fall over on her back with laughter and the old man laughed with her.

All this was in her mind as she ran along the path toward Sand Walker's hut.

A rabbit darted into her way, then zagged back to escape her pounding feet. A few branches, emboldened by the coming summer, strayed across her path and whipped her arm, leaving red scratches. Impatient with the marks, she ignored them.

At the final turning the old man's hut loomed up. He was sitting, as always, in the doorway, humming, and eating a piece of yellowed fruit, the juices running down his chin. At the noise of her coming he looked up and grinned.

"Hai!" he said, more sound than greeting.

Flower skidded to a stop and squatted in the dirt beside him. "You look tired," he said. "Did you dream?"

"I tried. But dreaming is so slow," Flower admitted.

"Dreaming is not living. You and I—we live. Have a bite?" He offered her what was left of the fruit, mostly core.

She took it so as not to offend him, holding the core near her mouth but not eating. The smell of the overripe, sickly sweet fruit made her close her eyes, and she was startled into a dream.

The fruit was in her mouth and she could feel its sliding passage down her throat. It followed the twists of her inner pathways, dropping seeds as it went, until it landed heavily in her belly. There it began to burn, a small but significant fire in her gut.

Bending over to ease the cramping, Flower turned her back on the old man's hut and crept along the trail toward the village. The trees along the trail and the muddle of gray-green wildflowers blurred into an indistinct mass as she went, as if she were seeing them through tears, though her cheeks were dry and her eyes clear.

When she reached the cliffside she saw, to her surprise, that the withy ladders went down into a great hole in the earth instead of up toward the dwellings on the cliff face.

It was deathly silent all around her. The usual chatter of children at their chores, the chant of women, the hum-buzz of men in the furrowed fields were gone. The cliff was as blank and as smooth as the shells of the eggs she had gathered that morning.

And then she heard a low sound, compounded of moans and a strange hollow whistling, like an old man's laughter breathed out across a reed. Turning around, she followed the sound. It led her to the hole. She bent over it, and as she did, the sound resolved itself into a single word: *bawenah*. She saw a pale, shining face looking up at her from the hole, its mouth a smear of fruit. When the mouth opened, it was as round and as black as the hole. There were no teeth. There was no tongue. Yet still the mouth spoke: *bawenah*.

Flower awoke and stared at the old man. Pulpy fruit stained his scraggly beard. His eyes were filmy. Slowly his tongue emerged and licked his lips.

She turned and without another word to him walked home.

Her hands cupped her stomach, pressing and releasing, all the way back, as if pressure alone could drive away the cramps.

Her mother was waiting for her at the top of the ladder, hands folded on her own belly. "So," she said, "it is your woman time."

Flower did not ask how she knew. Her mother was a woman of great power still and such knowledge was well within her grasp, though it annoyed Flower that it should be so.

"Yes," Flower answered, letting a small whine creep into her voice. "But you did not tell me it would hurt so."

"With some," her mother said, smiling and smoothing back the white stripe of hair with her hand, "with some, womanhood comes easy. With some it comes harder." Then, as they walked into their rooms, she added with a bitterness uncharacteristic of her, "Could your *healer* not do something for you?"

Flower was startled at her mother's tone. She knew that her association with the old man had annoyed her mother. But Flower had never realized it would hurt her so much. She began to answer her mother, then bit back her first angry reply. Instead, mastering her voice, she said, "I did not think to ask him for help. He is but a man. *I* am a woman."

"You are a woman today, truly," her mother said. She went over to the great chest she had carved before Flower's birth, a chest made of the wood of a lightning-struck panomom tree. The chest's sides were covered with carved signs of power: the florets of the tree with their three-foil flowers, the mouse and hare who were her mother's personal signs, the trailing arbet vine which was her father's, and the signs for the four moons: quarter, half, full, and closed faces.

When she opened the chest, it made a small creaking protest. Flower went over to look in. There, below her first cradle dress and leggings, nestled beside a tress of her first, fine baby hair, was the Herb Belt she had helped her mother make. It had fifteen pockets, one for each year she had been a girl.

They went outside, and her mother raised her voice in that wild ululation that could call all the women of power to her. It echoed around the clearing and across the fields to the gathering streams beyond, a high, fierce yodeling. And then she called out again, this time in a gentler voice that would bring the women who had borne and their girl children with them.

Flower knew it would be at least an hour before they all gathered; in the meantime she and her mother had much to do.

They went back into the rooms and turned around all the objects they owned, as a sign that Flower's life would now be turned around as well. Bowls, cups, pitchers were turned. Baskets of food and the drying racks were turned. Even the heavy chest was turned around. They left the bed pallets to the very last, and then, each holding an end, they walked the beds around until the ritual was complete.

Flower stripped in front of her mother, something she had not done completely in years. She resisted the impulse to cover her breasts. On her leggings were the blood sign. Carefully her mother packed those leggings into the panomom chest. Flower would not wear them again.

At the bottom of the chest, wrapped in a sweet-smelling woven-grass covering, was a white chamois dress and leggings. Flower's mother took them out and spread them on the bedding, her hand smoothing the nap. Then, with a pitcher of water freshened with violet flowers, she began to wash her daughter's body with a scrub made of the leaves of the sandarac tree. The nubby sandarac and the soothing rinse of the violet water were to remind Flower of the fierce and gentle sides of womanhood. All the while she scrubbed, Flower's mother chanted the songs of Woman: the seven-fold chant of Rising, the Way of Power, and the Praise to Earth and Moon.

The songs reminded Flower of something, and she tried to think of what it was as her mother's hands cleansed her of the sins of youth. It was while her mother was braiding her hair, plaiting in it reed ribbons that ended in a dangle of shells, that Flower remembered. The chants were like the cradle songs her mother had sung her when she was a child, with the same rise and fall, the same liquid sounds. She suddenly wanted to cry for the loss of those times and the pain she had given her mother, and she wondered why she felt so like weeping when anger was her usual way.

The white dress and leggings slipped on easily, indeed fit her perfectly, though she had never tried them on before, and that, too, was a sign of her mother's power.

And what of her own coming power, Flower wondered as she stood in the doorway watching the women assemble at the foot of the ladder. The women of power stood in the front, then the birth women, last of all the girls. She could name them all, her friends, her sisters in the tribe, who only lately had avoided her because of her association with the old man. She tried to smile at them, but her mouth would not obey her. In fact, her lower lip trembled and she willed it to stop, finally clamping it with her teeth.

"She is a woman," Flower's mother called down to them. The ritual words. They had known, even without her statement, had known from that first wild cry, what had happened. "Today she has come into her power, putting it on as a woman dons her white dress, but she does not yet know her own way. She goes now, as we all go at our time, to the far hills and beyond to seek the Word That Changes. She may find it or not, but she will tell of that when she has returned."

The women below began to sway and chant the words of the Searching Song, words which Flower had sung with them for fifteen years without really understanding their meaning. Fifteen years—far longer than any of the other girls—standing at the ladder's foot and watching another Girl-Become-Woman go off on her search. And that was why—she saw it now—she had fallen under Sand Walker's spell.

But now, standing above the singers, waiting for the Belt and the Blessing, she felt for the first time how strongly the power called to her. This was *her* moment, *her* time, and there would be no other. She pictured the old man in his hut and realized that if she did not find her word she would be bound to him forever.

"Mother," she began, wondering if it was too late to say all the things she should have said before, but her mother was coming toward her with the Belt and suddenly it was too late. Once the Belt was around her waist, she could not speak again until the Word formed in her mouth, with or without its accompanying power. Tears started in her eyes.

Her mother saw the tears, and perhaps she mistook them for

something else. Tenderly she placed the Belt around Flower's waist, setting it on the hips, and tying it firmly behind her. Then she turned her daughter around, the way every object in the house had been turned, till she faced the valley again where all the assembled women could read the fear on her face.

Into the valley, in the fear we all face,
Into the morning of your womanhood,
Go with our blessing to guide you,
Go with our blessing to guard you,
Go with our blessing and bring back your word.

The chant finished, Flower's mother pushed her toward the ladder and went back into the room and sat on the chest to do her own weeping.

Flower opened her eyes, surprised, for she had not realized that she had closed them. All the women had disappeared, back into the fields, into the woods; she did not know where, nor was she to wonder about them. Her journey had to be made alone. Talking to anyone on the road this day would spell doom to them both, to her quest for her power, to the questioner's very life.

As she walked out of the village, Flower noticed that everything along the way seemed different. Her power had, indeed, begun. The low bushes had a shadow self, like the moon's halo, standing behind. The trees were filled with eyes, peering out of the knotholes. The chattering of animals in the brush was a series of messages, though Flower knew that she was still unable to decipher them. And the path itself sparkled as if water rushed over it, tumbling the small stones.

She seemed to slip in and out of quick dreams that were familiar pieces of her old dreams stitched together in odd ways. Her childhood was sloughing off behind her with each step, a skin removed.

Further down the path, where the valley met the foothills leading to the far mountains, she could see Sand Walker's hut casting a long, dark, toothy shadow across the trail. Flower was not sure if the shadows lengthened because the sun was at the end of its day or because this was yet another dream. She closed her eyes, and when she opened them again, the long shadows were still there, though not nearly as dark or as menacing.

When she neared the hut, the old man was sitting silently out front. His shadow, unlike the hut's black shadow, was a strange shade of green.

She did not dare greet the old man, for fear of ruining her quest and because she did not want to hurt him. One part of her was still here with him, wild, casting green shadows, awake. He had no protection against her power. But surely she might give him one small sign of recognition. Composing her hands in front of her, she was prepared to signal him with a finger, when without warning he leaped up, grinning.

"*Ma-hane*, white girl," he cried, jumping into her path. "Do not forget to laugh, you in your white dress and leggings. If you do not laugh, you are one of the dead ones."

In great fear she reached out a hand toward him to silence him before he could harm them both, and power sprang unbidden from her fingertips. She had forgotten the Shaping Hands. And though they were as yet untrained and untried, still they were a great power. She watched in horror as five separate arrows of flame struck the old man's face, touching his eyes, his nostrils, his mouth, sealing them, melting his features like candle wax. He began to shrink under the fire, growing smaller and smaller, fading into a gray-green splotch that only slowly resolved itself into the form of a *sa-hawa*, a butterfly the color of leaf mold.

Flower did not dare speak, not even a word of comfort. She reached down and shook out the crumpled shirt, loosing the butterfly. It flapped its wings, tentatively at first, then with more strength, and finally managed to flutter up toward the top of the hut.

Folding the old man's tattered shirt and leggings with gentle hands, Flower laid them on the doorstep of his hut, still watching the fluttering *sa-hawa*. When she stood again, she had to shade her eyes with one hand to see it. It had flown away from the hut and was hovering between patches of wild onion in a small meadow on the flank of the nearest foothill.

Flower bit her lip. How could she follow the butterfly? It was going up the mountainside and her way lay straight down the road. Yet how could she not follow it? Sand Walker's transformation had been her doing. No one else might undo what she had so unwillingly, unthinkingly created.

To get to the meadow was easy. But if the butterfly went further up the mountainside, what could she do? There was only a goat track, and then the sheer cliff wall. As she hesitated, the *sa-hawa* rose into the air again, leaving the deep green spikes of onions to fly up toward the mountain itself.

Flower looked quickly down the trail, but the shadows of oncoming evening had closed that way. Ahead, the Path of Power —her Power—was still brightly lit.

"Oh, Mother," she thought. "Oh, my mothers, I need your blessing indeed." And so thinking, she plunged into the underbrush after the *sa-hawa*, heedless of the thorns tugging at her white leggings or the light on the Path of Power that suddenly and inexplicably went out.

The goat path had not been used for years, not by goats or by humans either. Briars tangled across it. Little rock slides blocked many turnings, and in others the pebbly surface slid away beneath her feet. Time and again she slipped and fell; her knees and palms bruised, and all the power in her Shaping Hands seemed to do no good. She could not call on it. Once when she fell she bit her underlip so hard it bled. And always, like some spirit guide, the little gray-green butterfly fluttered ahead, its wings glowing with five spots as round and marked as fingerprints.

Still Flower followed, unable to call out or cry out because a new woman on her quest for her Power must not speak until she has found her word. She still hoped, a doomed and forlorn hope, that once she had caught the *sa-hawa* she might also catch her Power or at least be allowed to continue on her quest. And she would take the butterfly with her and find at least enough of the Shaping Hands to turn him back into his own tattered, laughing, dismal self.

She went on. The only light now came from the five spots on the butterfly's wings and the pale moon rising over the jagged crest of First Mother, the leftmost mountain. The goat track had disappeared entirely. It was then the butterfly began to rise straight up, as if climbing the cliff face.

Out of breath, Flower stopped and listened, first to her own ragged breathing, then to the pounding of her heart. At last she was able to be quiet enough to hear the sounds of the night. The butterfly stopped, too, as if it was listening as well.

From far down the valley she heard the rise and fall of the running dogs, howling at the moon. Little chirrups of frogs, the pick-buzz of insect wings, and then the choughing of a nightbird's wings. She turned her head for a moment, fearful that it might be an eater-of-bugs. When she looked back, the *sa-hawa* was almost gone, edging up the great towering mountain that loomed over her.

Flower almost cried out then, in frustration and anger and fear, but she held her tongue and looked for a place to start the climb. She had to use hands and feet instead of eyes, for the moonlight made this a place of shadows—shadows within shadows—and only her hands and feet could see between the dark and dark.

She felt as if she had been climbing for hours, though the moon above her spoke of a shorter time, when the butterfly suddenly disappeared. Without the lure of its phosphorescent wings, Flower was too exhausted to continue. All the tears she had held back for so long suddenly rose to swamp her eyes. She snuffled loudly and crouched uncertainly on a ledge. Then, huddling against the rockface, she tried to stay awake, to draw warmth and courage from the mountain. But without wanting to, she fell asleep.

In the dream she spiraled up and up and up into the sky without ladder or rope to pull her, and she felt the words of a high scream fall from her lips, a yelping *kya*. She awoke terrified and shaking in the morning light, sitting on a thin ledge nearly a hundred feet up the mountainside. She had no memory of the climb and certainly no way to get down.

And then she saw the *sa-hawa* next to her and memory flooded back. She cupped her hand, ready to pounce on the butterfly, when it fluttered its wings in the sunlight and moved from its perch. Desperate to catch it, she leaned out, lost her balance, and began to fall.

"Oh, Mother," she screamed in her mind, and a single word came back to her. *Aki-la.* Eagle. She screamed it aloud.

As she fell, the bones of her arms lengthened and flattened, cracking sinew and marrow. Her small, sharp nose bone arched outward and she watched it slowly form into a black beak with a dull yellow membrane at the base. Her body, twisting, seemed to stretch, catching the wind, first beneath, then above; she could feel the swift air through her feathers and the high, sweet whistling of it rushing past her head. Spiraling up, she pumped her powerful wings once. Then, holding them flat, she soared.

Aki-la. Golden eagle, she thought. It was her Word of Power, the Word That Changes, hers and no one else's. And then all words left her and she knew only wind and sky and the land spread out far below.

How long she coursed the sky in her flat-winged glide she did not know. For her there was no time, no ticking off of moment after moment, only the long sweet soaring. But at last her stomach marked the time for her and, without realizing it, she was scanning the ground for prey. It was as if she had two sights now, one the sweeping farsight that showed her the land as a series of patterns and the other that closed up the space whenever she saw movement or heat in the grass that meant some small creature was moving below.

At the base of the mountain she spied a large mouse and her wings knew even before her mind, even before her stomach. They cleaved to her side and she dove down in one long, perilous swoop toward the brown creature that was suddenly still in the short grass.

The wind rushed by her as she dove, and a high singing filled her head, wordless visions of meat and blood.

Kya, she called, and followed it with a whistle. *Kya,* her hunting song.

Right before reaching the mouse, she threw out her wings and backwinged, extending her great claws as brakes. But her final sight of the mouse, larger than she had guessed, standing upright in the grass as if it had expected her, its black eyes meeting her own and the white stripe across its head gleaming in the early sun, stayed her. Some memory, some old human thought teased at her. Instead of striking the mouse, she landed gracefully by its side, her great claws gripping the earth, remembering ground, surrendering to it.

Aki-la. She thought the word again, opened her mouth, and spoke it to the quiet air. She could feel the change begin again. Marrow and sinew and muscle and bone responded, reversing themselves, growing and shrinking, molding and forming. It hurt, yet it did not hurt; the pain was delicious.

And still the mouse sat, its bright little eyes watching her until the transformation was complete. Then it squeaked a word, shook itself all over, as if trying to slough off its own skin and bones, and grew, filling earth and sky, resolving itself into a familiar figure with the fierce stare of an eagle and the soft voice of the mouse.

"Late Blossoming Flower," her mother said, and opened welcoming arms to her.

"I have found my word," Flower said as she ran into them. Then, unaccountably, she put her head on her mother's breast and began to sob.

"You have found much more," said her mother. "For see—I have tested you, tempted you to let your animal nature overcome your human nature. And see—you stopped before the hunger for meat, the thirst for blood, mastered you and left you forever in your eagle form."

"But I might have killed you," Flower gasped. "I might have eaten you. I was an eagle and you were my natural prey."

"But you did not," her mother said firmly. "Now I must go home."

"Wait," Flower said. "There is something . . . something I have to tell you."

Her mother turned and looked at Flower over her shoulder. "About the old man?"

Flower looked down.

"I know it already. There he is." She pointed to a gray-green butterfly hovering over a blossom. "He is the same undisciplined creature he always was."

"I must change him back. I must learn how, quickly, before he leaves."

"He will not leave," said her mother. "Not that one. Or he would have left our village long ago. No, he will wait until you learn your other powers and change him back so that he might sit on the edge of power and laugh at it as he has always done, as he did to me so long ago. And now, my little one who is my little one no longer, use your eagle wings to fly. I will be waiting at our home for your return."

Flower nodded, and then she moved away from her mother and held out her arms. She stretched them as far apart as she could. Even so—even farther—would her wings stretch. She looked up into the sky, now blue and cloudless and beckoning.

"Aki-la!" she cried, but her mouth was not as stern as her mother's or as any of the other women of power, for she knew how to laugh. She opened her laughing mouth again. *"Aki-la."*

She felt the change come on her, more easily this time, and she threw herself into the air. The morning sun caught the wash of gold at her beak, like a necklace of power. *Kya*, she screamed into the waiting wind, *kya*, and, for the moment, forgot mother and butterfly and all the land below.

JANE YOLEN

Born in New York City and raised in Westport, Connecticut, Jane Yolen graduated from Smith College, where she now teaches, while living with her family in Hatfield, Massachusetts. She went to work in the publishing business, first for *Newsweek* and then for the *Saturday Review*. Eventually, after learning the various parts of the publishing business, she became an editor while beginning to write and publish her own books. Since her first publication—*Pirates in Petticoats*, a nonfiction book about women pirates—Ms. Yolen has published nearly one hundred books, while also writing numerous essays, poems, songs, and two musical plays.

Known best for her science fiction, fantasy, and folk tales, she has written for all ages, although most of her work has been for younger children. Among her picture books are *Mice on Ice, No Bath Tonight,* and *The Seeing Stick,* which won the Christopher Award. Among her collections of original tales are *The Minstrel and the Mountain: A Tale of Peace* and *The Girl Who Cried Flowers and Other Tales,* which won the Golden Kite Award, was named a Best Book of the Year by the *School Library Journal,* and was a National Book Award finalist. Her nonfiction books include *Touch Magic: Fantasy, Faerie, and Folklore in the Literature of Childhood* and *World on a String: The Story of Kites.* Both written and oral storytelling are among Jane Yolen's favorite activities, along with folksinging. "Story," she says, "is what distinguishes humans from beasts."

Specifically for teenage readers, there is *The Gift of Sarah Barker,* the story of two teenagers who fall in love in a Shaker village in the 1850s. It was named one of the Best Books for Young Adults by the American Library Association. There is also the exciting and wonderful Pit Dragon trilogy: *Dragon's Blood, Heart's Blood,* and *A Sending of Dragons,* all ALA Best Books for Young Adults.

Among this prolific writer's latest publications is *Merlin's Booke,* a collection of nine short stories and four poems about the famous wizard of King Arthur's court.

Roses, bread, onions, spaghetti sauce, burning leaves all produce distinctive smells in our world. But there is only one fragrance in the world where seventeen-year-old Caroline is conducting a scientific investigation. . . .

THE SWEET PERFUME OF GOOD-BYE

M. E. KERR

Here nothing smells.

Almost nothing smells.

The roses are red beyond belief but give off no aroma. The lemons are as yellow as the sun, but there is no lemony fragrance, just a semblance of bitterness as you bite into one. The fresh-cut bright green grass where my lovers sit does not even smell, as it did summer mornings when I was on Earth and could smell it from my room while the boy cut our lawn.

I call them "my lovers" with a little smile. That is my sense of humor emerging (though I am thought to be a humorless young scientist). They do not make love to me, of course. They are mine only in the fact that I am studying them.

Here the only perfume is the sweet perfume of good-bye that comes on a person one hour before death. I cannot describe it accurately, even though I am a stickler for accuracy. Like our lilies? A little, but more rare and tantalizing, and people rush to be near whoever is dying, keeping a respectful distance (scores of them behind me as I write this), but still lingering nearby for a faint whiff.

Carlo, the boy, is dying. He has just begun to give off this haunting, beautiful scent. His girlfriend, Marny, is ecstatic as she breathes it in. They sit on the grass near me, having their last conversation.

I can hear them. It is love talk of the passionate variety.

The great advantage of being thought to be crazy is that I can sit near them and they ignore me. Let her be, they say. The poor thing, they say. We have so much and she has nothing but her mixed-up brain, they say.

It is important for you to know that there is no murder here, no suicide, no wars, no illness. The only way you can die is naturally, when your time comes, and no one knows when that will be.

Carlo is my age, seventeen.

I have a certain freak value here.

They ask me to be on late-night television talk shows of the kooky variety.

They pretend to treat me with respect, but no matter who the host is, there is always the slanted smile, the wink I am not supposed to see, the same questions.

"So what is Earth like?"

"Filled with the most magnificent fragrances!" I respond.

"Is everyone there an hour away from death then?" Ha! Ha! from the studio audience, but I persist. "No, listen! Our flowers smell. Our food smells. The very air smells. Not always good. We have bad smells too."

"So you spend all your time on Earth mesmerized by these odors, ah? How do you get anything done on Earth? How did your people ever build that fantastic spaceship you supposedly came here in, if you have all these odors to distract you?"

"We take our scents for granted, you see."

"Of course! Of course! And does your spaceship smell?"

The audience is bent double with laughter, and it is just as well in this phase of the interview, for I am not to disclose anything about the mission, not even in jest, not even here in this report.

I am to concentrate on Farfire.

That is what they call this place.

I was chosen because of my practical nature, my keen ability to be objective and unemotional. I am my father's daughter. Doctor Orr remarks on it often, telling me that I am rational and unstirrable beyond my years.

"Tell me, Caroline—is that your Earth name or your Farfire name—Caroline?"

"It is my Earth name. I am not from Farfire, so I have no Farfire name."

"Caroline's not too unlike a Farfire name, though, is it?"

"There is a lot of similarity between Earth and Farfire."

"Yes, well, tell me, Caroline, do you have death on Earth too?"

"Of course we have death."

"Of course you have death." His tone mocks me again. "Except when you Earth folks die, there is no odor." Big wink to the studio audience.

"Not a good one, no."

"What's a bad odor, pray tell?" and there is more laughter.

"I can't describe it. Burnt rubber. Dead flowers. Feces. Those are bad odors on Earth."

"Feces smell on Earth?"

"Yes, they do," and the audience is in convulsions again.

"Well, Earth must not be all that lovely. You must be glad to be on Farfire, hah?"

I was, in the beginning. I truly was. Anticipating it, before I left, with pleasure. Challenged when I arrived. All of it new. But I did not calculate this part of it, being taken for a laughable freak, the way on Earth we treat those who say they've seen flying saucers or been to Mars.

"You'll not be there long," Father reassured me. "The moment you hear three beeps in your earpiece, use your minimike to assure Doctor Orr you're going directly to the field where you were dropped. He'll get you home safely in about two years, just in time for your nineteenth birthday!" Father was excited. "There's no telling what you'll learn about your Farfire teenage counterparts!"

"But will I blend in?" I asked him. "Will they take me captive? Will I be in any danger?"

"They will treat you as interlopers have been treated from time immemorial."

"How is that?"

"They will find some way to trivialize you. They will not believe you. It's all to your advantage."

"Caroline, Marny and I saw you on television," Carlo calls over to me. If anything could ruffle me, it would be that exquisite fragrance, almost making me homesick, it's so voluptuous. "We want to ask you a question." His lopsided smile reminds me of the talk show hosts. "How," says Carlo, "do you know someone's dying on your Earth, if there is no perfume?"

I try to tell him, but his eyes glaze over as I start to describe traffic accidents, war, heart disease, all of it, and Marny giggles into her hands.

"How," Carlo interrupts me as though he is bored with my ranting and raving, "do you handle death then? Death sounds like something horrible."

"How," I come back with a testiness that surprises me, "do you handle the idea that in about forty-five minutes you won't ever be with Marny again?"

He laughs gaily. "We will have been together for as long as we were intended to be together. What more can anyone want?"

Marny asks, "On Earth, do people die at the same time?"

"No, but . . ." I have no ready answer. "But we don't like death."

"What sense does that make?" Carlo says. "Everyone must die. It can't go on forever."

In a while they prepare for his funeral.
They sing:

> *My! My! My! I smell good-bye!*
> *I know you've got to go*
> *So one last kiss*
> *The scent is bliss!*
> *Good-bye, the scent's to die!*

They all wear white and dance.
Marny can't stop smiling with joy.

There is nothing ever said about God here.
After the funeral I ask Marny if there is religion, God, what?
"All of that is after death," she says.
"But what exactly do you believe happens after death?"

"We don't know," she says, and her mouth tips in a grin. "I suppose on Earth you do?"

"We have certain beliefs," I say. "We have concepts. There is a concept of heaven, and a concept of hell. Now, heaven is . . ." and even as I talk, Marny wanders off from me, yawning, calling over her shoulder that she'd really like to hear all about it . . . some other time.

I have never been treated so rudely. That is the part that is so hard to bear: me, Caroline Aylesworth, winner of so many, many honors in science my bookshelves cannot hold all the gold statuettes, my walls with no room left for framed certificates. Not even *listened* to here on Farfire!

I cannot say that I am in any way disappointed when I hear the three beeps, even though this tiny taste of Farfire *has* provoked considerable curiosity in me . . . and even though there is no way ever again to have that curiosity satisfied, for there is no returning here.

"Hello, Caroline!" I hear Doctor Orr's familiar voice. "Do you think you got a good sample?"

"Not a comprehensive one, by any means, but enough about Farfire to make a highly interesting report."

"Excellent! And you know how to find your way to the field?"

"Of course I do."

"I'm here now, waiting for you."

"Give me about an hour and fifteen minutes."

"Gladly," Doctor Orr answers. "My God, Caroline, I'm almost overwhelmed by this wonderful fragrance here!"

"A fragrance, Doctor Orr? Not on Farfire. You see—"

He interrupts me with a whoop of joy. *"Un*believable! Almost like lilies! It's come upon me suddenly! Caroline? It's so all pervasive! It's on *me!* My hands, my face—it's the sweetest perfume!"

Of course, I cannot get to him in time.

I sit down right where I am and make my entry.

I write, *I think I've lost my ride home.*

In the interest of accuracy, I cross out "I think."

M. E. KERR

M. E. Kerr, born Marijane Meaker in Auburn, New York, is now a resident of East Hampton on Long Island. She published her first story in the *Ladies' Home Journal* in 1951.

Her earliest and best-known novel, *Dinky Hocker Shoots Smack!*, is about an overweight girl who "overdoses" on food to compensate for the lack of attention from her parents. In addition to being named one of the Best Children's Books of 1972 by *School Library Journal*, it was made into an ABC-TV "Afterschool Special."

Many of her novels—*The Son of Someone Famous; If I Love You, Am I Trapped Forever?; Is That You, Miss Blue?; What I Really Think of You;* and <u>*Him*</u> *She Loves?*—have more intricate plots and are peopled by more unusual characters than those found in many other young adult novels. Her most unusual characters are found in *Little Little:* a beautiful seventeen-year-old girl who is only three feet, three inches tall and her boyfriend, Sydney Cinnamon, another little person who plays "The Roach" in a TV pest control commercial. Kerr's own zany teenage adventures and the models for some of her adolescent characters are described in her recent autobiography, *Me Me Me Me Me: Not a Novel.*

M. E. Kerr's most sophisticated novel for teenagers, *Gentlehands*, begins as a summer romance between two mismatched teenagers and slowly unfolds as a hunt for an ex-Nazi war criminal.

Her most recent novels for young adults are *I Stay Near You*, a three-part story that examines teenage relationships in three successive generations, and *Night Kites*, which concerns the relationship that develops between Erick Rudd and Nikki, who is a Madonna imitator as well as the girlfriend of Erick's best friend, Jack. But as that conflict develops, Erick discovers that his older brother, Pete, is a homosexual who has contracted AIDS. M. E. Kerr conceived of "The Sweet Perfume of Good-bye" while writing *Night Kites*, where Pete is trying to write a story with the same title and plot but can't seem to finish it.

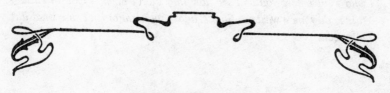

KINSHIPS

Grandpa Jeremiah loves to tell stories about the past. He says they form a bridge: "You can sneak across that bridge and see some folks who went before you and see how they didn't break." Cousin Ellie thinks they are a waste of time. The young narrator isn't sure what it all means. . . .

JEREMIAH'S SONG

WALTER DEAN MYERS

I knowed my cousin Ellie was gonna be mad when Macon Smith come around to the house. She didn't have no use for Macon even when things was going right, and when Grandpa Jeremiah was fixing to die I just knowed she wasn't gonna be liking him hanging around. Grandpa Jeremiah raised Ellie after her folks died and they used to be real close. Then she got to go on to college and when she come back the first year she was different. She didn't want to hear all them stories he used to tell her anymore. Ellie said the stories wasn't true, and that's why she didn't want to hear them.

I didn't know if they was true or not. Tell the truth I didn't think much on it either way, but I liked to hear them stories. Grandpa Jeremiah said they wasn't stories anyway, they was songs.

"They the songs of my people," he used to say.

I didn't see how they was songs, not regular songs anyway. Every little thing we did down in Curry seemed to matter to Ellie that first summer she come home from college. You couldn't do nothin' that was gonna please her. She didn't even come to church much. 'Course she come on Sunday or everybody would have had a regular fit, but she didn't come on Thursday nights and she didn't come on Saturday even though she used to sing in the gospel choir.

"I guess they teachin' her somethin' worthwhile up there at

Greensboro," Grandpa Jeremiah said to Sister Todd. "I sure don't see what it is, though."

"You ain't never had no book learning, Jeremiah," Sister Todd shot back. She wiped at where a trickle of sweat made a little path through the white dusting powder she put on her chest to keep cool. "Them old ways you got ain't got nothing for these young folks."

"I guess you right," Grandpa Jeremiah said.

He said it but I could see he didn't like it none. He was a big man with a big head and had most all his hair even if it was white. All that summer, instead of sitting on the porch telling stories like he used to when I was real little, he would sit out there by himself while Ellie stayed in the house and watched the television or read a book. Sometimes I would think about asking him to tell me one of them stories he used to tell but they was too scary now that I didn't have nobody to sleep with but myself. I asked Ellie to sleep with me but she wouldn't.

"You're nine years old," she said, sounding real proper. "You're old enough to sleep alone."

I *knew* that. I just wanted her to sleep with me because I liked sleeping with her. Before she went off to college she used to put cocoa butter on her arms and face and it would smell real nice. When she come back from college she put something else on, but that smelled nice too.

It was right after Ellie went back to school that Grandpa Jeremiah had him a stroke and Macon started coming around. I think his mama probably made him come at first, but you could see he liked it. Macon had always been around, sitting over near the stuck window at church or going on the blueberry truck when we went picking down at Mister Gregory's place. For a long time he was just another kid, even though he was older'n me, but then, all of a sudden, he growed something fierce. I used to be up to his shoulder one time and then, before I could turn around good, I was only up to his shirt pocket. He changed too. When he used to just hang around with the other boys and play ball or shoot at birds he would laugh a lot. He didn't laugh so much anymore and I figured he was just about grown. When Grandpa got sick he used to come around and help out with things around the house that was too hard for me to do. I mean, I could have done all the chores, but it would just take me longer.

When the work for the day was finished and the sows fed, Grandpa would kind of ease into one of his stories and Macon, he would sit and listen to them and be real interested. I didn't mind listening to the stories when Grandpa told them to Macon because he would be telling them in the middle of the afternoon and they would be past my mind by the time I had to go to bed.

Macon had an old guitar he used to mess with, too. He wasn't too bad on it, and sometimes Grandpa would tell him to play us a tune. He could play something he called "the Delta Blues" real good, but when Sister Todd or somebody from the church come around he'd play "Precious Lord" or "Just a Closer Walk With Thee."

Grandpa Jeremiah had been feeling poorly from that stroke, and one of his legs got a little drag to it. Just about the time Ellie come from school the next summer he was real sick. He was breathing loud so you could hear it even in the next room and he would stay in bed a lot even when there was something that needed doing or fixing.

"I don't think he's going to make it much longer," Dr. Crawford said. "The only thing I can do is to give him something for the pain."

"Are you sure of your diagnosis?" Ellie asked. She was sitting around the table with Sister Todd, Deacon Turner, and his little skinny yellow wife.

Dr. Crawford looked at Ellie like he was surprised to hear her talking. "Yes, I'm sure," he said. "He had tests a few weeks ago and his condition was bad then."

"How much time he got?" Sister Todd asked.

"Maybe a week or two at best," Dr. Crawford said.

When he said that, Deacon Turner's wife started crying and goin' on and I give her a hard look but she just went on. I was the one who loved Grandpa Jeremiah the most and she didn't hardly even know him so I didn't see why she was crying.

Everybody started tiptoeing around the house after that. They would go in and ask Grandpa Jeremiah if he was comfortable and stuff like that or take him some food or a cold glass of lemonade.

Sister Todd come over and stayed with us. Mostly what she did is make supper and do a lot of praying, which was good because I figured that maybe God would do something to make Grandpa Jeremiah well. When she wasn't doing that she was piecing on a fancy quilt she was making for some white people in Wilmington.

Ellie, she went around asking everybody how they felt about Dr. Crawford and then she went into town and asked about the tests and things. Sister Jenkins asked her if she thought she knowed more than Dr. Crawford, and Ellie rolled her eyes at her, but Sister Jenkins was reading out her Bible and didn't make no notice of it.

Then Macon come over.

He had been away on what he called "a little piece of a job" and hadn't heard how bad off Grandpa Jeremiah was. When he come over he talked to Ellie and she told him what was going on and then he got him a soft drink from the refrigerator and sat out on the porch and before you know it he was crying.

You could look at his face and tell the difference between him sweating and the tears. The sweat was close against his skin and shiny and the tears come down fatter and more sparkly.

Macon sat on the porch, without saying a word, until the sun went down and the crickets started chirping and carrying on. Then he went in to where Grandpa Jeremiah was and stayed in there for a long time.

Sister Todd was saying that Grandpa Jeremiah needed his rest and Ellie went in to see what Macon was doing. Then she come out real mad.

"He got Grandpa telling those old stories again," Ellie said. "I told him Grandpa needed his rest and for him not to be staying all night."

He did leave soon, but bright and early the next morning Macon was back again. This time he brought his guitar with him and he went on in to Grandpa Jeremiah's room. I went in, too.

Grandpa Jeremiah's room smelled terrible. It was all closed up so no drafts could get on him and the whole room was smelled down with disinfect and medicine. Grandpa Jeremiah lay propped up on the bed and he was so gray he looked scary. His hair wasn't combed down and his head on the pillow with his white hair sticking out was enough to send me flying if Macon hadn't been there. He was skinny, too. He looked like his skin got loose on his bones, and when he lifted his arms, it hung down like he was just wearing it instead of it being a part of him.

Macon sat slant-shouldered with his guitar across his lap. He was messin' with the guitar, not making any music, but just going over the strings as Grandpa talked.

"Old Carrie went around out back to where they kept the pigs penned up and she felt a cold wind across her face. . . ." Grandpa Jeremiah was telling the story about how a old woman out-tricked the Devil and got her son back. I had heard the story before, and I knew it was pretty scary. "When she felt the cold breeze she didn't blink nary an eye, but looked straight ahead. . . ."

All the time Grandpa Jeremiah was talking I could see Macon fingering his guitar. I tried to imagine what it would be like if he was actually plucking the strings. I tried to fix my mind on that because I didn't like the way the story went with the old woman wrestling with the Devil.

We sat there for nearly all the afternoon until Ellie and Sister Todd come in and said that supper was ready. Me and Macon went out and ate some collard greens, ham hocks, and rice. Then Macon he went back in and listened to some more of Grandpa's stories until it was time for him to go home. I wasn't about to go in there and listen to no stories at night.

Dr. Crawford come around a few days later and said that Grandpa Jeremiah was doing a little better.

"You think the Good Lord gonna pull him through?" Sister Todd asked.

"I don't tell the Good Lord what He should or should not be doing," Dr. Crawford said, looking over at Sister Todd and at Ellie. "I just said that *my* patient seems to be doing okay for his condition."

"He been telling Macon all his stories," I said.

"Macon doesn't seem to understand that Grandpa Jeremiah needs his strength," Ellie said. "Now that he's improving, we don't want him to have a setback."

"No use in stopping him from telling his stories," Dr. Crawford said. "If it makes him feel good it's as good as any medicine I can give him."

I saw that this didn't set with Ellie, and when Dr. Crawford had left I asked her why.

"Dr. Crawford means well," she said, "but we have to get away from the kind of life that keeps us in the past."

She didn't say why we should be trying to get away from the stories and I really didn't care too much. All I knew was that when Macon was sitting in the room with Grandpa Jeremiah I wasn't nearly as scared as I used to be when it was just me and Ellie listening. I told that to Macon.

"You getting to be a big man, that's all," he said.

That was true. Me and Macon was getting to be good friends, too. I didn't even mind so much when he started being friends with Ellie later. It seemed kind of natural, almost like Macon was supposed to be there with us instead of just visiting.

Grandpa wasn't getting no better, but he wasn't getting no worse, either.

"You liking Macon now?" I asked Ellie when we got to the middle of July. She was dishing out a plate of smothered chops for him and I hadn't even heard him ask for anything to eat.

"Macon's funny," Ellie said, not answering my question. "He's in there listening to all of those old stories like he's really interested in them. It's almost as if he and Grandpa Jeremiah are talking about something more than the stories, a secret language."

I didn't think I was supposed to say anything about that to Macon, but once, when Ellie, Sister Todd, and Macon were out on the porch shelling butter beans after Grandpa got tired and was resting, I went into his room and told him what Ellie had said.

"She said that?" Grandpa Jeremiah's face was skinny and old looking but his eyes looked like a baby's, they was so bright.

"Right there in the kitchen is where she said it," I said. "And I don't know what it mean but I was wondering about it."

"I didn't think she had any feeling for them stories," Grandpa Jeremiah said. "If she think we talking secrets, maybe she don't."

"I think she getting a feeling for Macon," I said.

"That's okay, too," Grandpa Jeremiah said. "They both young."

"Yeah, but them stories you be telling, Grandpa, they about old people who lived a long time ago," I said.

"Well, those the folks you got to know about," Grandpa Jeremiah said. "You think on what those folks been through, and what they was feeling, and you add it up with what you been through and what you been feeling, then you got you something."

"What you got Grandpa?"

"You got you a bridge," Grandpa said. "And a meaning. Then when things get so hard you about to break, you can sneak across that bridge and see some folks who went before you and see how they didn't break. Some got bent and some got twisted and a few fell along the way, but they didn't break."

"Am I going to break, Grandpa?"

"You? As strong as you is?" Grandpa Jeremiah pushed himself up on his elbow and give me a look. "No way you going to break, boy. You gonna be strong as they come. One day you gonna tell all them stories I told you to your young'uns and they'll be as strong as you."

"Suppose I ain't got no stories, can I make some up?"

"Sure you can, boy. You make 'em up and twist 'em around. Don't make no mind. Long as you got 'em."

"Is that what Macon is doing?" I asked. "Making up stories to play on his guitar?"

"He'll do with 'em what he see fit, I suppose," Grandpa Jeremiah said. "Can't ask more than that from a man."

It rained the first three days of August. It wasn't a hard rain but it rained anyway. The mailman said it was good for the crops over East but I didn't care about that so I didn't pay him no mind. What I did mind was when it rain like that the field mice come in and get in things like the flour bin and I always got the blame for leaving it open.

When the rain stopped I was pretty glad. Macon come over and sat with Grandpa and had something to eat with us. Sister Todd come over, too.

"How Grandpa doing?" Sister Todd asked. "They been asking about him in the church."

"He's doing all right," Ellie said.

"He's kind of quiet today," Macon said. "He was just talking about how the hogs needed breeding."

"He must have run out of stories to tell," Sister Todd said. "He'll be repeating on himself like my father used to do. That's the way I *hear* old folks get."

Everybody laughed at that because Sister Todd was pretty old, too. Maybe we was all happy because the sun was out after so much rain. When Sister Todd went in to take Grandpa Jeremiah a plate of potato salad with no mayonnaise like he liked it, she told him about how people was asking for him and he told her to tell them he was doing okay and to remember him in their prayers.

Sister Todd came over the next afternoon, too, with some rhubarb pie with cheese on it, which is my favorite pie. When she took a piece into Grandpa Jeremiah's room she come right out again and told Ellie to go fetch the Bible.

It was a hot day when they had the funeral. Mostly everybody was there. The church was hot as anything, even though they had the window open. Some yellowjacks flew in and buzzed around Sister Todd's niece and then around Deacon Turner's wife and settled right on her hat and stayed there until we all stood and sang "Soon-a Will Be Done."

At the graveyard Macon played "Precious Lord" and I cried hard even though I told myself that I wasn't going to cry the way Ellie and Sister Todd was, but it was such a sad thing when we left and Grandpa Jeremiah was still out to the grave that I couldn't help it.

During the funeral and all, Macon kind of told everybody where to go and where to sit and which of the three cars to ride in. After it was over he come by the house and sat on the front porch and played on his guitar. Ellie was standing leaning against the rail and she was crying but it wasn't a hard crying. It was a soft crying, the kind that last inside of you for a long time.

Macon was playing a tune I hadn't heard before. I thought it might have been what he was working at when Grandpa Jeremiah was telling him those stories and I watched his fingers but I couldn't tell if it was or not. It wasn't nothing special, that tune Macon was playing, maybe halfway between them Delta blues he would do when Sister Todd wasn't around and something you would play at church. It was something different and something the same at the same time. I watched his fingers go over that guitar and figured I could learn that tune one day if I had a mind to.

WALTER DEAN MYERS

Beginning with the attitude that "Children are our gifts to the future," Walter Dean Myers has chosen to write about the positive experiences of children and teenagers living in less than ideal environments. Almost all his earliest books for young adults were prizewinners: *Fast Sam, Cool Clyde, and Stuff; It Ain't All for Nothin';* and *The Young Landlords* were declared Notable Books by the American Library Association. *The Young Landlords* also received the Coretta Scott King Award, was named an ALA Best Book for Young Adults, and was made into a film by Topol Productions.

Also named Best Books for Young Adults by the ALA were *The Legend of Tarik*—the story of a young black knight who must face the merciless El Muerte—and *Hoops*—a basketball success story. In *Hoops*, Harlem basketball star Lonnie Jackson and his coach are pressured by some heavy bettors to throw the championship game. Lonnie, in *The Outside Shot*, finds that his street smarts do him little good in dealing with the demands of college classes, high-pressure sports, and big-time corruption.

Adventure is on tap for readers of *Tales of a Dead King*, in which two teenagers attempt to solve a mysterious disappearance on an archeological dig in Egypt. And in *The Nicholas Factor*, a college freshman, recruited to infiltrate an elitist right-wing student society, finds himself in the jungles of the Amazon.

In a more realistic vein, as well as in a more familiar location, Myers explores the pressures of life in Harlem through the experiences of a young woman who struggles to stay above the vices of the inner city as she—along with a homeless orphan—tries to save her brother from the clutches of drugs in *Motown and Didi: A Love Story*.

Born in West Virginia and raised in Harlem, Walter Myers now lives in Jersey City, New Jersey, where he also writes books for children—including *The Dragon Takes a Wife, The Golden Serpent,* and *Mr. Monkey and the Gotcha Bird*. His most recent books are *Adventure in Granada* and *The Hidden Shrine*.

Norman was definitely weird. For one thing, all he ever did was read. Willie, on the other hand, was "a real boy" who especially loved baseball. What these two had in common came about only because a mysterious stranger came to town. . . .

THE BOY WITH YELLOW EYES

GLORIA GONZALEZ

Only a handful of the residents of Preston Heights recall the actual events. And even then, years and conflicting accounts have clouded the facts.

Still, in some quarters, and especially during the relentless winters unique to the hillside village, the incident is spoken of with pride and awe.

Till today, if you get a couple of old-timers in the same room, a heated debate will erupt over the mundane detail of whether Norman was ten or going on thirteen. They'll also argue whether he lost one shoe or both in the scuffle.

What the parties do agree on is that it happened in Preston Heights and it involved Norman and his next-door neighbor Willie, whose age for some reason is never questioned—thirteen.

And of course . . . the stranger.

Opinions are equally divided on whether the stranger's limp was caused by a deformed right or left leg. But everyone, to a man, can tell you exactly what the Vice President of the United States was wearing when he arrived and what he ordered for lunch. (In fact, his discarded gingham cloth napkin, since laundered, is part of the local exhibit, which includes his signature in the hotel's register.)

The only other point of total agreement is that Norman was the least likely of heroes. He had none of the qualities that could have foretold his sudden fame.

Norman was not the kind of kid who would cause you to break out in a grin if you saw him ride your way on a bike.

1. He couldn't ride a bike.
2. He rarely emerged from his house.
3. He was considered . . . well . . . weird.

This last opinion was based on the fact that Norman would only be seen heading toward or leaving the library, and always hugging an armful of books. To the townfolk it seemed unhealthy for a young boy to read so much. They predicted a total loss of eyesight by the time he reached nineteen.

Willie, however, was a kid who, had there been a Normal Kid Pageant, would have won first and tied for second and third. A dynamic baseball player, daring bike rider, crackerjack newspaper delivery boy—he was the town's delight. Never mind that he was flunking all school subjects and had a reputation as a bully, he was, after all, "a real boy."

The differences did not escape the boys themselves. Though neighbors, separated only by splintery bushes, they never as much as shared a "Hi."

To Willie, Norman was simply the kid with the yellow eyes. Not that they were actually yellow—more of a brown-hazel—but often, the way the sunlight bounced off the thick eyeglasses, it seemed to create a yellow haze.

(Years later, in a rare interview, Norman was asked if he had missed having friends while growing up. He replied: "Not at all. I had Huck and Tom Sawyer.")

To Norman, Willie was exhausting. He talked fast, ran fast, walked fast, and, he suspected, even slept fast. (If such a thing could be measured.) It was tiring just to sit behind him in class and listen to his endless chatter.

If Norman was slow motion, Willie was definitely fast forward. Which brings us to the stranger, who fit somewhere in between.

Some say the stranger arrived one early summer day on foot. Others believe he came on the bus from Boulder.

One fact is undisputed: he took a room on the second floor of McCory's hotel. Not that he had much of a choice; it was the only lodging in town. The hotel dated back to the construction of the first railroad. It had been hastily thrown together to house the army of laborers that would lay the train tracks. Unfortunately, the hilly terrain stymied the work force and the project was eventually abandoned, leaving behind three passenger and two freight cars.

George McCory, the town's undertaker, purchased the hotel and soon found he could make more money by housing the living.

The hotel parlor soon became the common milling ground. Here you could always get into a game of checkers, buy stamps, mail a letter, or receive news of neighboring towns via the traveling salesmen.

That's why when the stranger first arrived, his presence went almost unnoticed. It was only after he was still visible over a period of weeks that others became aware of him. A tall, muscular man in his thirties with a ready smile, he made a favorable impression. Maybe it was the limp. Many attributed it to the war then raging in Europe. Too polite to inquire, the hotel regulars silently accepted his "wound."

Since the man was never seen during the day and rarely till after supper, his comings and goings drew much speculation. Local gossip had it that he was an artist who'd come to Preston Heights to paint the unusual terrain. This theory was fueled by the sight of the man always carrying a dark satchel. Some held that the man was famous.

Perhaps that legend would have endured except for three insignificant, unrelated events:

1. The library decided to paint its reading room.
2. Willie's baseball coach had a tooth pulled.
3. The stranger overslept.

On the day of the "incident," Norman headed, as usual, to the library. Mrs. Brenner, the librarian, met him at the entrance and explained that due to the cleanup work the library was temporarily closed.

The thought of studying in his stuffy bedroom (no air could circulate because of all the books he ordered from Chicago and New York publishers) sent him instead to the railroad yards.

The discarded railroad cars—which had been painted a zippy burgundy when new—now bore the scars of merciless winters and oppressive summers. Vandalism and neglect had added to the toll. For too many years, kids had deemed it their own amusement park. In recent time, the decaying cars had even been abandoned by the vandals. Rumor had it that rats and raccoons openly roamed the burgundy cars.

Norman knew it wasn't true. At least once a month, when the weather was nice, he would head for the rail yard, lugging his books, to settle comfortably in a cushioned seat in car #7215, his head pressed against the wooden window frame (now paneless). When the day's shadow hit the bottom of the page, he knew to close the book and head home.

On this day, the high position of the sun assured him of at least four uninterrupted hours of reading.

Across town, in the school yard, Willie stood with friends swinging his baseball bat at air. He looked forward to practice almost as much as to the games. That's why when the coach appeared to say he had to cancel due to an impacted tooth, the teenager found himself at a loss as to what to do.

It was too early to start his newspaper money collection. Knowing it was best to strike when families were seated for dinner, he wandered aimlessly toward the rail yards with a mind to picking up some chunky rocks and using them as balls to swat about the empty field.

And so it was that he found himself in the proximity of car #7215.

The unusually warm weather had its effect on the stranger who now dozed in the freight car, an iron link away from #7215. The heat had caused him to discard his usual caution in return for a slight breeze. He had lifted the huge steel doors that slid upward, affording him a welcome breeze from the quiet countryside. The cool air had lulled his senses, stretching his customary nap long past its normal half hour.

Perhaps it was his two months of success, his feeling of invincibility, or his unconscious desire for danger that caused him to be careless this day. In any event, when he awoke, he did not bother to lower the steel door.

He opened his black satchel and removed the network of tubes, cylinders, wires, bolts, and antennas which he expertly positioned in a matter of minutes. It was by now an automatic labor. His mind refreshed by sleep, he thought ahead to the coming week when he would be safely aboard the steamer that would carry him across the ocean. The lightness of his touch, as he twisted the spidery wires, reflected his carefree attitude.

Norman's first reaction was to ignore Willie's sudden entrance.

"You see my ball go by here?"

Norman didn't even look up from the book he was reading. "No."

"Not exactly a ball, more like a rock," Willie said, sitting on the armrest of a seat, with his legs blocking the aisle.

"No," Norman answered.

Normally, Willie would have stalked out, but it was cooler inside the car, and most appealing of all, Norman looked so relaxed and comfortable that he felt compelled to ruin it.

"What are you doing, anyway?"

"Reading."

"I figured that. That's all you ever do. Aren't you afraid you're going to lose your eyesight?"

Norman's lack of response did not still Willie.

"I think reading is dumb."

"I think hitting a rock with a stick is dumb."

"Oh, yeah? You ever try it?"

"No. You ever try reading?"

"When the teacher makes me. I'd rather hit a rock. It's fun."

"So is reading."

Willie didn't buy it. "When I hit a ball, I'm *doing* something. Reading is not doing."

Norman removed his glasses and closely regarded Willie with his full attention.

"Do you know what I was *doing* when you barged in here? I was running through a haunted castle being chased by a vampire who was very, very thirsty. If that isn't 'doing,' I don't know what is."

This led to Norman's explaining the plot of Brom Stoker's *Dracula*. Willie, totally engrossed, sat on the floor listening to the tale of horror.

Norman was telling him about Renfield—and his daily diet of

spiders and insects—when a distant clicking sound averted his attention.

"Probably a woodpecker," Willie said, urging the other boy to get back to the story.

Norman stretched his neck closer to the sound.

"If it is, it's the smartest woodpecker in history," Norman said, straining to hear.

Something in Norman's expression caused Willie to whisper, "What are you talking about?"

Norman swiftly signaled him to be quiet and silently crept toward the source of the tapping.

Willie, suddenly frightened for reasons he could not explain, followed closely. "What is it?" he asked, gripping his baseball bat.

The tapping was louder now.

"It's coming from the freight car." Norman dropped to the floor, his body hunched against the steel door separating them from the other car. Willie fell alongside him. "What is it?" he half pleaded.

Norman took a pencil from his pocket and began scribbling furiously on the margins of the library book. Willie noticed that he wrote with the rhythm of the clicking sound. Whenever the tapping stopped for a moment, so did Norman's pencil.

Willie glanced at the jottings, but it was difficult to make out the words. He did make out one short phrase. "End is near."

Norman and the clicking stopped at the same time.

"What does it mean?" Willie whispered, his fear growing. He had known fear once before, when a stray dog, foaming at the mouth, had cornered him behind the general store. But this was worse. Here the threat was unknown.

Norman quickly stashed the book under a seat and jumped to his feet. "We have to stop him!" he told Willie.

"Who?"

"The spy," Norman said as he slid open the heavy door and dashed outside.

A startled Willie sat frozen.

The bright sun slammed Norman in the face as he jumped

from the train car and rolled underneath the freight compartment. He was silently happy to see Willie join him seconds later.

"What are we doing?" Willie asked, frightened of the answer.

"Waiting."

"For what?" he whispered.

"Him," Norman said, pointing to the underbelly of the rusted car.

Before Willie could reply, the stranger jumped from above their heads, clutching his dark suitcase. They watched as his limping form started to move away.

Norman sprung from under the car, raced after the man, and —to Willie's horror—tackled him from behind. The satchel went flying in the surprise attack.

"Grab it! Grab it!" Norman screamed.

The stranger clawed the ground and struggled to his feet, fighting like a wild man. His eyes were ablaze with hate. His arms, hands, and feet spun like a deranged windmill. His actions were swift but Norman was quicker. Try as he might to grab the boy, the man kept slashing at the air. He managed to clutch the boy's foot, but Norman quickly wiggled out of his shoe. The man grabbed him by his pants leg and pulled him to the ground.

"Do something!" Norman screamed at Willie, who stood paralyzed with fear. The man was now crouched over the boy's body and was gripping his neck.

Willie, seeing Norman's legs thrash helplessly in the air, swung his baseball bat with all his strength and caught the stranger— low and inside.

"About time," Norman coughed, massaging his throbbing neck.

Hours later, sitting in the hotel lobby with the chief of police, the boys watched wearily as swarms of people dashed up and down the stairs. They knew the man's room was being torn apart.

In the hotel kitchen the stranger was surrounded by FBI agents who had been summoned from the state capital, seventy-eight miles away. More were en route from Washington, D.C.

By nightfall the hotel was completely isolated from the public and everyone heard of how Willie and Norman had caught themselves a real-life Nazi spy.

It took weeks for the full story to emerge, and even then the citizens felt that the whole story would never be revealed. (Norman's *Dracula* book, for instance, had been whisked away by agents.) What was learned was that the man had been transmitting information to a colleague in Boulder. That man had managed to slip away and was now believed to be back in Berlin. Two of the strangers' conspirators in New York—one a woman—were arrested and being held in a federal prison outside of Virginia.

Three months later, in a highly publicized visit, the Vice President of the United States came to Preston Heights to thank the boys personally. Film crews shot footage of the unlikely trio that would be shown in movie theaters throughout the country; Preston Heights would never be the same.

The cameras were there when Norman was asked how he had been able to understand the Morse code. "I learned it from a book," he said.

Asked how he had been able to overpower the man, Willie grinned. "Easy. I'm batting .409 on the school team."

Preston Heights blossomed under the glare of national attention. Tourists visiting the state made it a point to spend the night at McCory's hotel and gawk at the corner table in the dining room where the Vice President ate lunch with the boys and their parents.

Willie did not go on to become a major league slugger. Instead, he left Preston Heights to join the navy and rose to the rank of chief petty officer upon retirement.

Norman attended Georgetown University and went on to serve as press secretary for a New Jersey senator.

Every Christmas they exchange cards and a list of books each has read during the previous year.

Norman is still ahead of Willie, two to one.

GLORIA GONZALEZ

A native New Yorker who now lives across the Hudson River in West New York, New Jersey, Gloria Gonzalez began her writing career as an investigative reporter for various New Jersey newspapers. She is now best known as a playwright, many of whose works have been produced Off-Off Broadway as well as on television, in California, and in Europe. Among the published works for which she has won awards is the play *Curtains*, which was named one of the Best Short Plays of 1976. Among her unpublished plays is one called *Love Is a Tuna Casserole* and another called *Murder 101*, which has been optioned for Broadway.

Many young adult novels have been made into television movies, but Gloria Gonzalez worked the other way around. After her play *Gaucho* was produced on CBS television in 1970, she rewrote it as a novel. *Gaucho* examines the feelings and resulting problems of a poor teenage boy in New York City who is desperate to earn enough money to buy two plane tickets to get himself and his mother back to their native Puerto Rico. In the process of trying to make some quick money, he gets himself into a lot of trouble.

Like *Gaucho*, Gloria Gonzalez's first novel for teenagers is humorous and upbeat. *The Glad Man* is about the friendship between two young people and an old man who lives with his dog in a broken-down bus at the city dump and the clamor that results when one of the young people writes a letter to a newspaper about the old man's life-style.

Ms. Gonzalez's most recent novel for teenagers—*A Deadly Rhyme*, a selection in Dell Laurel-Leaf's Twilight series—concerns a girl in prep school who finds that events predicted in an old poem are starting to come true. Ms. Gonzalez is also working on a new mystery novel.

*Nobody felt good when Cousin Jessie died, but sorrow wasn't the
only emotion Roseanne felt at the funeral. . . .*

THE BEGINNING OF SOMETHING

SUE ELLEN BRIDGERS

When Mama said, "We're all going home for Cousin Jessie's
funeral," I said, "Not me," but here I am. We rode all night with
static blaring off the radio to keep Mama awake so she could
nudge Daddy. Nothing keeps him awake except an elbow, not
even static. He's so tone-deaf, it sounds like music to him. Buddy
and me stayed all tangled up in the backseat. He can sleep
through anything, but I was restless and uneasy. It was hot, too.

We left right after supper. Mama already had a chicken stew-
ing for pastry when the phone rang. She started crying right there
on the phone, a big wailing sob with her mouth open like she was
getting ready for a high note. Mama sings.

After a while, she settled down enough to find out when the
funeral was going to be—Sunday at two o'clock—and she still
wanted to get in the car that minute and go. She would have, too,
except for the chicken and Daddy's navy blue suit somebody had
to get out of the cleaners and having to think of something I
could wear. I'm still outgrowing clothes—well, actually, my shape
is changing. One day I'm pudgy-looking, and the next I've got
this waist that nips in just perfect. Not like Melissa's, of course,
who was born with a good body and no brains.

Melissa is Cousin Jessie's daughter. Cousin Jessie was Mama's
first cousin and her best friend besides. They grew up together
and they've always loved each other the way people do who remember all grades of silliness and mischief between them. I've
heard some of the things they used to do, baby stuff like sneaking
out after the house was locked and smoking Camels on the front
porch. Big deal. Before Cousin Jessie got so sick, the two of them
would start giggling and whispering behind their hands and hug-

ging each other. Used to make Melissa and me sick. We've never liked each other all that much, mostly I reckon because we're supposed to. Two weeks at her house every summer, two weeks at mine. The longest month God ever made.

Mama was crying all the while she rolled out the dough for the pastry and then the whole time she hunted through the closet for something I could wear. She already had a black dress. People like Mama keep a black dress all the time, just in case. Fourteen-year-old girls don't wear black unless they've got loose morals, except for a T-shirt or something minor like that. Finally Mama found this tacky midnight blue dress I'd pushed to the back of the closet because every time I look at it I about puke, that's how unattractive it is. Mama bought it on sale and anybody can tell it, too. I just about died the one time I wore it. Kept my coat on all through church and it was one of those late winter days that turns out to be positively springlike. Now I've got to wear it to a funeral in July. They might as well lay me out right next to Cousin Jessie.

At this minute I'm sitting here on the porch swing next to Melissa, who won't say a word. I reckon while it's quiet like this, I could tell you what she looks like, and I'm going to try to tell the truth. She's been crying off and on ever since she got up this morning. I think she must of woke up not remembering anything but all of a sudden it came to her because she moaned real loud and pulled the sheet over her head. I could see the sheet trembling like there was a poltergeist under there. I hadn't been asleep more than two hours and my mouth felt scorched and my eyes wouldn't half open but I couldn't leave her like that so I went over to her bed and put my hand on the jerking sheet. I pressed right on her chest till her breathing slowed down. There wasn't any point in saying anything, was there? She kept on crying but at least she wasn't wearing herself out with it. Holding onto her like that was like calming a scared animal, but I don't think Melissa would ever think about it that way. She used to want me to rub her back all the time, just a couple of years ago. She expects things like that of people, but it always embarrasses me. Melissa is spoiled.

She's pretty, though. Even right now with her eyelids swollen and her cheeks puffed up and not a smidgen of lipstick in sight— nothing done to get ready for the world but her teeth and hair brushed—she looks darn near perfect. Like a model. Like she doesn't have to do anything but just *be*. I know you've seen people like that. I think you ought to consider yourself lucky if you don't know any.

So she's sitting here in the morning heat—it's hot down in the flatland at nine o'clock in the morning. There's no haze to burn off so the sun just comes on out at five A.M. and everything's cooking by ten. When Melissa stays with us in the mountains, she sleeps in a double bed with me and she curls up right tight next to me about daybreak when the air turns as chilly as it's going to get. She sleeps under a blanket every night. I think that's the only part about coming to our house she likes—snuggling under the covers like that.

Anyway, we didn't visit this summer because her mama was so sick, hardly walking and needing to be looked after every minute. Cousin Jessie had diabetes from the time she was first married. She gave herself those shots every day and even with doing that, sometimes she'd start shaking and jerking and finally just fall down unconscious. Everybody in the family carried Life Savers around in their pockets. Diabetes is what killed her, Life Savers or no.

When the news came, Mama was brokenhearted. Even knowing Cousin Jessie's time was coming and praying about it and fretting over it, Mama wasn't one bit ready. The look on her face when she was on the telephone was a sight—like she was hearing something terrible and truly unexpected instead of word that Cousin Jessie was at rest.

She looked wild, Mama did, like the time she pulled Buddy out of the path of Mr. Bowdine's Ford when he reversed by accident. Then there was the time she lost a baby in the bathroom. Felt it passing while she clutched a bloody towel between her legs, but nothing was going to stop it. I sneaked a look in the toilet when I was helping her to bed, but there wasn't anything but bloody water. I didn't even know it was a baby until that summer when I heard Mama and Cousin Jessie going over the details and put two and two together. The point is, that was the look on Mama's face, a look of being ripped apart and so startled she didn't know which was worse, the surprise or the pain.

Diabetes runs in the family. Cousin Jessie's daddy had it and one of his sisters did, too. Mama's always telling us to watch our blood sugar, although Cousin Jessie's daddy wasn't a blood relation to us, her mama was. So it's Melissa who ought to be watching her blood sugar and I reckon she knows it. There's not an ounce of fat on her. She's wearing white shorts and a pink skinny top that shows everything. Mama didn't even let me bring shorts, even knowing how hot it is here. I've got seersucker slacks and this cotton skirt and that infernal blue dress. Of course, there's nobody to tell Melissa what she ought to be wearing. I mean, who's going to say it? Her daddy is in the throes of grief, so I think Mama's going to end up in charge. Already this morning she's cleaned out the refrigerator to make room for the cold dishes she's expecting. She's cleaned off a pantry shelf on which to put fried chicken, boiled vegetables, and ham. The buffet in the dining room will take care of cakes and pies and, I hope, some brownies. I would die for a brownie right now. And a Dr Pepper. Melissa and I skipped breakfast.

I think she's just going to sit here until one o'clock, when we're supposed to go down to the funeral home and view the body. I told Mama I wasn't going and she said all right, I could take care of Buddy. He's nine and doesn't have any business at a funeral home. Melissa is going, though. She and her daddy are suppose to see if Cousin Jessie looks all right before they let other people view her. It seems to me it ought to be the other way around. Let some objective people get the first look. I think funerals are sick.

"Melissa, let's get something to eat."

She's pushing the swing with her bare feet so it trembles a little. She's got the prettiest toenails. I swear it! They curve just perfect and she's put this pink polish on them that turns silvery when the light catches it right. I guess fixing her toenails gave her something to do last night. You can spend hours messing with your nails if you want to. Well, I couldn't, but I bet Melissa can. Her feet are the kind somebody's going to want to kiss. It won't be long either, because Melissa's been going out with boys for a year or more. She's older than me, already sixteen, and there were boys after her when she was twelve. Cousin Jessie was fighting them off with a stick. Mama's never had that trouble with me.

"No, thanks," Melissa says about the food like I'm offering to fix her something. "Jamie's coming over here in a few minutes. He said he would."

That's the boy she's been going out with all summer. He'll be a senior next year, and for their first date he took her to the Junior-Senior Prom this past spring. Their picture's taped smack in the middle of her dresser mirror so you have to look around it to do your face. They're standing in front of a blue curtain with silver stars on it and she's got her back up against his chest and he's got his arms around her. I'm going to borrow that dress she's wearing if my figure settles down by next spring. I know Melissa's not intending to wear it again even if it cost one hundred and fifty dollars, which it did. Cousin Jessie told Mama Melissa's got expensive taste. She tried to sound like she was complaining, but I heard the pride in it. Melissa was everything to Cousin Jessie.

"Well, I'm eating something." Mama told me to stay with her. Comfort her, Mama said. "You want me to bring you a sandwich out here?"

We're eating peanut butter and jelly with milk. Melissa nibbles at hers and leaves the milk glass half full on the porch floor. This old tomcat of hers starts nosing around it, trying to get his face down to the milk. She doesn't even notice when he turns it over. I've got to remember to clean up the sticky place when he gets through. Mama wants everything clean, just like Cousin Jessie used to keep the house before she got weak and bloated and the medicine quit doing any good.

"Finished?"

When Melissa nods, I take her half-eaten sandwich and the empty glasses into the house. It's cooler in the house, especially in the living room, because the blinds are shut and it's dark in there. The kitchen's warm, though, and Mama's beading up while she scrubs the countertops and the cabinet fronts just like she was home. I think this is nervous energy working because she didn't sleep at all in the car and I don't think she closed her eyes after we got here. She and Cousin Roy sat down together at the kitchen table first thing, and that's where they were this morning when I came down. They'd been talking for hours, Uncle Roy telling Mama step by step what happened. I heard bits and pieces of it and I don't see how anybody remembers everything like that. It's like three days are marked in his brain, minute by minute. Looks like it would all be a blur.

Cousin Roy couldn't of picked a better person to tell it to, because Mama wanted to hear every word of it. I know she wishes she'd been here, but when Cousin Roy first called her to say Cousin Jessie was back in the hospital, practically in a coma, he told her there was no need for her to rush across North Carolina to see her. Cousin Jessie wouldn't know she was there, he said, hoping, I think, to relieve Mama's mind. But she wanted to come, she told Daddy, who agreed with Cousin Roy that she should save her strength for the end. "You can't help Jessie now," Daddy said, "but you can help Roy and Melissa later on if you don't wear yourself out. Jessie'd want them to have plenty of attention."

Mama gave in, but like I say, she fretted about it and prayed and cleaned her own house like we were expecting company ourselves. The older Mama gets, the more nervous she acts. I always thought when you got about forty, nothing much would worry you anymore. I mean, everything ought to be settled by then. But it's not so. Mama's a bundle of nerves under the best of circumstances.

Now she's perspiring through the housedress she brought to clean in. "Your daddy's still asleep," she says, aggravated by everything.

"He drove all night," I say in his defense.

"I know it." Mama wishes she weren't mad with Daddy. Her irritation weighs heavy on her, like it's a sin to feel anything but sad. "Your daddy's a fine man," she says, to get rid of her bad feelings. It's what she always does when she catches herself being upset with him. Mama always feels what she calls remorse, which I don't know a thing about unless you call remorse what I felt when Candy Hooper and I got caught copying each other's algebra problems. She'd done half and I'd done half so I don't call that cheating, but Mrs. Siler did and Mama did when Mrs. Siler sent me home from school at ten o'clock with a note saying I was suspended for the rest of the day and for Mama to either come see her or sign the note proving I'd done at least one honorable thing. I think I spent that afternoon in remorse.

"Can I help you do anything?" I ask her, because she's sniffling again. This crying is getting to me. I haven't cried a tear. Not that I don't love Cousin Jessie. She was always more fun than Melissa, but I just don't feel like crying about her. She was real sick and now she's not sick anymore, if you believe what you hear in church. And you're supposed to believe it, aren't you? Preachers talk about faith all the time, but right now I don't see much of it around here.

"Just keep an eye on Melissa," Mama says, scrubbing hard at a spot I could of told her was at least a three-year-old stain. "I haven't had a minute to be with her and I know she's distraught."

"She's sitting on the porch swing waiting for Jamie Fletcher to come see her. He's her boyfriend." I say that harder than I should have. Sometimes I can see where I've got a streak of meanness in me a mile wide.

Mama pauses in her scrubbing to consider the appropriateness of this. Mama's always worrying about what's appropriate.

"Well, maybe it'll do her good," she decides finally. She doesn't have any authority over Melissa anyway. I could of told her that, too.

When I come back to the porch, Jamie Fletcher is here and he's got somebody with him.

"Hey, Roseanne," the other boy says like he knows me, and all of a sudden, I know him! It's Travis, who lives three houses down from Melissa and used to play with us. I haven't seen him in three summers—last summer I didn't come, and the summer before that Travis was at a camp at the beach, where he learned to sail and high-dive and got muscles. Some things I can't describe, not with any amount of trying, and one of them is how Travis Cuthbert looks now that he's filled out and got muscles and a dynamite tan and hair on his legs. He's gorgeous. He's not that tall, blond, golden type like Melissa's Jamie, but he's handsome in a way that suits me better. He's kind of short and tight and his hair is dark and wavy and he's got brown eyes instead of this washed-out blue everybody in our family got stuck with. He's got on cut-off jeans and a green T-shirt from Myrtle Beach and those worn-out looking mocassins that cost a fortune but people never polish so they'll look like they can afford to abuse them. Daddy always polishes my shoes, even if I don't want him to. I hate him doing that.

"How you doing?" Jamie says to Melissa and sits down beside her on the swing. Travis and I are just standing here.

"Fine," Melissa says, but she grabs his hand.

I'm still looking at Travis even though I know I'm making a fool of myself. I'm glad I put my face on.

"How you been, Roseanne?" Travis wants to know. He turns a little away from Melissa and Jamie, like ignoring them will give them privacy in broad daylight.

I take myself over to the steps and plop down on the top one. I can't think of a thing to say. Have you ever been struck dumb like this so you make a fool out of yourself doing absolutely nothing?

"Come sit down," I say when I find my breath. I think my lungs have collapsed on me because no air's going in. I try pushing out and there's a great big sigh like somebody gives to show they're bored, which I definitely am not. "Whatcha' been doing?" I ask when he's sitting next to me.

"The usual. Working at the pool. I earned my senior lifesaver badge so I've got a lifeguarding job."

That accounts for the tan. I look pasty beside him, but some people like a delicate look, even in the summer time. I smooth my flowered skirt over my knees and rub my hands down my calves. I've got good calves, tanned or not.

"You've changed a lot," Travis says, noticing my calves. I do baton twirling for a hobby and go to jazz class twice a week. Mama let me take it up when I refused to go to another piano lesson.

"It's been more than two years," I say and wish I hadn't. He'll think I've been keeping track.

"Too bad about the circumstances," he says, nodding toward Melissa, who's got her head resting on Jamie's chest right here on the front porch. Mama's going to have a fit.

"Well, she was real sick," I say like I'm suppose to comfort him or something. "We've got to go to the funeral home at one o'clock and look at her. I'm going with Melissa in case she breaks down over it. She's been so brave." Well, a person can change her mind, can't she?

Travis is looking at me like I'm God's gift to the bereaved. That's the truth. He's got this expression of awe on his face I wish I had a picture of. "Whatcha doing later?" he asks me.

I think to myself, this is how a date gets started. Here I am on Cousin Jessie's porch with her dead in the funeral home and her own child crying on her boyfriend's shirtfront and Mama in the house scrubbing everything in sight and I've got to think of the right thing to say. "Well, there's the visitation . . ." I begin.

"Oh, yeah." I can tell he's disappointed.

"But that's over at nine," I slide in.

"I don't suppose you and Melissa'd want to go somewhere, just out for a ride or to get something to eat," Travis says, brightening up. "Jamie and I were talking about it. Maybe it would do her good to get out of here for a while."

Ever since late this morning, I've had this fever. There's a cool dampness inside my clothes but my cheeks are burning. I feel like I've been on fire inside my face all this time but nobody seems to notice. I have a date!

I can't believe Melissa straightened herself up from Jamie Fletcher's arm and went right in the house to her daddy and said to him, "It'll be all right if Roseanne and me ride around awhile after the visitation." Didn't ask him. Told him in that sweet way of hers like her mama had somehow already given her permission, and he just nodded while my mama stared holes through both of us. I kept looking at Mama and after a long minute she sort of half nodded her consent to me, too. She was giving in and her face sagged with it like she was grimacing before the next blow, waiting to be struck down.

I'm burning up. Ever since that minute when Mama gave in, I've been hot under my skin, so I keep thinking about water. About how Travis must look at the pool. I bet during the rest periods he practices his dives. We used to run through the lawn sprinkler spray when it was hot like this and Travis would come over and aggravate us. He'd sit on the jets or chase us with the hose. He'd make Melissa so mad. One time he held the sprinkler on my head so I was surrounded by whirling spray with colors in it, like a crown shooting off diamonds. I remember it like it was yesterday. I have always thought a lot of Travis.

In a few minutes I'm going off with him. I ought to tell you this is my first date in a car. I call riding around a date, don't you? I mean, it's likely we'll go somewhere and get a cola or a soft cone. That would make it official. I believe somebody has to spend some money to make it a date. Craig Watkins comes and sits on our porch sometimes in the evenings after his American Legion baseball practice. He's on his way home and he sees us there and he comes and sits. Sometimes he and Buddy roughhouse or toss a baseball around until it's too dark to see. Most of the time, though, he leans against a porch post and watches the sky with me. It's the only time I like to be still—in that little while between sunset and true dark when the world is closing up and after a while there's nothing to see but our street, the house full of yellow light across the way, and our own porch. The cool smell of night is coming but there are no stars yet. I know just where I am then. Craig Watkins sitting on the porch is not a date.

This afternoon I went with Melissa to view the body, but I didn't look. I went about halfway up there to the casket, which was at one end of a long room lined with vinyl sofas and straightback chairs. There were lights in the ceiling along the molding and some plants on endtables that separated the sofas from the chairs. There were flowers on either end of the casket, too. Wreaths of carnations and mums and gladioluses. I kept looking at them so I didn't have to look at Cousin Jessie. I don't believe Melissa wanted to look, either, but I reckon she felt like she had to.

"Do you think what she's wearing is all right?" she asked Mama, like clothes were the important thing. Well, they are to Melissa. She's always had everything she wants. You ought to see inside her closet.

"It's fine," Mama said and put her arm around Melissa's shoulder. They were both trembling. You could see their shoulders jumping. Cousin Roy came in with Daddy then, and Mama and Melissa opened a place between them and hugged him, too. Cousin Roy looked weak and sick, not giving his full height, which is more than six feet. I have never liked tall men. Five eight or nine is good enough for me.

By the time we got home, the house was full of people and flowers and food. Melissa wouldn't eat a thing. She wouldn't talk to people either. I don't know what gets into her. I mean, she knows everybody in this town so it's not like anybody expected her to greet strangers. Most of them are unknown to me, however, and I was polite. Even Mama commented on it. I wish I'd brought that mint green top that's cut low in the back. I'd put it on right now if I had it.

Lord, it was hot at the visitation. You'd think a funeral home could keep itself cool, but the place was packed with people, even backed up in the hall, waiting to view Cousin Jessie and pay their respects. Some people were so glad to see Mama they acted like it was a reunion, but Mama held herself back. I heard a woman ask her if she was going to sing something at the funeral. She wanted to hear Mama because it had been such a long time. Mama said she wasn't, but the thought of it brought tears to her eyes. She sang at Cousin Jessie's wedding and was the maid of honor besides.

I feel like I'm going on and on. Diarrhea of the mouth. That's what happens when a person gets feverish. You feel like you've got to get everything said before you pass out of heat exhaustion. My mind's been racing for hours. It's like I've got a top spinning in there, whizzing and making heat. Everywhere I've been it's been so hot and tomorrow I've got to wear that dress. I ought to take some aspirins or something.

When we got home from the visitation it was dark, and Travis and Jamie were waiting on the porch. Mama invited them in to have a piece of cake—we've got six kinds—but they wouldn't. I came upstairs just now to fix my face and see how bad I look. I look flushed and my eyes are shining, just like a person with a fever. There's something pretty about it, though. I mean it's better than looking washed-out and sickly. Melissa, who stayed downstairs with the boys instead of fixing herself, is not as pretty as she used to be. If you saw her baby pictures, you'd think she should have been on the Ivory Snow box.

Now that we're finally riding around, I can tell you that I thought Mama would never let us out of the house, she kept being so social. She's beside herself with worry about every little thing and I could tell she didn't want us out of her sight. Jamie and Melissa are quiet in the backseat. I don't know what they're doing and I don't intend to look. I watch the asphalt running up under us. If you watch the lights on the road long enough, you'll get dizzy and pass out. Travis is a fantastic driver. He's got one hand on the wheel and the other elbow resting out the window. Every now and then he changes hands. Once he put his hand down on the seat between us and I thought to myself, this is it, but then he made a turn. I think we are riding in circles.

I have noticed that Travis likes to talk about himself, which is all right with me. He tells me all about his job, what time he goes to work, when he closes, and the details of several incidents of disciplinary action he's been involved in. Nobody has drowned in his pool. He tells us about the camp he went to. He won lots of certificates and awards. Football practice starts in three weeks. He is first-string running back and ran nine hundred yards for eight touchdowns last year. All this he says in a half whisper so I have to lean a little toward him to hear. If it weren't for my seatbelt I could slip over.

I am absolutely light-headed. The breeze gusting past my head is hot and oily like we are trailing in someone's exhaust. The air down here doesn't breathe good like at home. I feel as powdery as used charcoal and every breath I take turns prickly in my throat.

"Let's get some burgers and drinks and go out by the river," Jamie says from the backseat.

He and Melissa are stretching and sighing just like they're waking up. "I could eat a horse," Melissa says with a little laugh. And we've got all that food at home.

The boys go in McDonald's while Melissa and I wait in the car, so I turn around to talk to her. She's rumpled and relaxed looking. Her lips are puffy and her hair looks tangled in the back.

Around her face it's as smooth as silk where she's combed her fingers through it.

"Travis is nice," I say. I have always wanted to be sitting in a car at McDonald's waiting for my date to come back. People going in always glance at you and know there's somebody inside getting you something.

"He's all right," Melissa says, sighing. She used to talk a whole lot more than this.

"What's at the river?" I ask.

"Nothing. Just the river bank and trees and stuff. It's where people go to park, Roseanne."

"You mean we're going to park? We can just eat the burgers and talk, can't we?"

"You can do anything you want to," Melissa says.

I think what I'll do is faint.

We rode up here to the church in a black Cadillac limousine, but there wasn't a thing fun about it. I mean, you ought to be going to a party in a car like that. I rode in front with Melissa. Mama, Daddy, Cousin Roy, and Buddy were in the back. Cousin Roy's family from Wilson was in the car behind and I think his sister Esther is put out about it. After all, she's more kin than we are. Sometimes kin is not what matters, I don't reckon. Cousin Roy knows how it was between Jessie and Mama, so we got to ride in the limousine behind the hearse. The air conditioner was blowing full blast between my legs but I was hot anyway. We waited in the limo outside the church until they'd slid the casket onto this folding stretcher contraption and rolled it in. Then we got out, and right there I started sweating because the sun could boil water today. This church is not air-conditioned either.

The organ is playing, and we're sitting on the front pews, our backs to everybody. Melissa is between her daddy and my mama. She's wearing blue, but it's a soft color. Soft summery material, too. She looks like an angel, all glittery and shiny, while the rest of us are black and gray and midnight blue. I'm between Daddy and Buddy, but I can see Melissa's hands working a Kleenex. In a minute she's going to have it torn up, the way she's twisting and squeezing it. Mama has a pocketbook full.

The organ is sending out mournful notes, too draggy to follow. I think we ought to sing. It would be better than sitting here, holding the words in our heads. I'd like to blast right out "j-us-s-t as I am-m-m" so that woman would pick up the beat, but Mama would die. I feel like I'm going to jump out of my skin. I've never been good at waiting.

Anybody with eyes can see how I'm fidgeting. My mind won't stop whirring, trying to make sense of all that's in it. Travis Cuthbert kissed me last night! We rode out by the river with me holding the cardboard tray with four drinks and a sack of burgers in my lap. The smell of hot onions and pickles was enough to make a well person sick. I sipped on my Pepsi all the way out there, trying not to throw up, although I am not a person with a weak stomach. Travis parked the car and distributed the food. He kept the switch on so we could listen to the radio. It was dark except for the green dials on the dashboard, so Travis opened the pocket so the little light in there showed. The burger tasted a lot better than I thought it would. When everybody was finished, Travis turned the switch off and shut the pocket so everything was quiet and still and dark around me. I couldn't even see the river, but I could hear it, just this little stirring movement and, now and then, a plopping sound like someone throwing a stone or dipping a cup into the water. Our rivers at home are always moving, rushing and slapping rocks, going somewhere in a hurry. They sound cool and fresh and busy. These rivers down here hardly move at all and the air around them is sticky and sour.

"Let's get out," Travis said. We left Melissa and Jamie in the backseat and walked down to the water. It wasn't any cooler there and mosquitoes were hovering in the grass, but we sat down on a big flat rock right on the water's edge and pulled our feet up.

I didn't get a whole lot of warning. I always thought when I got kissed it was going to be with eye contact, in slow motion, you know, so expecting it would be just as exciting as the kiss itself. It wasn't like that. Travis kissed me hard and flat at first, like it was an attack or something, but right away I knew that wasn't how he meant it. When I didn't pull back, he softened up and we kissed for a while. Little kisses and a couple of big ones. I think he was practicing as much as I was. I felt as weak as water and clammy in my chest and my head was full of light so I just wanted to keep my eyes shut like when you wake up suddenly and the sun's too bright in your room. I didn't want to move or wake up or anything.

We didn't talk much going home. I don't mind admitting I'm tongue-tied in some situations, and Melissa and Jamie were keeping to themselves.

Melissa is not such a bad person. After we got home, she was so quiet and sad looking. I think she'd hoped going out with Jamie would make her feel better but it didn't. Nothing's going to make her feel better for a long time.

We were standing in front of her dresser mirror. She was brushing her hair and I was just looking at myself. I reckon I expected to see some difference but there doesn't seem to be any. Anyway, Melissa and I happened to look at each other in the mirror. It was truly strange because it was like we were seeing each other for the first time. I mean, I think she saw that I was there with her. And I saw—well, I saw that something terrible had happened to her, had been happening most of her life. Her mama had been dying for a long time, and her being pretty and popular hadn't changed that. Melissa knows a lot of things I don't know.

Later on, I could tell she wasn't asleep. I wasn't sleepy either but I was thinking about Travis, about how a person's life can be changed so quick. I felt good inside, cooled down and calm but excited, too, like some wonderful adventure was just getting started. All the while, Melissa was tossing around, trying to find a comfortable position. Sometimes there's just nothing you can do to stop being miserable. I waited a little bit to see if she'd settle down. When she didn't, I got up and got in bed with her and rubbed her back like she used to want me to do. I wasn't one bit embarrassed.

This preacher is talking about what a good woman Cousin Jessie was. Everything he's saying is the truth. This church feels dark like there's a cloud stopped over it, but I know it's a bright, sunny, July Sunday outside of here. We've got to go to the cemetery next. I'm going to melt out there in this dress, but I'm going to stay as long as Melissa does. I'm going to tell her how sorry I am. I'm going to tell Cousin Roy, too, because I haven't told him yet. But I'm not going to tell anybody except you about Travis Cuthbert kissing me. It's as private as grief but it doesn't need sharing. Just Melissa knows and someday when we're all grown up and married, we'll probably talk about it just like Mama and Cousin Jessie used to talk about things just they knew about.

As soon as I get a chance, I'm going to hug Mama.

SUE ELLEN BRIDGERS

North Carolina is the general setting for all of Sue Ellen Bridgers's novels. It's not just because she was the daughter of a farmer, born and raised there. It's more because the land and the rural way of life are so important to her. Today she lives with her husband in the Blue Ridge Mountain town of Sylva. Families, too, are very important, and Bridgers's novels contain important adult characters with whom the teenage characters interact, as they do in "The Beginning of Something." Her stories are also hopeful ones. They deal, as she says, "more with head and heart than with adventure and intrigue."

Her books have another element in common: they are all prizewinners. Each of her first three novels for teenagers has been named a Best Book for Young Adults by the American Library Association. In addition, *Home Before Dark* was named a *New York Times* Outstanding Book of the Year, *All Together Now* received the Christopher Medal, and both *All Together Now* and *Notes for Another Life* were nominated for the American Book Award.

Home Before Dark explores the feelings of Stella, a daughter of migrant farm workers, who finally finds a place where she can settle down, where she can *belong*. *All Together Now* concerns one summer during which Casey, a motherless girl, lives in a big house in a small town with a wonderful grandmother and a retarded man named Dwayne. A grandmother also plays a central role in *Notes for Another Life*, about a sister and brother who must cope with their mother's leaving the family and their father's mental illness.

Bridgers's most recent novel is *Sara Will*, an adult novel which older teenagers will appreciate. Sara is a middle-aged spinster whose solitary life is disrupted by her sister Swanee, her dead sister's brother-in-law Fate Jessop, his unwed teenage niece Eva, her baby, and Eva's "boyfriend."

In 1985 Bridgers received the ALAN Award for her "outstanding contribution to the field of young adult literature."

DONALD R. GALLO is a former junior high school English teacher and reading specialist who is now professor of English at Central Connecticut State University, where he teaches courses in writing and in literature for young adults. In addition to editing *Sixteen: Short Stories by Outstanding Writers for Young Adults* (which is available in a Delacorte Press and a Laurel-Leaf edition), he is also the editor of the 1985 edition of *Books for You,* a former editor of the *Connecticut English Journal,* a member of the editorial board of the National Council of Teachers of English, and president of the Assembly on Literature for Adolescents of the NCTE (ALAN). He lives in West Hartford, Connecticut.